Fractured Fairy Tales of the Twilight Zone
Volume One

by J. Cafesin

Entropy Press
2021 (First Edition)

Second Edition
July 2024

Library of Congress Cataloging-in-Publication Data is available.

ISBN-10: 0615978444
ISBN-13: 978-0615978444

Cover design by TargetMediaDesign.wordpress.com

Contents

Tales of

Finnegus
Boggs

Lessons from a Marid Djinn

✦

Billy & Tyron

A fractured fairytale by

j. cafesin

Tales of Finnegus Boggs;
Lessons from a Marid Djinn:
Billy and Tyron

The Setup
❖

It was Billy's idea to rip off the liquor store. He heard brotherabe on his cell say the place was ripe.

Bounce was good— take Fruitvale or Foothill outta there. Heart of the hood, where this kinda crap happens all the time. And Lucky Liquors is run by this old chink. Gook's at the mart from opening til closing cuz he too damn cheap to hire help from the Projects. Serves him right getting tagged every couple of months.

Slide convincing Ty to do the deed. Bluds since Sunshine Daycare, they bled enough and shredded enough to earn respect as the cracka/nigga posse not to jack. No fools in their faces since 5th grade, or on their streets edging the rim of the Hood. Only their jank address and the popo's keeping em down.

Lunchroom Thursday, Billy goes on spouting about taking what they deserve for being dissed since they was kids. From jacking construction sites at seven, to ripping music, movies and apps off the net and selling it on Marketplace at eleven, Tyron is always angling for money. To Ty, it buys respect. To Billy— freedom. He be flipping off his hammered old man and dick-head brother on the way outta town, and his mom too, if she'd stuck around.

"One strike gets us a sled and elevates us the rest a high school, blud. Then we outta here, down to Hollywood, man, do some rappin, some actin, be whoever we wanta be, Ty. And even if we get caught, but we won't, the most we'd get is maybe a short stint in juvie since we ain't got no rap sheets. And if we don't get caught, and we won't, I heard Chris say the gets around five large."

Tyron stares at Audrey across the lunchroom, the hoodrat who brought him out, now slumming with the cracka slanger, Baker. "Five grand would get us some respectable treads," Ty says. "We be legally stylin by the weekend if we did the deed this week." And Ty's sly, white-tooth grin spreads like a crack in a cave against his dark skin. "Late afternoon, tomorra," Tyron says. "Before the chink stashes his cash from the day in a safe or at the bank. Hoodies and caps, keep our mugs down, away from cameras, and we be golden."

"We ain't gonna just glide in there and ask for cash, blud. And copin a gun's gonna take time, and it ain't gonna be cheap," Billy feels a need to reality check him.

"We don't need no gun. Never liked em anyway. I'll thinka

somethin."

No shit Tyron hates guns. Took his old man out in a drive-by in their driveway when he was nine and his dad's brains landed all over him.

They're rifling through Tyron's shared closet for old baseball caps after track Thursday afternoon. Action figures missing body parts, busted Transformers, remoteless remote control cars once Ty's, now part of his four younger half-brothers and sisters collection. Most of the toys were used when he got em, but now they're all trashed, except for the hard plastic stuff, like shields and swords, and his old toy gun, the black and silver Beretta M92 pistol he got for his tenth birthday from Uncle Mike, a replica of the ones in the The Matrix. Tyron holds it with both hands, points it out in front of him towards Billy still ripping through the pile of junk.

Billy looks over at Tyron and his freckled face goes white. "What the fuck—." Then he grins, his blue eyes laughing. "Dope, home. I remember that, when you brung it to school and Guard Dog Jackson almost shot yo ass."

"Guess it's real enough," Ty says checking out his old toy. "And this way we in control, get what we want and no one dies. Now all we need is caps and we tight on gear, but we gonna need treads to haul ass outta there. Stupid runnin round the Hood—ever— but retarded after popo's get called out on the hit."

Billy's bushy brows bunch, then his eyes light up like there's a bulb in his head. "I'm for liberatin my brother's Charger from the Costco parkin lot. Jack it right after he starts his shift. Bring it back before his dinner break and he'll never know we copped it."

"And how we gonna cop his keys, homes?" Ty asks.

"Chris made an extra set of keys after that time he shredded me for losin his."

"Even though ya didn't, and he found em in the fuckin couch cushions after crackin yo ribs for losin em."

Billy can't help grinning. "Asshole laid out $150 for a new set he didn't need, which he keeps in his box of stash under his bed."

Tyron nods, but Billy sees his eyes glazing, his minds churnin. Ty's brain is always workin.
"I gotta hold the gun, since it's mine, well, was. And I'm way more harsh than yo cracka mic mug." Ty's plan— he points the toy gun at the chink, covers most of it with his monster paws so it looks real, then shouts for the paper. Billy snags it and they haul ass. "And with a bogus gun no one gets drilled. And that keeps us in juvie if we get nailed."

"But we won't get nailed if we do this right, Ty. Then we be stylin with our own treads, right on outta here."

The Hit

❖

After track next day, Billy and Tyron walk the mile and a half to Costco. Parking lot is crawling with Kardashian's swarming into Oakland since the tech invasion. Chris' Charger is parked at the far right side of the lot, bordered by trees lining the canal between Oakland and Alameda. The boys cut through the grove to either side of the car, get in casually, and drive away.

They share a J on the way to Lucky Liquors, listening to Live105 to chill. Billy parks across the street from the gook mart. Storefront windows is stacked with boxes, bottles of booze, cases of water and soda right up to the glass door with iron bars. White bird crap spots a blue cloth awning that runs along the top of the old brick building and shades the sidewalk below.

Casing the joint, they wait across the street for the store to clear out of customers. Sun's setting when Billy finally swings the Dodge round and parks in front of the liquor store. They put on tattered Oakland A's caps, pull down the rim to their brows, then hoods over their heads to the brim of the caps. Tyron grips the toy gun inside the long pocket of his hoodie and holds it pressed to his stomach as he follows Billy's lead out of the car and into Lucky

Liquors.

Billy goes to the cold cases in the back and pulls a six pack of Bud. Tyron grabs a bag of pretzels and Lays and brings them to the register as Billy comes up behind him.

Chink stands behind the counter, seen only through the small space not packed with crap for sale. He don't look at Tyron as he scans the bags. The slant deserves to be messed with. Payback for the neighborhood he's pretending don't exist while they fork over their welfare checks to buy his shit.

He pulls the toy gun from his hoodie. "Gimmy every fuckin bill in the register. NOW!" Tyron demands as he points the gun at the Chinaman who just stands there. "I said now, foinky!" Ty's rushing, feels like a speed buzz. Scared, but something else too… Smart. Powerful. Heart pounds hard, but beats steady, filling his chest like music does.

The chink finally looks up at him, speckled gray eyes wide. Then he looks at Billy.

"Ya heard da man." Billy's voice is deeper, angrier than Tyron's. "Give em the cash now or my blud here splatters your brains all over your booze." He eyes a golden bottle of Jack Daniels on one of the shelves along the wall behind the chink, and goes to get it.

"Sup, hom?" Tyron gets tense, with Billy not following the plan.

"I'm elevatin us above the crap we been drinkin." Billy rounds the counter to get the whiskey behind the old man.

There's a loud bang! Tyron's stomach is suddenly burning, like he's been stabbed, some unseen force slamming him backwards into the stack of plastic bottles of soda behind him. Then he's on the floor, and tries scrambling to his feet but the pain is so blinding, ripping through his guts, his chest. And there's blood everywhere, on his hands, his gray hoodie…

…Billy's yelling in his face but it's hard to hear, to breathe. The chink's still behind the counter. He's pointing a silver gun at them, a six shooter like in old movies, and screaming about something, but Tyron can't hear what with the burning in his guts. Then Billy has the toy Beretta, holds it by the barrel waving it around, his voice suddenly blasting.

"—it's FAKE! It's fuckin plastic!" Billy yells at the chink, then throws the toy gun at the old foinky, but Tyron can't see if he nailed him.

Then Billy's pulling on him to get up, helps him to his feet but he can't feel them and his legs fold. Billy practically drags him outta the liquor store to the Charger, opens the back door and drops Tyron on the back seat, stuffs his legs in and slams the door, then gets behind the wheel and hauls ass outta there.

The Doctor

❖

"How bad you hit, Ty?" Billy glances back at Tyron, then watches him in the rear view as he moves with the traffic on Fruitvale, hoping to blend. "Talk to me, blud."

Tyron slumps in the middle of the back seat, hands numbing now, watching tagged houses of west Oakland pass in slow motion. "He shot me. Why'd he do that?" He looks down at his hoodie soaking with blood. "Oh God, I'm bleedin bad." Tyron curls on his side. He holds his stomach with both hands trying to hold in his blood. "I'm gonna fuckin bleed to death. I don't wanna die, man. I'm only 17. I don't wanna fuckin die."

"You ain't gonna die, Ty." Billy's blowing smoke up Ty's ass. Even in the rear view he can see blood all over the beige bench seat. Chris is gonna split his skull open this time. "I'll take you to the 12th Street Clinic—"

"NO! They have to report gun shots. I can't get 5-0'd. It'd kill my mama." Tyron starts crying then. He can't help it. "God, it hurts. My stomach's on fire, man." He groans, curled on the back seat shivering. "I'm cold...I'm scared, Billy. Whata we gonna do?"

Billy cruises at the speed limit, but his mind is racing. He continues across the short bridge onto Alameda Island, where chedda and green rules. He and Ty used to bike to Crown beach all the time when they was kids just to screw with the natives and popos, since they don't take kindly to Oakland teens invading their slice of paradise.

"Oh Christ, I'm bleedin all over the place. I'm gonna be sick. I swear to God I'm gonna puke." Tyron's talking to himself, but it's making Billy crazy. "It fuckin hurts, man. You gotta help me, Billy."

"What the fuck do you want me to do, Ty? You don't wanna go to 12th Street then you gotta tell me what to do, man." Billy yells into the rear view mirror.

"I don't know. I don't fuckin know!" Tyron manages to yell back.

Fast turns into slow motion as Billy cruises at 25mph along tree-lined streets, passing big green lawns of luxury cribs. Even the apartments are nicer than anything in or even near their hood just over the little bridge. He drives toward the beach, as if moving to the past, wishing like hell he could go back there, to when they was kids, or at least to before they came up with this fool plan.

Billy notices the stop sign when he's less than two feet from it and slams on his brakes. Tyron moans as the Charger lurches forward and halts a few feet over the crosswalk. No other cars at the intersection. No curtains or shades move in the windows of the houses on three of the four corners, and no one is outside the big white buildings across the street on the right.

"Yo, Ty! Ya with me, blud?" Billy moves slowly through the intersection, trying to see Tyron in his rear view, but it's almost dark out and dim inside the car. "Ty!" No response. "Tyron! Talk to me, man!" Still no response. "Fuck!" He pulls the Dodge to the curb alongside the parking lot in back of the white buildings, kills the engine and turns around.

Tyron's usual dark chocolate skin looks almost... milky, the red surrounding his black eyes sinking them even more. A strobe of headlights and Billy spins back forward. He slides low as a white Beemer pulls out of the gated lot then passes by the Charger. Only then does Billy see the 'Doctors Only' sign on the parking lot entrance, and realizes where he is.

Deserve it or not, Jesus must be watching out for them. And down or not, if Ty's hit bad enough, Billy's taking him inside Alameda Hospital he's just parked on the side of.

Billy turns back round, leans towards Ty between the two front seats. Blood's all over the bench seat Ty's curled up on, and Billy thinks he might hurl but swallows it back. He moves Tyron's bloody hands from his stomach, then lifts his blood soaked hoodie real slow to see the damage. Tyron gasps, opens his eyes halfway, like he's toasted, and moans.

"Sorry. Gotta check it out, Ty." Billy's never seen a bullet wound before, except in video games and movies. Looks pretty much like that— a sea of bright red surrounding a dark hole oozing thick red juice.

"It's fuckin freezin." Tyron mumbles then sorta laughs. "It's true, just like on TV, when someone is dyin, ya get cold…" He drifts, thinking on what he's just said.

"Ya ain't dyin," Billy deems, but compulsively shivers because he don't believe it.

Ty seems like a little kid, curled up and holding his guts in like he is. Blood's dripping off the bench onto the floor now. And it's all over the back of the bench too. Billy was sure he'd only heard one shot. He pulls Ty's hoodie up along his side carefully to check out his back. Tyron sucks in hard, like he's hitting a bong, then groans loud.

"Sorry. Gotta see your back, home. Lean towards me."

Tyron does, but he practically screams as he rolls towards Billy.

Billy spots a hole oozing blood in Ty's lower back, just inches from his spine, and he's suddenly sure the grace of God is watching out for them. "The bullet went straight through, blud! You golden, Ty. Gotta guardian angel lookin out for ya, man. Now

all we gotta do is get you stitched up and you'll be smack, home."
And Billy's convinced it is now God's will that Ty won't die.

"I'm fadin, man. I think I'm dyin, Billy." Tyron is crying
again, his tears making long dark streaks across his face. He looks
like a scared little kid after getting called out.

Billy takes off his hoodie and folds it up. "Press this against
ya, man, and hold it there," and he pushes his hoodie into Tyron's
bloody hands and presses them against his friend's stomach. Tyron
moans, and curls tighter, but keeps hold of Billy's hoodie.

"Keep pressure on it! Slow the bleedin, man." Billy turns
back forward, shivers in his thin black t-shirt as he pops the glove
box hoping to find some herb to calm their nerves. No Js, or even
loose bud, but nestled among crumpled receipts and manuals is a
small gray P99. His brother has crossed the line from dealer to
thug, and a stupid one at that. If Chris gets tagged with a 9mm-
semi, he'll blow his parole and be facing hard time.

"If I die... ya gotta make some shit up to my mama... how
I saved somebody... or some bullshit that'd make her proud," Tyron
says between deep quivering breaths. "Ya hear me, blud?"

"Bullet went straight through, home. You ain't gonna die,
Ty! Just gotta get yo sorry ass sown back up." Billy's fingers are
sticky with blood. He looks around, taxing his brain for a way to
get help without getting them both snagged.

The hospital lot is packed with cars, but Billy don't see no one. Then a cracka— no, darker, maybe a raghead—comes strutting through the glass doors at the back of the hospital and crosses the lot towards their Charger parked curbside. His doctor coat flares with the wind. He looks tall, at least as tall as Billy. And he's thin, dressed in all black under his white coat. He moves smooth, almost like he's gliding. Getting closer Billy can see the doc is a slumdog. Dark, wavy hair that's all there. And this dude is pumped, especially at his age. Billy's sure he's too young to be talking to himself, then he notices the blue light blinking in the dude's ear from his wireless earbud.

Fifty feet away, now forty, the doc is coming towards the last row of cars parked in the lot. Billy can tell he's headed for the black Ferrari just the other side of the four foot high, ivy-covered fence separating the lot from the sidewalk, and their Charger parked on the street. He crouches low, hoping he's invisible beyond the fence, in the dark, and to pedigree like a doctor.

"—don't care what the market price is, Marty." Doc's voice is deep, and as smooth as his groove, and gets louder the closer he gets. "The gold has been among my assets for generations. It's only a trifle of my holdings, and I don't need the capital." He switches a small, bulging black bag from one hand to the other, then reaches in his pants pocket. Doc's probably got all Ty needs in that black bag of his.

It'd take that sand monkey like ten fucking minutes to sew up Ty's two small holes, then Billy'd let him go, even drop him back to his car for the owe. No reports. No one gets snagged. No one dies. All good. Like none of this ever happened. Billy looks back at Tyron. He's out, eyes closed but surrounded by dark like hollow black holes. Makes Billy shiver, like a ghost passing through him.

Ferrari alarm chirps. "I get it," the dude says. "I do. But I'll ride it out, Marty. Don't worry. I have the time."

Now or never. Billy pops the glove, grabs the gun, gets out of the Dodge and shuts the door quietly. He'll jack the slumdog before he makes the gate.

The sand monkey opens the Ferrari's door and gets in.

Nowhere to pocket the gun, and his jeans hanging too loose to hold it in his waistband. Billy grips the gun tightly as he moves around the back of the Charger, then onto the curb and across the sidewalk in a few quick steps. His heart hammers in his chest and ears. He tries pretending he's a shooter in Halo but it ain't really working to pull him from the reality slam. MOVE! MOVE! MOVE! is yelling in his head. He's waiting to hear the Ferrari ignite, and rushing to get in front of it before it leaves the lot. But that fine machine just sits there, silent.

Slide jumping the fence—way easier than the hurdles in

track. He lands silent as a puma behind the Ferrari, then moves to the driver's door, yanks it open and points the gun at the doc he saw get behind the wheel a minute ago.

"Freeze mothefucka—" Billy growls into the milky void inside the Ferrari.

Glowing smoke swirls in greenish mist, then suddenly gathers like a coiling snake and rushes towards him. And as it surfaces Billy sees a face, the face of the Indian doctor, and then the doc's sitting behind the wheel of his Ferrari, the blue light from his cell earpiece mixing with his door light making him look blue/green, almost like water.

The doctor looks at him casually, and laughs, bringing Billy back from one fucked up flashback.

"Get out!" Billy grips the gun with both hands now and points it at the doc's head. "Get your black bag and get out."

"Bizarre as it seems, I believe I'm being car-jacked, Marty." He talks to his earpiece but stares up at Billy, beyond the gun two feet from his face, looking right into Billy's eyes. "No. No," he chuckles. "I'm fine. It's just a kid, no more than a teen."

"Lose it or I blow it off." Billy points the gun at the slumdog's ear.

"Marty, I'll have to get back to you." He smiles, indulgent-like as he takes the wireless from his ear, closes it in his weirdly long fingers then like a magician opens his hand at Billy and the earpiece is gone.

Billy almost shoots the prick, except the safety is still on. "Get out! Get the fuck out of the car." Prickling rush when the doc just sits there, like Billy's some sorta joke or something. He pushes the safety forward so the gun can fire. "I said get your black bag and get out. Don't make me pop ya."

Doc grabs his black bag sitting on the passenger seat and gets out. Billy keeps the gun on him as he backs up, suddenly filled with a massive dose of chill since there's no way in hell Billy could've forced this jacked dude out of his car.

"I've had many strange experiences in all my years, to be sure. But I don't believe I have ever been carjacked. Isn't that remarkable?" Doc stands by his open door, towering over the low Ferrari, eye-to-eye with Billy, not three feet between them. "If it's my car you desire, I'm afraid it only responds to my commands. I've had it customized to my—"

"I don't want yo flash treads. Ya think I'm a moron? It's a goddamn billboard screamin, *Look at me!*" Billy shoves the doc forward. "I need some doctoring. Move!"

"Where are we going?" the sand monkey asks, like he's excited or something being shoved along by Billy.

"Black Dodge on the street." Billy resets the safety, holds

the gun at his side but keeps his finger on the trigger, and his thumb on the safety. They come round the fence at the lot's entrance and onto the sidewalk. He shoves the gun harder in between the doc's shoulder blades pushing him towards the Charger, which looks empty parked at the curb.

"Get in. Do it now!" Billy commands as he opens the passenger door, glancing at Ty, curled like a suckling baby on the bloody back seat, dead maybe. And with this thought comes a choking, suffocating weight, as if Billy's being buried alive.

Doc eyes Ty laying in the back as he gets in the Charger without Billy needing to convince him. Again he's flooded with that sense of relief, knowing he couldn't have made the doc get in if the dude resisted. He sits all chill, even laces his big fingers together, puts his hands in his lap and looks up at Billy, like they was buds or something. No fear that Billy can see, or even sense. He slams the door in the slumdog's face, but keeps the gun pointed at his head as he walks around the front of the Dodge, gets behind the wheel, and locks them all in.

"What would you like from me?" He looks at Billy, stares, like into him, stopping Billy cold. His black eyes seem to change then, to deep, emerald green, and they practically twinkle, like he's laughing again, except he's not. "I would say: 'Your wish is my command,' but that is so cliché, don't you think?" His deep voice practically echos, the vibration in Billy's chest jarring. He points the gun less than a foot from the doctor's head, but doesn't release the safety.

"Shut the fuck up. I'll do the talkin." Billy's sure Doc's playing him a fool, acting like they is all down. Billy don't care. "You fix my friend, sew him up, and you outta here, back at your car like yous never here."

Tyron moans, and both of them turn to see him open his eyes, but they only open halfway, like he's seriously baked.

"He took a bullet. It went straight through. Sew him up, front and back, and you gone. Ya got my word." Billy manages to keep the gun on the Doc as he starts the car and puts it in gear with his left hand then pulls from the curb real slow, heading for the beach, where it's quiet and empty at night.

The Genie

❖

"I'm Finnegus Boggs. Dr. Boggs, if you'd like. I also go by Doc Finny, but mostly to children, which you clearly are not."

"Don't give a shit about your name. We get to the beach and you're gonna fix up my blud here." Billy drives past the apartments and the bay suddenly spreads out in front of him. "When ya get Ty right, we say ga-night." He turns onto Shoreline Drive, cruises slowly along the beach front for a space between the Beemers and monster SUVs. The Bay's a deep violet void, but the hills across the water, the Bay bridge and the city beyond it all twinkle.

"Ah. Hunza," Doc says, all over the top, like he's seeing Oz or something. "San Francisco is a sparkling jewel, is she not?" He looks at Billy like he's waiting for an answer. "Well, it's important to acknowledge beauty, even in troubling times. Especially in them, don't you agree?" He stares at Billy, waits.

"I ain't squawkin with ya, man." Billy pulls the Dodge to the curb in front of the Seaview Apartments. "I nabbed ya to sew up my man here, so shut the fuck up and get back there and fix him up."

"How droll. Don't be a stereotype, son. It's deathly dull."
Doc sighs heavily, like he's a father calling out his kid. "Let's have a
look at your friend then, shall we?"

And suddenly Billy's outside, sitting cross-legged on Crown
Beach under a blanket of stars brighter than he's ever seen. Feels
like he's in a dream. Tyron lays in front of him on sparkling golden
sand, except not on the sand, but floating just above it, his eyes
closed, his hands holding onto Billy's blood-soaked hoodie. Billy
scrambles to his feet, tripping in the warm glittering sand as he
moves toward the empty Charger parked across the street, then
wheels back round to Tyron, and the sand monkey's in front of him
blocking his way.

His gun is gone, so with closed fists Billy shoves Boggs'
hard in the chest. The doc glides backwards like he's on ice, but
doesn't fall. "What is this? What the hell's goin on?!" Billy shoves
him again, only this time it feels like he's slamming a wall. His
knuckles burn, like he's shredding skin, and Boggs doesn't move at
all. "Who are you? What the hell are you?" He practically whispers,
afraid of the answer. "Some kinda magician or somethin...?"

"Not a magician. A typical guess, that, or some sort of god,
but that's neither here nor there." Boggs' smiles slow and wide, like
that cat in Alice In Wonderland. "I am a Marid, a djinn, a *genie*, as
you may refer to me, though I find that expression rather vulgar,
don't you?" His black eyes sparkle, for real. Light

twinkles from them, like coming from inside of him.

Ty's inert body starts to rise slowly. He groans, then opens his eyes halfway, totally blank he's floating four feet off the ground now. Boggs moves to his side and shines a pen light into his eye. He stares up at Boggs, then grabs the collar of the Doc's white lab coat with his bloody hand. "You're real." Ty mumbles, gripping the clean white collar. "Billy always said you was fake, that there ain't nothin gonna save us, but you's real." He stares into the Doc's eyes sure he's seeing the angel Gabriel, and even with his blurry vision he's equally sure the spirit is glowing. He lets go of the Doc's coat, blinks out some tears and sighs gratefully. "Am I dead?"

"Not yet," Doc says kind of gentle, like the way he puts his fingers on Ty's neck.

"You ain't dead, blud. I'm here." Billy moves to Ty's side opposite the Doc. He grabs Ty's bloody hand and holds it in both of his, right then getting what Ty meant when he said he was cold. His hand is freezing, his grip so weak Billy can barely feel him squeezing. "I got this doc here, man, and he's gonna fix ya right up. We ain't gonna let ya die, Ty." Billy looks at Boggs, pleading, still unsure if he's dreaming. It all seems so real, except Boggs' white coat is lit up against the black Bay and makes it look like he's kind of glowing.

"Don't tell my mama how I died, blud," Ty begs, gazing up at Billy now. "Tell her I took a bullet tryin to stop it. Make me a hero, Billy. Please man…" Tears are streaking his face again.

"You ain't gonna die, man. Ya hear me, Ty?!" Billy glares at Boggs. "Tell em he ain't gonna die."

"I will not." Boggs looks at Billy, shakes his head slowly. "I do not lie. I could, of course, like most do. It took me many millennia to learn that lying about facts to spare feelings ultimately serves no one."

Then Ty's grip goes slack in Billy's hand and his eyes roll back in his head.

"Where's your black bag? Where the fuck is it?!" Billy's all up in Boggs' face, yelling over Tyron. "Ya need to sew him back up and stop the bleedin!" He lays Ty's hand back on his bloody hoodie. It stays there, like his elbows are on the ground instead of floating feet above it, but blood drips from Ty's back and hits Billy's left Converse before he backs up. "Where's your black bag, Slumdog? Ya need to sew him up before he bleeds out, man. You need to stop the bleedin—" Billy stifles a sob with short breaths, afraid the sand monkey sees how scared he is.

"No. I don't." Boggs looks Billy straight in the eyes, but his eyes ain't sparkling now.

A jumbo jet taking off from Oakland airport rumbles the earth and makes the golden sand shimmer as it flies over the black Bay.

Boggs looks down at Tyron, puts his hand on top of Ty's

hand, still holding Billy's bloody hoodie. "Your friend has lost a lot of blood. Even if he gets sewn up there is only a marginal chance this boy will survive without an infusion of hypertonic saline along with a viscosity enhancer like Hextend or—"

"Talk fuckin English." Billy starts shaking, hoping this wacked out asshole don't see.

"Well, I am, of course. You're inability to understand me is perhaps your own ignorance." Doc looks at Billy like he's waiting on directions.

"Then we go back to the hospital, and ya get him the medicine—"

Doc shakes his head. "Too late for that." He brings his hand to Ty's neck and presses two fingers into the side of Tyron's throat. "His heart rate has accelerated." Boggs closes his eyes, like he's trying to feel inside Ty. "Pressures dropping. Vessels are starting to clamp down to try and maintain perfusion." He sighs real deep, like he cares. "He may have three minutes, maybe five, before he has a heart attack, or strokes out, or if he's lucky goes into an irreversible coma."

Billy feels hot tears running down his cheeks. And dissing himself for being a pussy ain't stopping em. "You tellin me Tyron's gonna die? Right here? Right now?" He feels dizzy, like the ground ain't under him anymore.

"It's not possible to predict the future with consistent

accuracy, regardless of the recent claims by your data science community." Boggs' smiles but just for a sec. "The future is dynamic, ever changing, and solely your making. Whatever hand you've been dealt, your choices chart your course, your journey through life, which is why one can only move backwards on any given time line—"

"Shut the fuck up, slumdog!" Billy stands a few feet from floating Ty, eye-to-eye with Boggs. "What yo rappin 'bout, dickhead? Take ya a fuckin second to pop us back to the hospital, fix up my man, and be done." He wipes his tears away with the end of his t-shirt as they fall, but he can't stop them. "Why ya talkin at all, Doc? If he's dyin, why ain't ya tryin to save him? You a goddamn doctor, ain't ya? Ya took a oath on a fuckin bible to cure people, didn't ya?"

"I'm not a priest. And I've learned there is no such thing as holy men. You are all born solipsists, and most of you never seem to grow out of it. Too bad too—"

"Shut up!" Billy barely stops himself from clocking the sonofabitch in his snug face, but that won't help Ty none. "Ty dies. You die," he growls, glaring at Boggs. "Fuckin get us to a hospital like ya got us on this beach, or I make it my mission to come for yo fam if his mama has to bury him."

The ground vibrates but there ain't no planes that Billy can see. The gold sand starts rising in sparking flashes of light. He feels his body hair rise off his skin. Not exactly sparks, more like pops of golden light, like glitter is swirling around their ankles now, and way beyond them, as far as down the beach Billy can see.

"As... *unique* as this experience is, being diverted from a rather dull evening by, well," and Boggs waves his hand in the air as if swatting a fly, "you, I imagine if I were mortal it would not be. Either way, it's unwise to push me too far." Boggs turns away, moves a couple of steps from Ty and stares out at the Bay.

Billy's coming unhinged, can't think, can't stop shaking, fighting himself not to move on this asshole the longer he just stands there letting Ty bleed out. "I don't care what ya are, or if this is even real, but if this is, and you's some kinda angel, like Ty says, or devil, which it'd be more my luck, then," and he stops cuz he's shedding in front of this sand monkey now. "Take me..." Billy stifles another sob. "No one gives a shit about me anyway." He wipes his dripping nose with the bottom of his t-shirt again. "Ty's got a mama who loves him, and brothers and sisters too. You fix him up, and take me instead if ya need someone dead. Please, I'm beggin ya, man, take me."

Boggs turns and faces Billy again, standing a few feet from floating Tyron. He's smiling, not like that grinning cat, but halfway, like suddenly he gives a shit. His black eyes go soft, like warm, welcoming black holes sucking him in, freezing him in place.

Golden glittering light swirls and pops round them rising

in slow motion, up past where Ty lay floating, almost to Bogg's and Billy's chests now. It's fucking awesome, like nothing he's ever seen, not YouTube, not gaming, not anywhere.

"This likely will not save your friend," Boggs says as the glittering light continues to rise around them. "And if he dies, his timeline is effectively over. Complete." Glitter starts spinning all around them. "Tyron's life will have ended, and can not be resurrected." Flashes and pops of glittering light sparkles around them faster and forms a circular vortex of sparkling gold. The vortex brightens as its speed increases, lighting up the three of them, the golden sand, the beach beyond and out over the Bay, making the black water shimmer with light, brighter and brighter...

Then everything goes white.

The Wish

❖

Billy is standing next to Tyron laying in a hospital bed. Before he can even register where they're at, he's being pushed aside by the nurses coming in. They gather around Ty, put an IV in his arm, then stickers on his chest, and the heart monitor beeps on. Billy don't know how Boggs got them there. He don't know why. He don't care. They'll fix Ty up for sure in here.

Blue curtain surrounding them sweeps aside and Boggs' comes in, his doctor's coat all bright white, like he ain't never left the hospital tonight. The nurse moves away as he stands over Ty and shines a penlight in his eye.

Tyron stirs, groans, blinks his eyes open, but just barely. Boggs stares down at him and Ty fixes his gaze on Finnegus. Tears fall, making a dark line, like mud streams in dry dirt, down the sides of his face. "I'm sorry!" Ty sobs to Boggs. "Tell Jesus, I'm sorry! Gabriel please forgiv—" Then he starts chokin. "Forgive me my sins—" and then his eyes roll back in his head and the heart monitor starts beeping real fast.

Billy moves towards Tyron but a nurse pushes him back. "Please leave now," she demands and is literally pushing him out of the draped enclosure as he hears Boggs' say, "Get me 15ml hypertonic saline and 500ml Hextend stat."

Billy stands stone still against the drapes where the nurse left him to attend to Tyron. He hears Boggs giving orders to the nurses about stuff to do, and while he hears the words, Billy don't get what the hell he's talking about, using doctor speak like he is.

Then it's quiet except the rustling of the nurses and Ty's heartbeat on the monitor. And suddenly Boggs' is standing next to him and Billy nearly jumps out of his skin.

"What the fuck's with you? What are you? You a real doctor, or just a mothafuckin wacked out psycho that slipped me some shit and this is all some fuckin head trip? If this is real, then why ain't you in there tryin to save him?"

"I did, just as you asked, in fact," Boggs' says.

The curtain sweeps aside. Boggs, then Billy looks over at Ty, all hooked up with tubes up his nose and needles in his arms, laying like he's dead, eyes closed, still as stone in the hospital bed.

Boggs kinda laughs. "And you are not the first to accuse me of insanity. For most indictments, I am proud— standing up against madness rather than succumbing to it. As for my credentials, I've been practicing medicine on and off for the last five millennium. I find it very satisfying. Except in times like these, of course. Such a tragic waste of grand potential."

Loud tone sounds and stays as the green line on the heart

monitor flatlines. It looks and sounds just like it does on TV.

Boggs just stands there, but the nurses spring into action, one pumping Ty's chest with her hands on top of each other, while the other nurse is grabbing paddles from the top of a box on the wall. "Clear!" she says real loud, then slams the paddles down on Ty's chest. His body bucks but the flat tone remains, and the green line's still straight after the spike from the shock.

Billy can't breathe. This is happening. Ty is dying. He can't stop it. And this dickwad doctor won't stop it. He can't stop his lower lip's quivering now, and Billy feels warm tears running down his cheeks again. He wipes them away with the back of his hand and looks at Boggs, pleading. "Please, please save my buddy, man. I don't give a shit if you is the fuckin devil. I'll agree to anything you say, do anything you want. Please save my friend! He's only 17, man. Please—" Billy can't help crumbling then, letting lose the sobbing been stuck in his guts. He don't even try to stop it.

Finnegus Boggs eyes Billy. "I can not." He looks at Tyron, then looks back at Billy, his eyes again like black holes, and don't reflect, but seem like they're sucking light in. "I can not save your friend, Billy. But you can."

"Clear!" the nurse says again, making Ty's body buck on the bed. The monitor bleeps in rapid secession, the green line jagged, not like a normal, rhythmic heartbeat.

"His heart is going into arrest. He's almost dead," the doc

says.

"Why ya still messin with me? He's dyin, for fuck sake. How the hell am I supposed to save him if you can't?"

"You'd call it magic. But it's really just physics." A smile cuts across the genie's face like some Yoda. "While going forward is only a predictive model, as the future is undetermined, certain beings, like myself, for example, can go backward along a timeline. Say the words and I can, well, put you in a position of saving your friend, essentially give you the opportunity to reset your lives on a different path which does not lead to this particular outcome."

Something weird starts happening with time, like it's slowing down. The nurses are moving slower, the tone on the heart monitor is deeper.

"C...l...e....a....r...." The nurse's voice is low and slow. Instead of slamming the paddles onto Ty, it looks like she's moving in super slow motion and just placing them on his chest.

Billy inhales a shaky breath. "Just fuckin tell me what the hell ya want me to do," he says, but not with any clout, suddenly tapped, like he may pass out.

"I just told you what to do," the Doc says like a bummed coach. "Clearly you have learning issues. So, I'll tell you again, but PAY ATTENTION BOY," Boggs booms, his voice deep, echoing with reverb.

And suddenly they're all back at Crown beach, still standing together watching Ty just like in the hospital. Billy tumbles back, nearly falls, recovers, then glares at Boggs just standing there watching him fumble like some fool. "What the fuck?!" Then Billy sees Ty. He's not in the hospital bed, and he ain't floating either. He's laid out on the golden sand this time, his arms across his chest, like he's in a casket, looking real peaceful like. "Is he dead?" Billy dare ask just above a whisper.

"Not yet," Bogg's says like he doesn't really care anymore. "However, I can give you the power to save him, Billy, but only before he is dead, as I've said." He moves to where Ty lay, points two weirdly long fingers down at him then flicks them upwards. Tyron starts rising, slow, until he's four feet off the ground, but he's laying like he's still on the sand. "I am a Marid, the first in the line of my kind, and the most powerful, and respected of Djinn I may add. When you opened the door to my Ferrari, you essentially summoned me, like Aladdin's mother rubbing the oil lamp. Ah, but then you're probably unfamiliar with the tale of One Thousand and One Nights."

"I fuckin know who Aladdin is. And I ain't him." He glares at Boggs. "Aladdin's a fuckin fairy tale. My mom is gone and there ain't no such thing as genies."

"Aladdin is a legend, a fable, to be sure. But I am not." Doc smiles, like Ty's mom when she's telling him how it is from what he thinks. "Scheherazade told of us more eloquently than I, but I'll

36

try and translate into twenty-first century, guttural American slang." He cracks the slightest smile. "In layman's terms, contrary to legend, Djinn's can live anywhere we like. We possess the authority to grant one wish to whomever calls us out, you might say, which is why most of us don't live in houses, with front doors." Boggs smiles, but it sags when Billy doesn't. "I keep the car doors locked most of the time, and, other than valets, for which I prepare my exit beforehand, not many people open the driver's door of a vehicle other than the driver. In fact, you are only the third in over 90 years."

"Lucky me." Billy says and looks at Ty floating like he's dead, his posse, his homedog, his blud, more blood than any fam ever was.

"Ah…But you are, Billy," the smug sonofabitch says.

"Losin the one good thing bout my fuckin existence ain't lucky." Billy looks out over the black Bay to the beaded lights on the bridge to the city he and Ty never cross.

"Luck is what one creates with opportunity, Billy. And I'm giving you an opportunity now. While I'm not obligated to grant requests when called out, I am choosing to award you one for giving me this unique experience, which is rare for me living as long as I have. As payment for this adventure, I grant you one wish. It must be stated clearly, and concisely, and without multiple components. And you have my word, the outcome will be to your exact specifications. No refunds, exchanges, or repeats. And there is no wishing for more wishes. I'm honor-bound to grant only one per client I take on—"

Tyron moans, then's suddenly starts screaming like a zombie. Shocks the shit outta Billy and seems like Doc too cuz he hovers over him with two fingers on Ty's neck. Ty's mumbling something Billy don't hear till he moves closer.

"I see the light, B," Ty says, but he don't open his eyes and he don't seem to notice he's floating. "I see it, man. I see the light, blud. God damn, it's beautiful, all sparkly and shit…"

"Anoxia is affecting his optic nerves." Doc stands straight, within slugging distance, and looks at Billy. "His right temporal lobe is malfunctioning from oxygen deprivation. His brain is shutting down."

"Where's Gabriel?" This time Ty's eyes open but a slit so small his eyelashes stay woven together. "Oh no! No! He left me. He's gone. I'm goin ta hell, Billy. I know I am. I'm going to hell for all the bad shit we done…" and he's wheezing by the time he stops talking, gasping to breathe, tears carving up his face with wet lines again.

"Not to worry." Boggs says real casual like. "There is no place, or any reality known to me as humanity's religious constructs of hell. Only in life does one create it, or choose to avoid it."

"I'll make it my mission to prove ya wrong if ya don't save my friend." Billy glares at Boggs who frowns back at him like he's stupid. He tries to chill instead of kill the mothafucka, runs his hand through his hair and looks at Tyron, glowing in blue moonlight and floating like he's already a spirit.

Then Tyron starts jerking and gurgling like he's being strangled. His eyes spring wide open and he's glaring up at Boggs, begging, desperate. His red mouth's gaping and he's gasping in every breath.

"No. No. *Shhh*. It's all good, blud. Ya gonna be good—" Billy says, and he would've taken Ty's bloody hand in both of his but Boggs bends in front of him, his ear to Ty's chest forcing Billy to step back.

"Blood's accumulating around the lungs in the hemothorax," He straightens but rests his left hand real gentle on Tyron's chest. A deep red glow surrounds Boggs' hand and Ty's eyes close, his breathing settles some, wheezing instead of choking now.

"He should be dead soon," Doc says real matter of fact as he turns to Billy. "And, again, I can not reverse death once beyond it along this timeline."

Billy's trembling so hard everything's jittery. Was this really happening? Or it really be Thursday night, and he's just dreaming about the lunchroom today when they was squawking about hitting the liquor store. "This is wacked." Billy says out loud, trying to talk himself into waking up. "I'm havin a nightmare, or doin some nasty trippin…"

"Oh, this is happening, boy," Boggs says. "Reality does not go away because you choose to ignore it." He shakes his head like

Billy's stupid. "Change your life tonight, Billy, or choose your rage over reason and blow yet another opportunity. Your life, your choice, as always." Boggs eyes go from black to yellow, like eagle eyes, freezing Billy in terror where he stands. "You may request the tiresome 'riches beyond your wildest dreams'?" Boggs' flashes his *Alice in Wonderland* cat grin.

"Billy," Ty says real soft like, but his eyes stay shut. "Billy where ya at, blud? Help me..." Almost a whisper as Billy moves to Ty's other side opposite the doc and grips Ty's stone cold forearms folded cross his chest, hoping Ty can feel him.

"I'm here, blud," and Billy squeezes his forearm tighter. "I'm sorry, Ty. I'm so fuckin sorry about alla this..." He can feel heat coming off Doc's hand on Ty's chest, only inches from his before Boggs takes it off, steps back and looks at Billy.

"What's it going to be, boy?" Boggs stares at Billy like coach does when he's saying something complicated. "I can provide you with a steady, rather generous source of income allowing you to pursue your ambitions with all the trappings of wealth— a nice home in a prosperous neighborhood where the kids are destined for success." Again he cracks his big cat grin. "Or, I can send you back along your timeline, ensure you meet Tyron. Perhaps you will reconsider your choices, change these events and alter this outcome, cinch this opportunity to continue your long friendship, which, even with my assistance, only you can really do." His yellow eyes go red, then deep red then black, and he ain't smiling no more.

Billy lets go of Ty and steps back. Boggs is the devil, Billy is sure now, the red eyes just like the preachers say, and how they show Lucifer on TV.

"It's your choice, Billy, limited only by your vision, as is so much of life." Doc sighs. "Make your wish now, boy, or lose this opportunity."

Tyron starts breathing real loud, gurgling like he's choking again. His eyes pop open, black balls floating in liquid red. He's gazing up at Boggs like he's blazing— seeing God or something.

Dream or not, devil or angel, Billy don't give a shit now. "I don't know who or what the fuck you are, but if you can save him I'll play. I wish my friend is gonna live, gonna be fine, was never shot, like this never happened. That's what I wish."

"That was four wishes." Doc holds up his index finger. "'He's going to live.'" Boggs holds up two fingers. "He'll 'be fine,' whatever that means." He holds up three fingers. "He wasn't shot during the holdup; or go back in time to some unspecified date before you both committed robbery? I'm unclear on that last bit." He holds up four fingers. No blood on his hands or his white lab coat. Freaks verging on sparkling clean. "Which wish do you want, Billy? You only get one." Finnegus Boggs frowns. "Without fail, everyone always angles for more."

"You fulla shit, man. Yo docs is so fuckin proud but ya don't save nobody. Not my sister, not my blud, not me, not even you." Billy holds his hand up and points two fingers like a gun at Boggs' head. "You ain't nobody, like everybody else, just like me. Tyron dies, I smoke you, then me, and the world loses nothin."

Boggs shakes his head. "Your infantile whining is becoming tedious. When do you stop blaming everyone but yourself for where your choices have led you?" He looks at Tyron floating in front of him, now gargling in air, body jerkin, eyelids spazzing, his lower lip quivering, drooling foamy white shit running down his cheek and dripping on to the sand. "Watch your friend die, or make a wish, boy, one wish, and I'll make it so."

"I'll fuckin kill ya if you's playin me, man. But if you're what ya say you is and givin me a do-over," Billy knew exactly where he'd go. "I wish I could go back to the lunchroom last Thursday, right when we sat down and Tyron and me started talkin bout doin the hit. I wish we could go back to right then."

Boggs eyes pulse bright white light from inside him, like Billy just won the slots at Vegas. "Your wish is my command, sir."

Time slows then, like it did in the hospital. A plane leaving Oakland moves through the starry sky over the black Bay in super slo-mo. Tyron's still spazzing, the white foam coming from his mouth bubbles out slowly, and drips even slower down his cheek and onto the golden sand.

"There is only one addendum." Boggs pulls a see-through monitor the size of a tablet right outta the air as he moves around floating Ty towards Billy.

Something above the twinkling hills across the Bay, beyond

Boggs now next to him, catches Billy's attention. The starry sky is… disappearing, going black, in tiny squares, kinda like a busted computer screen.

"Your signature is required." Doc pulls a thin silver stylus from the breast pocket of his lab coat. Billy stands frozen, barely breathing. Everything around them is going black now. The hills beyond the Bay, then the city lights of downtown, and now part of the Bay bridge is vanishing in tiny squares to a black void.

"It acknowledges you understand the outcomes of your choices are solely your responsibility, in your control, and therefore I am not liable for any and all events that transpire after the stated request is executed, at which time our contract is terminated, and I am released from any and all obligations to you," Boggs says, just like the popos squawk when they busting yo ass. "Sign it, and I'll make your wish reality." Boggs' black eyes twinkle from inside again as he holds up the translucent screen for Billy to see. "Initial here, and here, and sign here," he points with the stylus, then hands it to Billy.

The pen is warm, and vibrates with energy like the transformer on a laptop cord. The Bay is being gobbled by black squares now, along with the rest of the Bay bridge, part of the beach they're on, the street and the apartments beyond.

Boggs sighs, like he's getting pissed, and points at his tablet again where Billy needs to sign. A deep blue light, sharp like a laser shoots from the tip of the stylist as Billy puts the pen to Boggs' glowing tablet. He puts his mark where Boggs said, then again, and the blue tip gets brighter, almost sky blue now, like a brilliant sunny day. The laser lights up the three of them, and the golden sand where they stand, but beyond their halo of light is only blackness now.

"Just your signature now and you'll have what you wish. And I'll throw in this bit of wisdom upon my leave… Regardless of the hand you've been dealt, to get the life you truly desire, Billy, you will have to make better choices. You are the god of your own destiny." He taps the screen where Billy should sign.

Billy's trembling so hard he can barely hold the pen. He says a silent prayer while signing his name that Boggs ain't selling his soul, and this nightmare will end. Right as he finishes scrawling his sig, the tip of the stylus goes white and floods the tablet with blinding light that burns his eyes. Billy squeezes them shut against the brightness, the afterimage in his head is his wonky signature scrawled across Boggs' glowing tablet.

The Do-Over

❖

"I dunno, home. Seems like it could get kinda wacked if it goes down bad," Ty says.

Daring to squint, the bright light is gone. Billy blinks several times to focus and sees Tyron wolfing the last of the small pizza that comes in a styrofoam box, along with a carton of milk, a bag of Cheetos's and a tiny cup of applesauce. The school's 'healthy' meal for welfare kids.

"Brotherabe's a dickhead, blud." Tyron speaks with his mouth full, his prime white teeth just about glinting against his dark skin. "Can't trust shit Chris squawks—" Tyron's eyes narrow on Billy. "What yo grinnin at fool? Ya totally wasted or what?"

Billy laughs, and can't wipe his big ass grin even after he stops laughing. "I'm good, def, man. Extra fine and right on time."

Ty stares at him. "Yous dope, homeslice." He tries to look cranked but Billy's grin is catching. Tyron can't help smiling back. "I ain't goin 'long with this 'cuz yo grinnin at me, B. Thought we gave up the stare down shit when we was in 3rd grade, blud." Tyron takes a few gulps of his milk then wipes the white mustache on his sleeve and scopes the humming lunchroom. "Audrey's been pumpin

45

Baker for like a month now." He stares at Audrey all decked—
tight red sweater and brown leather skirt that matches her long
legs but barely covers her ass. She's standing behind Tim Baker
sitting on a bench across the room, a cracka punk dealer with a Z9
Beemer. She's rubbing his shoulders while he rambles with some
runner in his crew. "The bitch is only doin him 'cuz he's got the life,
livin large off all that tax-free cash."

"Maybe..." Billy says, reliving the first time they did this
scene. He was supposed to say, 'We could too. And we ain't gotta
pimp to get it." He hears the words leave his mouth in his head,
knows he said them the first time, and then spouted on till he'd
convinced Tyron to do the deed. It was easy. 'One strike gets us a
sled and elevates us the rest of school, blud. Then we outta here,
down to Hollywood, man, do some rappin, some actin, be whoever
we wanta be, Ty. I heard Chris say the gets around five large.'

Tyron stares at Audrey, now sitting next to Baker on the
bench. "Five grand gets us respectable treads." He's talking to
himself, figuring it out. "We be legally stylin by the weekend if we
did the hit this week."

Billy shudders, glares at Ty. He said the exact same words
he used the first time they was here, like Billy'd gone on convincing
him, like the first time, even though he was sure he only just said,
"Maybe..."

And like a brick to his head he gets it right then. The

twisted freak screwed him. Finnegus Boggs sent him back to after he wagged on about hitting Lucky Liquors. Flash of rage, at himself, really, makes him sweat. His wish to go back to "right when we sat down and Tyron and me started talking about doing the hit." Now Billy has to tell Ty the crap he was slinging in the lunch line was brain dead, without being marked a pussy. If Ty nails him for slinking, the hit will be left dangling, and Ty'd always be angling, and one day maybe even convince Billy doing the deed was righteous.

"Hold up, home. I'm razzin ya, Ty, just yankin yo chain." Billy don't sound near as chill as he wants to. He feels dizzy, like he might puke, looks around the room for a grip. Michelle sits on the bench across from Audrey. She'd been good, but not as good as she thinks she is, or his brother had shouted. "Ya spoutin wisdom bout brotherabe. Dickhead's a dropout, base-baked ex-con with his head so far up his ass he don't see he's goin nowhere. We prowlin to score treads, blud? We don't need to be thievin like Chris, or pushin crap like Baker to get one."

"Where we gonna be our last year here with no wheels, home?" Tyron talks to Billy but stares at Audrey. "And we don't have time to earn the dime to cruise outta here by graduation. How we gonna get us the goods without no cash?"

"I don't know, man. Find a junker and rebuild it. Ask Coach, or Principal Conner to turn us on to a payin gig after school couple days a week. Pull better grades and we won't need no car to break out. Ms. McClellen says scholarships are a one way fast pass outta here." Billy glares back at Tyron who's eyeballing him like he spinning jive. "I'm serious, Ty. Nixin treads for now beats endin up with records, or in juvie, or one of us capped."

Ty scrunches his big bushy brows together, like he's trying to figure Billy out. "What sup, blud? Ya fried or wiggin or what?"

"We ain't doin the hit, home. Be Chris' bullshit idea and we ain't doin it."

"Ya put it on the table and now ya wussin on me?"

"I ain't wussin. I finally got it right. A car ain't gonna prove who we are, Ty. And it ain't no sanctuary to save us from here. We gotta do that— by gettin it on with how things is— workin for somethin, at being somethin other than just blattin on like we been doing, blud. Jackin Lucky Liquors just proves we dickhead losers like Brotherabe. No crime, no time— live long and large down the line if we do it right." And suddenly Billy flashes on the afterimage of his signature on the translucent screen and remembers Boggs saying, "…to get what you truly desire, Billy, you'll have to make better choices. You are the god of your own destiny." And Billy smiles right then, and can't help laughing, till Ty's eyeballing him mostly shuts him up. "I finally get it, blud. We can be whatever we want, man, have the life we want. We really do get to choose."

Outcome [of Choices]

❖

Chris Connolly was killed in an attempted robbery of Lucky Liquors later that week. The Chinese owner had recently armed himself after being robbed to his insurance limit. Billy got his brother's Dodge Charger and his job at Costco. He advanced quickly from stock boy to cashier while finishing his senior year at Castlemont High School.

His final English assignment was to write a short story. Billy considered blowing it off, be satisfied he'd turned his F to a C this last semester. He played with the idea of writing the story of Finnegus Boggs. He'd never spoken of that night, not even to Tyron, afraid he may be crazy. Half the time Billy could blow it off as just a dream, the other half he was sure his night with Boggs had happened.

It was Ms. Mallory that talked him into submitting a story, pumping him up about his stellar storytelling on recent assignments. He considered it a parting gift to his high school English teacher for helping him catch up without making him feel stupid. Writing about what happened that night was hard, getting the words to even make sense. He wrote and rewrote night after night till he got it out of his head and on the page right— made the tale seem possible, almost real. Of course, everyone in class thought it was made up, but most agreed, even applauded along with Ty when someone said Billy should write a book of "Twilight Zone fairy tales" to sell online.

Ms. Mallory proudly serialized his short story in the Oakland Patch where she worked as an editor part time. It was picked up by the Associated Press as a feel good story, and published nationally. Billy got offers from colleges all over the country for full scholarships to their writing programs. He finished his first novella, *Fractured Fairy Tales of the Twilight Zone* during his four year free ride at NYU. His book was picked up shortly after graduation, along with a three book deal from Random House, and a movie deal from Dreamworks for a screenplay and the rights to *The Tales of Finnegus Boggs—Confessions of a Marid, Djinn.*

—

Bored after Billy took his brother's job at Costco, Tyron got an afternoon job at a neighborhood preschool on Coach Russo's recommendation. Tyron's years of experience helping care for four siblings made him well suited for the childcare role. He quickly became a surrogate father to the many kids at the Sunshine Day School without dads— fathers that had left, or like his, were barely seen.

Mrs. Jackson, the director of the preschool, was so impressed with Tyron's rapport with the kids, and his talent for assisting her and the staff with all things technological, she recommended him for a state-funded childcare management certificate program. He was scared to take a test after barely graduating high school three months earlier, but chose to attend the program with Mrs. Jackson's pushing, and a shove from Billy in a text sent from college in New York assuring him it was his ticket out of there, where Tyron still lived with his mama on the rim of the Hood.

Tyron did not leave Oakland on his 18th birthday as he'd planned. He attended night classes at Laney JC in early childhood development after graduating the childcare program with honors. He got his Master's in Education at Stanford four years later. His thesis outlined the inequity and racial bias in our education system, then introduced a K – 6th grade STEM learning platform he was developing with fellow graduate students that dynamically detected bottlenecks in learning, then alters the presentation of material to improve engagement and retention. No elementary school or even college student, regardless of location or socioeconomic status would need fall behind with Growing STEM Online.

A year after graduation, with generous financial support from Billy and his Hollywood friends, Tyron and his team launched their online STEM education platform. With documented learning outcomes over 90% in most cases, even with low-performing students, the program was adopted for public schools nationally within a year of launch. Today, Growing STEM Online helps balance inequity in the early learning experience, educating kids, regardless of where or how they learn, in science, coding, math, on their own level, allowing them to achieve beyond their per-conceived limits and be whoever they choose to be.

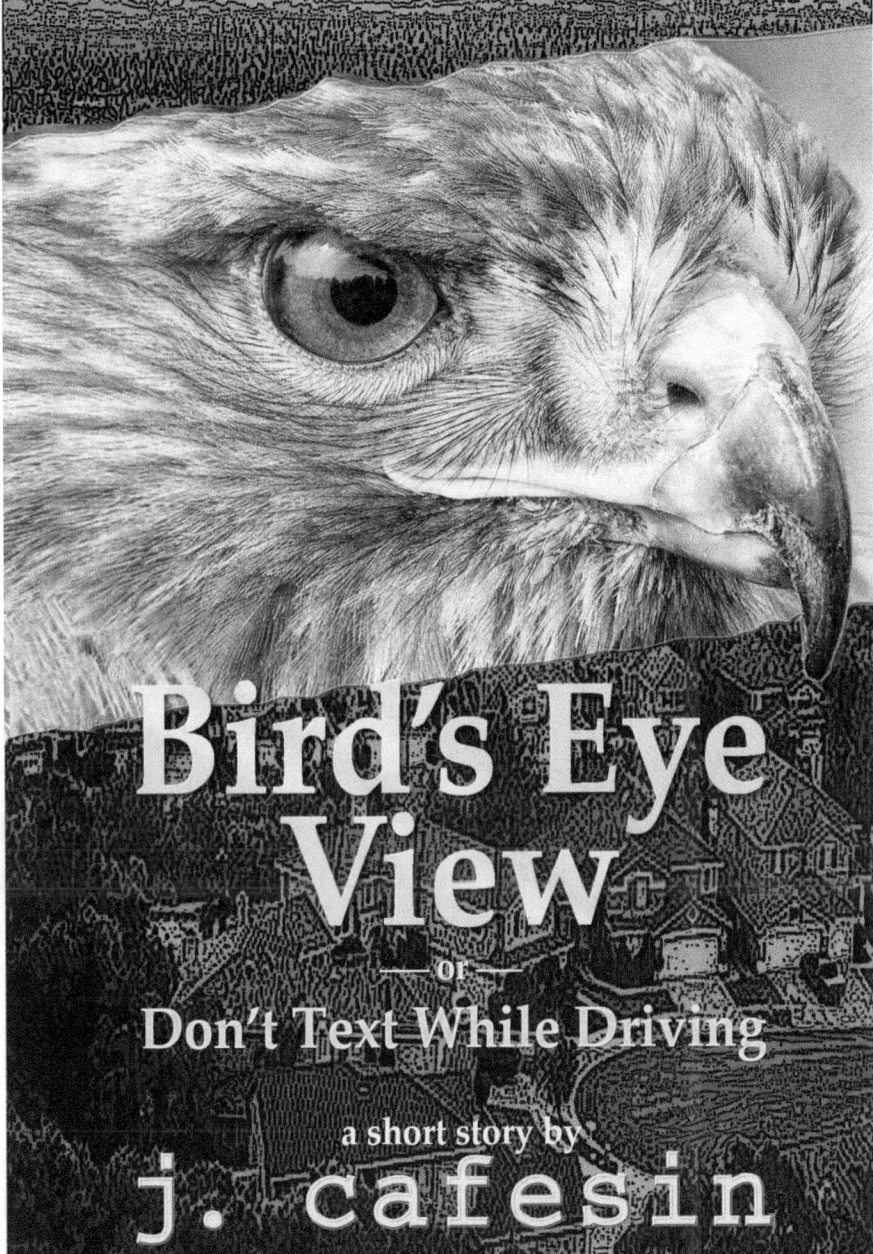

Bird's Eye
View

— or —

Don't Text While Driving

a short story by

j. cafesin

Bird's Eye View

or

Don't Text While Driving

Hawk

He spots his first meal in days from up high above the treetops. The gray furry mass hops across one of the open patches of green below, *always* green around the big hollow nests that popped up like mushrooms many cycles ago. Lazily riding a thermal, Hawk watches the prey feed on a line of flowering plants.

"Damn it, Mitchell!" Familiar high-pitched screeching drifts up from one of the creatures in the hollow nest on the green below. The furry gray prey freezes. "I told you *green tea*, not Tetley."

The prey springs up on its hind legs and turns toward the hollow nest. Even from up high Hawk can see its nose and whiskers twitching.

"What the hell's the difference?" Lower, deeper screeching comes from the opening in the invisible wall of the nest. "Can you *please* keep this door shut? It's freezing in this house." Then the creature is there, in shadow— long and narrow— behind the clear wall, closing the gap. Screeching fades to soft chirps sealed inside their hollow nest.

The prey goes back to feeding. Clearly, it too has heard the creatures screeching and chirping at each other before.

Stretching his wings all the way out to the tips, he angles them to earth and glides downward, silently closing in on strike range. Hawk likes the early light best for gliding, effortlessly riding the warm circular currents, cutting the morning chill with the rising sun. And prey comes down from the hills with the light in search of easy pickings off the brightly colored foliage that line the green patches of the hollow nests.

Flexing his talons as his prey strips a plant of purple flowers, Hawk circles into position, tilts his five primaries towards the sky, tightens his secondaries for greater speed and control, and dives. Still tree lengths from his prey he hears screeching again.

"...won't be there? I told you four times the amnio is at 1:00." The high-pitched creature from the hollow nest is suddenly at the clear wall opening it.

The prey sits upright, jerks its head towards the hollow nest, setting up Hawk for an easy kill.

Take it on the back of the neck and it'll never see me coming...

"Do you actually hear *anything* I say?" Screeching is clear, sharp. Close!

An instant from the kill and the prey suddenly hops under a plant and vanishes from view. Hawk barely misses crashing into the flowering bushes. His talons clip some leaves before he tucks them in as he returns to the sky.

"Wow... Look at that. The hawk is back, Mitchell." Screeching fades as he rises.

Hawk catches a thermal, and rising up on the warm air he circles back around, scanning for his prey to reappear. Unlikely. Even if it hadn't seen him coming, the screeching inside the hollow nest continues and is clear even up above the treetops.

"I told you to keep the damn door shut. It's 45º outside!" The bigger creature appears at the opening in the invisible wall, and with five long, clawless talons closes the gap without looking up at Hawk, then disappears inside their hollow nest.

The smaller creature stays by the invisible wall staring up at Hawk gliding. Its big, round brown eyes are on him, tracking him as he circles above. He knows these eyes, has seen them watching him many times, along with the longer creature inside. They used to stare up at him from the green patch beside their nest at the end of long light days. He'd not seen them since the cold set in, many light cycles past.

The smaller creature opens the wall again and steps out of its nest and onto a patch of gray stone. "I want to get away. I want to flyyy away...yeah, yeah, yeah..." Melodic chirping, like songbirds come from the creature's mouth. It's big eyes watch him, but he's safe above, able to move freely in the sky, sated that the spreading blight of long, narrow creatures below can not yet fly.

Megan

The hawk almost looks arrogant, effortlessly soaring above. I wish I could see its eyes (as it can most assuredly see mine with its enhanced vision). I'm certain they'd have the same proud 'twinkle' as Mitchell's.

"Where do you want to fly to, Megan?" Mitchell comes up behind me. He doesn't touch me. I wish he would, but am glad he doesn't. If he did, I'd crumble.

"Hawaii. Cozumel." I turn to look at him, eye to eye. "Even a weekend in Monterey would be nice."

"You know I can't get away right now, with the—"

"Telephonica deal," I sigh. "I know. Doesn't matter, I guess. Going somewhere else probably won't be any different from here. The rare occasions we're together lately, you're not really with me anyway."

His expression darkens, thick brows slightly furrowed. Eyes veil. I've lost him. Again. He's crawled into himself with my contentious rejoinder. "I'm going to work."

His words hurt, sharp, piercing. I shiver from the cold outside and in, desperately searching for something to say to get him to stay. We could talk. Find a space to connect again. Make love until mid-day, then take BART into the city for Dim Sum like we used to. I'm conjuring this outcome as I watch him turn and walk away.

Mitch disappears into the house without even glancing back. Vertigo with the cognitive dissonance— simultaneously relieved he's left and we've avoided a fight, yet suddenly reminded how inconceivably lonely I feel. I'm pushing him away, but don't know how to stop, wanting so much more than what we've settled into.

We met in Psych 101. He took the class to find out how we think, to help him figure out how to create software that modeled the brain with algorithms. I was there to discover why we feel, and better understand our emotions to become a more effective teacher. Our first 'date' he asked me to Drakes beach, and after a long walk and great talk along the shore, I discovered I was there to record the launch of his latest mini-drone. He was testing the remote control for distance, and planned to fly it to Sausalito and maneuver it to look into windows of homes, storefronts and cars. And he really didn't get why it was completely inappropriate, regardless of his need for *'proof of concept.'* If nothing else, Mitchell's never been boring.

Something rustles in the bushes. A gray fluffy fat rabbit hops out and freezes just under the hedge. It's beady black eyes stare at me. Damn rabbits. They eat all the herbs, strip all the flowers. City rats of the suburbs. "Get! Scat!" It scurries back into the bushes.

I hear the hawk cry from above and look up. He's circling over our lawn. I smile with the connection. He's here for the rabbit. "Have at it, hawk." And I exit the scene to let it play out.

Go back inside wondering if the hawk has a mate and chicks back in his nest. I read somewhere hawks mate for life. I ponder their primal relationship, revel in what I imagine to be glorious simplicity, devoid of the complexities people create.

I've spent the last 5 yrs of our marriage missing my husband. Weekend road trips and nightly talks have become scheduling each other since he's joined MoblX to grab the start-up brass ring. And even with a baby on the way, the chasm forming between Mitch and I isn't worth the anticipated financial windfall. The hall is narrow, and dark, and mirrors how I feel as I go to our bedroom to get dressed. I'd rather live minimally than lonely.

Clicking of computer keys practically stops my heart as I come up on the guest bedroom Mitch converted into his home office. He's sitting at his desk, but focused on his laptop and doesn't see me standing in the doorway. "What are you still doing here?"

"I had to back up some files I was working on last night." He shuts the laptop and stands, unplugs it and buries it in the leather briefcase I gave him for his 35th birthday last spring. "I'm going now."

Perhaps Fate is giving me another opportunity to communicate with my husband. "I'm sorry for what I said outside. It's just...well, am I the only one here having a problem with what's happening between us?"

Mitchell's shoulders sag, his lanky form weighted by my words. "Do we have to get into this now? I have a meeting with Steve at 9:00. I need to leave."

I'm chilled again, wishing I was dressed already, wearing more than just Mitchell's flannel shirt. "Why are we always back here, Mitch? Until I turn into a raving bitch, I'm at the end of the line for your time and attention. Why am I always your *last* priority?"

"What do you want from me, Megan?" His delivery borders irate. "I negotiate an hour of traffic to get to work every day to then deal with everyone's petty little issues at the office all week long. To accommodate you that I'm home most nights, I have another hour of traffic to get back here and then work all night, to get up at sunrise and do it all again. The baby isn't due for another four and a half months and I'm already exhausted."

"Well, so am I Mitchell. I teach three classes a day—"

"But you don't have to. We're doing fine. You can take leave any time. I'm making enough now to support us, *all* of us. I don't get what you're waiting for if you're still on the page of staying home with the baby the first few years."

Dead silence between us every second I don't respond. I suddenly feel naked under his scrutiny and pull at the bottom of his shirt to hide the crotch of my black satin panties. "I just want to make sure we have enough, you know, that we're all taken care of in case anything happens..." I hesitate, afraid I've hurt him again.

"Yeah, I get it. You're afraid I can't hack it, I'll screw up and get fired again, or worse, quit when I get bored. Well, let me tell ya, Meg, I'm already bored. Out of my friggin mind. I have been since getting pigeonholed into management instead of doing development."

"I know, Mitchell, which is why I'm not sure taking a sabbatical right now is a good idea. You tell me virtually daily how much you hate your job. Quit, then. I'd rather live tight until you find something you like than have you pissed off, exhausted, and on your damn cell the rare times you're around."

He looks at me like I'm clueless and shakes his head. "I'm not quitting, Megan. We've been over this. We agreed no latchkey kids if we could afford it. Well, we can. And even without the pending IPO, I make three times what you do, so I can't be the one staying home with the baby. Maybe walking away from your career to play mommy is the *real* issue here?"

Ouch. He's right, of course. It's hard to fathom, how, without paying attention, Mitchell is usually dead on about me. I'm momentarily humbled. It's fleeting though, knowing my husband's trick of diverting the conversation away from the real issue, this time by directing the focus of our exchange onto me. "Yes, Mitch. I feel scared of becoming a mom, and a teacher to just our child for the next few years. I have no idea how you feel about being a dad, though. Love to talk about it before you disappeared into your office. Any night this week is good."

He shakes his head and shoves a few more papers in his briefcase, retrieves his leather jacket from the back of his swivel chair and puts it on. Even with my blood boiling with irritation from his lack of response, he's still adorable, his black T showing off his muscular build, blue jeans hanging loosely on his hips, kept up with a thin brown belt. He's watching me, his full lips set in a pout. He pushes his wire-rim glasses into place and picks up his briefcase. He'll walk out the door this morning with issues between us left dangling one more time. I'll text him later, apologize for this morning's rancor, share how I feel again, why I said what I did. We'll have our typical text exchanges throughout the day, but his responses will be short, with promises to discuss in depth at home later. But I'll likely be asleep by the time he gets in.

"Text me after the amnio and let me know how it went." He gives me a peck on the lips and passes me in the hallway. "I'll be home late, after 8:00. We have a presentation to Samsung this afternoon at 4:00, and the wrap up meeting directly after will be at least an hour or two." He stands at the doorway threshold, not two feet from me, his striking green eyes are on me but hard to see behind the glare of his glasses.

Pull me in. Hold me. Kiss me... But he doesn't.

Mitchell

I want to tell her that I'll miss her tonight, that I'd rather be home then on the freeway late at night hoping not to get shot in some gang initiation, or into a collision with some idiot driver on their cellphone. I want her to know that I too miss spending time together, making dinner and sharing our day over the meal, then hanging out and watching TV before bed, her head in my lap, stroking her hair, silky like a cat, and as relaxing to pat. "Have dinner without me. I'll pick up something at the office or when I get home."

Her full lips frown. Her crystal blue eyes darken. I feel the weight of her disappointment, and the magnetic pull of her longing, but I have to go. It's past 8:00 and if I don't leave now I'm going to be late. I move down the hall.

"Why come home at all? Avoid the commute and sleep with Steve at the office. You're already in bed with him way more than me, honey."

I open the front door and look back at Megan, now moved into the office doorway. Her eyes pierce me. She looks small near the end of the hallway, her slight build hardly showing signs of pregnancy yet. Her slender legs reveal a gentle curve of muscles under her smooth skin and proffers her physical fitness. Her determination not to cry in front of me proves her inner strength. She is as beautiful as the day I met her, and I flash on her long tawny hair moving like a wave around her as she turned to look at me in the Rodin Sculpture Garden on that windy day at Stanford twelve years ago.

Hawk & Mitchell

High up, way beyond the treetops for a wide view, Hawk searches for prey. This morning still holds the chill of the dark days and he wants to be nesting instead of hunting. But a deep longing, an ache in his chest and emptiness in his belly had him take flight with the glowing sky. Hawk's mate left him to nest with a rival. Had he been paying more attention to her than his love of soaring, he probably wouldn't have lost her.

Hawk spots the furry creature from earlier, venturing out from under the line of bushes. It moves onto the green patch of the next hollow nest in the row. He circles out of the warm thermal, angles his wings for maximum speed and dives. The small gray meal stops in the center of the green, sits up on its back legs, its nose and whiskers twitching. No way Hawk will miss this time.

He angles for the back of the neck, flexes his talons wide. The prey jerks its head around towards Hawk just as he digs his claws into the mass of thick fur.

The prey screeches and jerks but Hawk holds tight and lifts it while it kicks and claws at the air. Heavier then expected, it's hard to hold on to, squirming in his talons and throwing him off balance. He struggles to hang on to the fluffy mass, furiously pumps his wings for lift. The prey in his claws stares up at him with small, round black eyes. He digs his claws deeper, closing them into skin. He takes no pleasure in the killing. The victory is in the eating.

—

I see a hawk above Howard's house as I'm getting into my car. It has something in its talons, a kitten or rabbit maybe, and it's flying erratically, trying to rise and hold on to whatever it's got. I know how he feels, and I smile to myself at the analogy.

Meg mentioned she saw a hawk this morning. Maybe it's the same one we used to watch riding the evening thermals from the lawn chairs in the back yard last summer. I can't help but smile with the sweet memory of holding hands under the emerging stars, watching the majestic bird's striped wings spread six feet wide as the raptor soared casually on the rising heat of the day.

I back the Prius out of the driveway. Put it in gear and see the hawk fly off awkwardly towards the hills I'm about to enter on my way to work, his meal still dangling from his talons. Only then do I realize I've left the house without having any breakfast, and feel a flash of anger at Megan for diverting me from my routine this morning. My grumbling stomach fuels my grumbling thoughts. Want more of my attention, Meg? Well, so the hell does everybody else. I've got to *be* there, plugged in, aware, and accessible 24/7. Startups are not the cloistered life of an academic, my dear.

I picture Meg in my office doorway at the end of the hallway watching me leave this morning. She seemed far away, like confirming the distance she'd said was between us. Flash on her blue eyes, dimmed with disappointment I had no time for her this morning. I get that she was scared, probably over having to face the amnio alone today. It's just routine, since she's only thirty-three and in good health. More for peace of mind than anything else. I'd been with her to a few ultrasounds and the baby's developing just fine. Meg doesn't really need me there. Still, I could have checked my schedule and slated the presentation for another day. And even through my ire, I feel the weight of my shame.

—

The prey still screeches and twitches in Hawk's talons making it difficult to fly. He's never been very good at air to ground attacks. Too hard to get lift after making the strike. He generally sticks to above the treetops and goes after smaller prey. Easier to go for lessor winged meals, or pick off the tree climbers if he gets really hungry, though they've become harder to find since the trees started disappearing with the screeching creatures hollow nests began blanketing the earth.

It's more than just a matter of pride to hang onto the meal. He must bring it back to his nest to show off his superior skill, to impress a mateless female and entice her into nesting with him, put an end the perpetual hollow that came when his mate left. Hawk's been seeking a new mate for some time. He misses the warmth, and the pleasure and power of coupling. The two of them becoming one, he was able to fulfill his function of reproduction. Can't blame her for leaving, really. He was hardly there to protect her while he soared all day, patiently waiting for in-flight kills and small prey to climb up what was left of the trees.

—

I catch sight of the hawk barely hanging on to whatever it's got as I drive up the steep slope of Norris Canyon. The bird follows alongside the highway, probably on the way back to his nest with his grand catch, if he can hold on to it. I still can't make out what the gray mass is, but it hangs low, nearly touching the earth as the hawk flies along the hillside. I wonder if he's taking the meal to his mate and chicks, if he ever feels afraid, like I do, and weighted with the responsibility of being a father, and the sole provider for the next few years.

It's more than just assuring we're taken care of, it's a matter of pride hanging onto this job, proving I can, and not just to Meg. But she's right, of course. Truth is, I've been leaving her lonely for years now, way before MoblX, maybe forever, since I tune out and into my head so often. I've always done it, drove my mother nuts, though she pridefully jokes it was a sign of genius.

I'm no genius, mom. I'm selfish. You let me be. Meg lets me too, but she doesn't deserve it. I'm failing my wife, like your husband did you, and me too, mom. I'm giving more of myself to my career than my marriage.

She said this morning she wants to take a vacation together. But *when?* Steve would have a meltdown if I took off right now, but it's highly doubtful he'd fire me. He needs me more than I need him. And it occurs to me that it's probably the same between me and Megan, except the other way around. I rely on her strength, her vision, her wisdom. She's a beautiful, accomplished woman, and even with a kid could likely get most any guy she wanted. I'm the nerd that never dated, and I still feel awkward around most women. A sudden wave a panic I could lose her stops me from breathing for a second.

—

The prey stills and Hawk pumps his wings with renewed vigor. Clearing each rolling peak is a monumental effort, straining his wings to their limit, feels like he's snapping his tendons, flattening every feather and closing them together for greatest lift. Hawk's sure he can clear the next slow rise, almost back at the nest atop the tallest red bark tree, but then the furry meal in his talons suddenly starts screeching, kicking and clawing again.

———

Something falls from the sky to the hillside on my right and I see the hawk swoop around, almost vertically on one wing, and catch it again, sweeping it off the grassy plateau. The bird manages to hang onto what I can now see is a rabbit as it lifts away from the hills, moving over the road ahead of me and up the canyon— the easiest route over the rising hills.

"Wow!" I say aloud, wishing Megan was with me to witness this. And I'm struck with a wave of sadness by the truth in what she said this morning about how separate we've become.   Then the hillside was suddenly directly in front of me and I swerved to avoid hitting it, over-correcting and crossing over into the oncoming lane just barely missing colliding with an SUV before I get back into my own lane.

I see the SUV driver flip me off out their sunroof in my rear view mirror. My heart is racing, though I'm not. I drive slowly, glad no one's behind me getting pissed at my pace. My palms are sweating greasing the wheel. A different turn of the wheel—a flip of the coin—and I could have killed someone, and/or be dead.

What is the sum of our lives if our only impact with those

we purport to love is contention? What is the point of amassing wealth if I lose my wife in the process? It's time to start making Megan my priority. And from the 10,000 ft level it's suddenly strikingly obvious what I need to do. I retrieve my cell from the outer pocket of my briefcase on the passenger seat and slide my finger across the glass surface to unlock the phone, then call home. Coming out of a sharp curve I spot the hawk again. The rabbit still dangling from his claws, he's maybe 30 ft above the road and 50 ft ahead of me, but I'm gaining on him fast.

—

Though still again, the weight of the prey in his talons feels like it's pulling them out. But Hawk's not letting it go. This kill matters. Keep this fat meal and prove to his next potential mate that he can hunt for the best, feed them when need be, and be with her at night in the nest. He's ached for his life-mate and her flock since she left. Now with another, she's stronger than he is without them. Hawk can now see that strength is not diminished, but gained with a mate and family.

—

Megan must be in the shower because her phone goes straight to voice mail. I bring up a text screen and begin typing. 'I LOVE U!! Sorry 4 this morning, and all these yrs. Im here w u now! Fly away with me—'

A loud thud and the front windshield shatters. I slam on

the breaks and something rolls off my hood and onto the road in front of my car as the Prius goes into a tailspin, and I catch a glimpse of something gray and furry scampering off the roadway as I careen off the steep edge of the hillside embankment.

Megan

My parents and brother tell me it's twisted I haven't erased the text message from Mitch yet. It's been *two years*, everyone I know has some need to keep reminding me. Beth is twenty months in September. I see Mitchell in her, her pouty lips, her almond eyes, set wide and vibrant green like his. She lines up her toys and Lego blocks in perfect rows. I wonder if she'll be a math wiz like he was.

I miss him everyday. Mostly all day still. Family and friends tell me I should go back to teaching, maybe get back into research, but Mitchell and I agreed no latchkey kids if we could afford it. Between his personal life insurance and the stock payout from the MoblX IPO, I can afford to stay home with our daughter, bond with her these first few years of her life instead of relinquishing the joy of raising her to some daycare.

Most days are filled with parks and play dates, trips to museums, the city, hikes in the Marin Headlands. I want to turn Beth on to her world. Like Mitchell, she craves stimulation. It was one of those great things about him. I loved his curiosity, and work hard at promoting our daughter's. We talk all the time. Question. Wonder. I try and be the mom Beth needs me to be, and the mother Mitchell believed I would be.

Writing helps me through most nights. I'm on the sequel to my bestseller *Making the Most of Your Relationships*. This new one, *Love Them While You Can*, goes over the difference between just *saying* we care—passing in the hall, or at the kitchen table on our cells or tablets—to *actualizing* love. It delves more into lifestyle organization with how to create focused, intimate time for each other in our busy lives. It give specific steps to consistently being there for the other, with trust building exercises that continually nurturing the relationship. Sharing the experience of living turns out to increase lifespan, overall health, and reported happiness.

Replayed my last scene with Mitchell a thousand times (a day sometimes), see the hawk circling, wonder if he ever caught that rabbit, brought it home to his mate and chicks. I imagine them cozy in their nest, feel envious, then the profound longing for Mitchell, and the black awareness he'll never come home to us again. Read somewhere that Red-tailed hawks are monogamous, like people strive to be. Perhaps they've thrived for millions of years because they innately understand the magnificent power of *love*— not the word—but the *actions* required to create and maintain it.

♥ **The End** ♥

Summer camping trip

The Activation

A short [campfire] tale by
j. cafesin

THE ACTIVATION

*A cautionary campfire tale for bickering children, and
the parents who fail to silence them...*

Close Encounter

✳

"Give it!" Michael demands.

But she doesn't. Amy sits next to him in the back seat of the SUV clicking through songs on his iPhone.

"Give it back, Amy! It's mine and I want it back NOW!" She completely ignores him so he grabs it out of her hand, pulling her earbuds and her head with his phone.

"Oww, you little brat!" Amy grabs her headphones back. "These are mine, you jerk—"

"Hey! Cut it!" Dad turns their SUV onto the small road to Hindley State Park. "Amy, give your brother back his phone."

"He's got it, honey," Mom says. "It's just mind-boggling you two are still at it at your age." She doesn't look at her son behind her but turns back to glare at her daughter.

"What?! He started it." Amy glares at Michael who glares right back at her. "You're always getting me in trouble. We wouldn't even be here if it wasn't for you. I hate you."

"Amy! Not appropriate." Dad catches them scowling at each

other in his rear view mirror.

Michael leans toward his sister. "I hate you right back," he says, louder than he wants over his father's protest.

"Knock it off! Both of you. Apologize to each other." But they don't, knowing there will be no repercussions. Dad sighs, shakes his head in disappointment as he slowly passes through the park entrance, the fee booth already abandoned for the day. "Your mother's right. Twelve and fourteen is way old enough to stop this incessant bickering." He follows the loop road that leads to their usual campsite. "Be cruel and thoughtless to each other long enough, and you'll create a chasm between you won't be able to bridge."

It's after 7:00, but still light out so close to summer solstice. Horizontal bands of golden sunlight filter through the huge redwoods. Dad turns into the small dirt parking area, and Michael opens the back door before his father stops their SUV.

"Michael James White," is the last thing he hears Mom say as he jumps from their car into the dust cloud from the tires as the SUV skids to a stop.

He runs along the narrow dirt path to the vacant campsite. The clearing is surrounded by a forest of hugely tall redwoods. They stand guarding the rusted barbecue, the dilapidated fire pit, and the splintering picnic table, the only signs of humanity having been there. Nothing's changed since last year. Michael breathes a deep sigh of relief then continues on towards the forest.

Deep in the old grove, the late sun lights only the treetops now, the tips of the giant redwoods glow orange, like torches, against a deepening blue sky. The rich smell of pine and dirt fill his nostrils and mouth, like sucking on candy. He moves quickly and quietly through the shadows. Warriors and wizards are surely hiding in the woods. He may be short for his age, but he's light, and fast. He runs nimbly, sprinting over fallen branches, leaves and twigs crunching in a soft, even rhythm with his quick steps.

A crackle of branches close by, and Michael senses something in the forest pacing him. He runs faster, his heart pumps harder and echos in his ears. Crunching near him speeds up too. He tears through the forest dodging massive tree trunks, the spongy ground vaulting him over small saplings, and Michael's absolutely sure whatever is chasing him is getting closer.

He spots it! Right side, through the maze of trees. Silhouette of a horse and rider. Warrior sees him, and turns his mammoth black stallion in pursuit. Michael runs faster then barrels past the last of the forest and onto the grainy white sand beach along the rushing, crystalline turquoise river. He stands gasping for breath, looking back at the edge of the redwood grove, half expecting the warrior he'd conjured to come galloping through the tree line.

The roaring melody of the river draws his attention and

Michael moves to the water's edge. Just the other side of the turbulent river, beyond the sandstone bluffs, the elk are probably grazing in the big, grassy meadow.

No crossing here. Fifteen feet is too wide, the water too deep and too fast this early in June. Have to cross upriver, or down. He scopes the area for spots where a tree's fallen, or rocks have gathered for a natural bridge.

Several yards downriver at waterline, fifty or more steely gray rocks the size of baseballs, nah, bigger, like softballs, and almost as round gather in a small inlet. Stones look almost identical in size, and kinda metallic, though the fading sunlight on their wet surface may account for that. The collection of rocks overflow around the lip of the inlet, each settling along the riverbank downstream, forming a quickly growing single beaded line. Really more deep blue than gray, the stones are worn almost smooth, with no large chips or craters. And it's really weird how round they are—

"Michael!" Amy's shriek cuts through the forest and rises above the river's song. "You'd better answer, you little freak. Dad says you're on dishes the rest of this stupid trip if you don't help set up."

Michael drops onto his stomach. He lays flat on the warm sand and peeks at his sister through the tall grass reeds that grow in patches where the sand turns to dirt. She's in her black minishorts and little red t-shirt—the one that shows her belly button. Pink streak in her short dark hair makes her look more goth than pop star. She seems so plastic to nature's grandeur all around her. She doesn't see him. Yet. He shimmies on his belly into the reeds and freezes, hardly breathing.

"Michael!" Amy passes him on a narrow dirt path within six feet of where he lay as she moves towards the river. "You'd better come on. Mom is totally pissed!" She moves awkwardly across the sand in her flip-flops. "Damn it, Michael..."

He spies her through the reeds scanning for him. She looks in his direction. His breath catches in his throat and he holds it until she looks away, towards the river. His sister moves along the water's edge, downstream a few yards. Michael has to kneel to keep her in sight. Amy stops at the waterline, staring at something. He moves quietly along the reeds' edge and stops a few yards behind her before he sees what she's looking at.

Fifty round stones have become well over a hundred, now bunched together in small inlets, and gathered along the riverbank in beaded strings. Like seaweed in the tide, the strings of rocks move in the water, gaining and losing stones with the surging river. And they seem to be...glowing, radiating a soft, blue-white light from inside of them.

Amy bends to pick one up.

"Don't!" Michael says before the word registers in his head.

His sister straightens and spins to face him. "You jerk! You almost gave me a heart attack! Where have you been? Mom is totally pissed you're not helping. Again. I am so sick of everything being about you all the time." She scowls at him.

Michael scowls right back. "You should talk, Amy, little miss teen queen. Too hip to care about anything but being popular and..." The rocks are glowing brighter behind his sister now, and he forgets the rest of his come-back.

"God! You're such a space cadet. ADHD kickin' in, Michael?" Amy shakes her head, disgusted.

"Is it puberty, or all those soccer balls to the head that's turned you into a psycho-bitch, Am?" Michael shakes with anger at her ADHD cut, which she's not allowed to bully him about.

The round rocks glow even brighter, as if they're agitated too, or activating— coming alive before his eyes.

"Get your ass back to camp and help us set up. Now!" Amy practically stomps past him, across the small beach and onto the dirt path towards the shadowed forest. She doesn't even glance back at the rocks.

Michael can't take his eyes off them. Phosphorescent blue/green lights up the water around the brightly glowing round stones, and laps along the long, waving strands of rocks overflowing from the inlets. The blue/white light inside the stones begins to fade. An instant later they're back to asphalt gray, and they no longer glow. Michael stares at them, hoping for some indication he hasn't imagined what he's sure he'd just seen.

"Come on, Michael!" Amy's shrill voice is distant, drowned out by the roaring river as she enters the redwood grove.

Michael stays fixed on the swaying strands of rocks another moment then follows his big sister. Trotting behind her sucks the fun right out of him, and the dim forest seems daunting now, the pine needle carpet feels slick under his sneakers. He's glad to see the light of the campfire through the huge old redwoods, even knowing mom is gonna be tweaked.

Actual Encounter

✳

The barbecue glows orange with hot coals. Mom pulls a plastic container from the ice chest and puts it on the portable table she's set up next to the grill. She glances at Michael as he enters the campground, then shakes her head, her expression almost a frown. "Michael James White, are you part of this family or what? Dad didn't even stop the car and you're out the door and gone."

"Sorry mom. It's just been a whole year since we've been here and it's almost grazing time and I thought maybe I'd get to see 'em at the meadow before it got dark."

"You have all weekend to see the elk. I expect a team effort in setting up this campsite. Your father and I are not your personal slaves." She says it mad, but gently. Mom has that tough outside but a soft center. Her long, wavy brown hair is pulled back but the ponytail falls forward, over her shoulder as she takes raw, dripping red chicken pieces out of the container and puts them on the sizzling hot grill.

Michael's stomach growls. He pulls the bag of corn chips amid the burger buns and condiments strewn across the picnic table. He glances around the campsite shoving chip after salty chip in his mouth. Amy has disappeared into their tent, the glow from her cellphone just barely silhouetting her lying on her sleeping bag through the blue fabric of the dome. Dad's finishing putting up the second dome tent for him and mom, setting the last of the stakes to secure it. Tall and skinny, with wire-rim glasses, and clean, white tennis shoes, dad's more nerd than mountain man. Mom fits into the scene better, in her dark flannel shirt, faded blue jeans, and old hiking boots.

Slaves or not, his parents obviously have everything under control. There's no actual reason he'd been called back from the river, and his annoyance blossoms quickly into outright frustration. He releases a heavy sigh, loud enough for mom to hear. "Well, what do you need me to do?"

She looks around the campsite. Her eyes finally stop on the fire pit. The heavier logs are just catching fire from the perfect pyramid of twigs she'd set ablaze beneath them. "Before those branches get going, find some big rocks and build a border around the fire pit. Make a nice, tight circle around the edge for a wind block to keep sparks inside."

"Think you can manage that, dude?" Dad, carrying a bottle of wine and two plastic wine glasses, winks at his son, then kisses his wife.

Michael sees them smile at each other and smiles too, though he says, "Yuk. I'm outta here." He runs off into the forest, excited to get back out to the river.

It's dusk. The sky's indigo, but the trees are silhouetted black. Michael isn't afraid. He knows his way by heart. The family has come to Hindley State Park the last seven years in a row to mark the official start of summer. This year's probably their last though, since Amy doesn't want to come anymore. She'd begrudgingly agreed to join the family, but is likely to be miserable all weekend so they'll nix the trip next year. She really is a killjoy now.

He's at the river in three minutes. The stones are still there, along the waterline and gathered in the shallows, though they don't appear to be glowing. Outnumbering the normal rocks among them ten to one, and no longer in waving strings, they fill the small coves and line the riverbank in multiple rows, clacking like pool balls as the water bumps them against each other.

Twilight is setting in and everything radiates midnight blue. Michael kneels to examine a large cluster of stones gathered in an inlet along the shoreline. They look to be granite, speckled with quartz. The glowing effect he'd seen earlier had to be from the crystals reflecting the last of the day's light. Years of flowing down rivers could account for their spherical shape and smooth surface. These rocks aren't really so strange after all.

He reaches out and pokes one. No shock. Feels like a rock. Michael snatches one, stands and examines it. It's surprisingly light, more like a Nerf ball then solid stone. It feels warm, really warm, already dry though it's been only seconds since he's lifted it from the water. He rolls it from hand to hand examining its almost metallic surface. Could be geodes, hollow with crystals inside. And all he has to do is crack it open for the treasure...

Michael hurls the stone down against the cluster of rocks in the inlet with as much force as he can. Sparks fly with the stone's impact, and continue to crawl over its round surface as it clatters across the tightly gathered rocks beneath it. He thinks he hears a low, electronic hum over the rushing river, but Micheal knows he's not imagining the noise after the rock he'd thrown settles among the others, instantly amplifying the fuzzy hum now emanating from all the round stones. The rock he'd thrown begins radiating a vibrant cobalt blue. The net of sparks over its round surface sends rogue arcs of lightning that seem to ignite the rocks it touches, which alight the rocks they touch, quickly alighting the round stones along the riverbank with sparks as far as he can see.

Run! NOW!

But Michael can't move, frozen in terror, and wonder. The hum resonating in his chest sounds almost like music, violins blending with the river's rhythm. The rocks begin pulsating, brightening from cobalt blue to white with each throb. Michael backs up slowly as their pitch gets higher, the melodic hum more a buzz now, like a swarm of bees. He continues to distance himself from the shoreline and is almost to the reeds when he feels the exposed hairs on his legs and neck rise. The stones become brilliant balls of light, like tiny suns—impossible to look at directly, then a flash of white light steals his sight momentarily.

Still standing, and seemingly unscathed, Michael forces himself to breathe. OMG! What the hell was that!? He gives a nervous laugh as he blinks back in his vision, pacing a few steps forward, then back. The ravine is dark and silent. Clouds pass by the half moon making it hard to see. Flash could have been dry lightning. Moving slowly to the river's edge again, Michael can make out many softball size rocks along the shoreline, some round, most not, and none of them are glowing. Most likely they never did — just some weird effect of lightning in the quartz. The roar of the river sings on, but the hum is gone, probably no more than resonance from the wind through the canyon.

He takes a deep breath and releases it slowly. Like the warrior in the forest, he'd imagined it all. He's being a jerk, freaking himself out again. He really has to grow the hell up, like Amy constantly nags; get out of his own head, like his mom says.

A tiny light flickers in the grove of spruce lining the cliff's edge across the river. Another tiny flicker. Then another. Within seconds there are hundreds buzzing around in the old grove, lighting up the wide trunks of the sleeping Redwood sentinels. Fireflies. They come out at twilight for only a couple of weeks in mid-June. Michael stands on the beach staring across the river taking in the magical moment. Then a sharp, cold wind whips down the ravine. A chill passes through him as the fireflies suddenly scatter and are gone. It's time to get out of there.

He strips off his hoodie and lays it on the sand, kneels and collects rocks for the fire pit from the riverbank, avoiding the oddly round ones, unable, or unwilling as dad would say, to escape his imagination. Better safe than sorry. He piles several normal rocks in his hoodie, bundles it, and then drags it back to the campsite.

The grove seems denser in the dark, and ominous in the middle. It's here where evil lurks at night, and in the real world where coyote and mountain lion hunt. Michael shivers in only his thin t-shirt, wishing he'd brought his flashlight. The glowing light from the campfire appears through the trees ahead, and he slowly releases the breath he feels like he's been holding since the weirdness at the river.

"I'm going to help him right now, mother." Amy's whining pitch cuts through the forest. "Relax. That's why we came up to the great outdoors. Right?!"

Michael clears the forest around the campsite dragging his heavy hoodie filled with rocks behind him.

"Don't talk to me that way, Amy. I don't talk to you like that." Mom stands at the barbecue flipping the chicken parts on the grill.

"Watch your tone, Amy." Dad stacks the bundles of wood he brought near the firepit. "And mom wouldn't be on you all the time if you took the initiative without us having to prod you. Where did my little go-getter go?"

"She's going to get rocks for the fire pit, dad. Oh joy." Amy's beyond sarcastic, sounds closer to snide, until she starts screaming in her shrilly girly tone while trying to shoo away a bug. She gets the bug spray from the picnic table and sprays it in the air all around her.

Michael spills the rock from his sweatshirt beside the fire pit. "You're the one that needs to chill, Amy. We are here to relax. So why don't you give it a try."

"Shut up, dork." She slams the bug spray can on the table.

"Keep out of it, Michael," Mom warns. "And Amy, you really need to settle down and watch the attitude."

"You certainly do, young lady." Michael imitates his father. Dad smiles to himself, suppresses a laugh.

Amy glares at her brother, then at mom waiting for her retort, but none comes. Michael grins at his sister.

Amy grabs the flashlight off the table and stomps into the grove without apology.

Michael follows the bouncing beam of her flashlight into the forest, runs to catch up to his sister and does so within moments but she doesn't acknowledge him. She keeps stumbling and cussing and grumbling about being out there.

Even in the dark, Michael's nimble on his feet. He's always been a good runner. Amy used to be too. They raced all the time, until he started winning. He doesn't even want to try goading her into racing as he trudges beside his sister out to the beach. Amy never talks to him anymore. And she makes him feel like everything he says is lame, so Michael stays quiet too. They make two trips to the riverbank, work in silence for fifteen minutes until they have enough rocks to line the fire pit.

Back at their campsite, Mom puts the barbecued chicken on a serving plate. Dad sets the table for dinner. And Michael is about to help Amy build the rock ring, but spies his iPhone on the end of the picnic table when dad lifts the package of paper plates off it. Battling Syphans on Bendelia is way more fun than working with his sister on the firepit.

They're Here...

✳

The great outdoors somehow makes food taste better. The barbecue chicken is sweeter, tangier on an open grill. It doesn't even bother him that the sweet golden corn he bit from the smoky cob sticks between his teeth. Stars glimmer above the black treetops, 'like diamonds on black velvet,' mom likes to say. She breaks out the marshmallows, graham crackers and chocolate bars. Even Amy can't resist. Dad hands out steel skewers and Mom, Amy, and Michael gather on the logs around the campfire while dad cleans up the remains of dinner.

S'mores are another favorite of summer, and Michael scarfs down his first sugary, gooey, crunchy creation before noticing the rock ring around the fire pit. Though he'd avoided getting the round rocks from the river, Amy had not. Several of the softball sized stones are among the irregular shaped rocks in the tight circle she'd created. Michael counts five in all, randomly placed around the ring.

The wind kicks up and fans the flames. Sparks flare and hot ash blows towards them. Mom gets up, collects the skewers and hands them to dad as Michael and Amy move to the picnic table to get clear of the smoky campfire. Mom joins them at the table, sits next her daughter, her back to the blaze to avoid the heat, since she's hot all the time now, she claims.

"TMI, mom. No one wants to hear about your aging issues." Amy scolds her mother for sharing too much.

"You're walking that thin line again, Amy. Be nice," Dad scolds, as he dries and stacks plastic dishes in the bin.

Mom scowls at her daughter, but her expression softens as she looks at her son on the bench across the table from them, waiting eagerly for one of her many excellent campfire tales.

"It was a dark and stormy night," mom speaks softly, but in a low, menacing tone, her eyes wide with wonder and twinkle with humor.

"Ah, come on," Michael protests the cliché.

"Just wanted to see if I have your attention." Mom smiles broadly and then launches into this story about going to the desert with this weird boyfriend of hers when she was younger. He'd heard there was a place where alien ships landed, and he wanted to see for himself. So she goes out to the middle of the desert with this guy, and they lie on his car hood and look at a hill in the distance at some blinking lights, and the guy is positive it's a UFO.

"But before I could convince him it wasn't," mom says, "the lights moved off the hillside towards us. And Darryl and I are off his car and get inside it as the light gets closer, and blinding. And the wind is whipping around us. Darryl puts his car in motion and we get about ten yards before he practically runs into an army jeep." The UFO turned out to be a helicopter. Darryl had mistakenly driven onto a military base north of L.A. somewhere.

Michael knew the ending would turn out okay. Mom always starts out scary and makes it safe in the end.

"That is soooo lame!" Amy sits straddled on the bench facing Mom. "I can't believe you went out with such a loser, mother. I mean, what kind of idiot believes in aliens from outer space. He probably just wanted to get you out there to cop a feel."

"Amy!" Dad interjects, standing over a pink plastic tub filled with soapy water trying to scrub the skewers clean of marshmallow with a steel wool pad. "Completely inappropriate. Apologize now, please."

But she doesn't. Doesn't have to, knowing Dad will just drop it.

"Is 'cop a feel,' like sex," Michael asks. "Or is it just sucking face, like you do with Stuart?"

"Shut up, you jerk. What is wrong with you? Are you retarded or what?" Amy glares at him across the table.

"You shut up! I was just asking a question," Michael shoots back.

"That is such bull," Amy shrieks. "You're trying to get me in trouble—"

"Both of you shut up," Mom literally yells. She's mad now. Really mad. And Michael tries to listen to the rest of her lecture on how lucky they are to have each other, but something's shimmering in the campfire just over his mother's shoulder "...absolutely must stop this perpetual sniping..."

The five round rocks Amy had set among the ring around the fire pit glow a rich, radiant blue. Michael stares at the campfire, checking this reality. The blaze is big, two feet high, three foot around, but contained in the pit. All the other rocks, the normal rocks he got, radiate a soft blood-orange light from the flames. Only the round rocks are blue, reflect no firelight, almost seem to absorb it as the light emanating from their center appears to be getting brighter.

"Mom—" Michael begins.

"I don't want to hear why it's all your sister's fault, Michael," Mom glares at him across the picnic table. "What is it with the two of you?" She and Amy face him, away from the fire, and don't see what he sees. Dad's engaged in finishing the dishes. "I can't believe you both still don't get that world peace begins at hom—"

"Mom!" The five round rocks glow red hot, though not that much brighter than the normal rocks next to them in the ring, awash with heat. They actually blend better then when they were blue, look as if they're simply reflecting more light from the campfire than the other rocks lining the pit.

Both his mother and sister turn to follow his line of sight to the campfire behind them. They both glance at it a moment, then Amy turns back to her brother.

"See! He's totally not listening," Amy whines, then looks at her mom. "And you let him get away with it. You'd be all over me if I was blatantly ignoring you and then interrupting you—"

"Shut up, Amy!" Michael yells.

"You shut up!" Amy screeches, glaring at her brother across the picnic table. "You're not the boss of me, dork!"

The round stones go from red to white, and start to vibrate, look almost blurry as they rise up slowly, and float a couple inches off the ground.

"Uh...guys..." Michael starts.

"Look at him, Mom. He's totally zoning again! I think he needs his meds now."

"Amy!" Dad and Mom yell simultaneously.

"Keep it up, and you'll lose screen time for the week when we get home," Mom says, clearly annoyed.

"Me!? Are you kidding me," Amy practically yells at their parents. "Your son is doing his zombie impression, and you're calling me out?"

Michael's suddenly aware of the melodic hum from earlier by the river, now coming from the fire pit, though it's barely distinguishable over Amy's shrill voice, or the wind through the trees. He glares wide-eyed at the floating white stones, his view suddenly blocked by his mom getting up.

"Oh, forget it. You two are just exhausting lately." Mom doesn't even glance at the campfire as she joins her husband in putting the remaining pots and utensils into the big plastic storage bin.

The round rocks seem to cool, from white hot to blue/white to glowing red, and they settle back to the ground in their place within the ring of rocks around the fire pit.

"Remind me why I'm supposed to feel glad to be here when I have to walk a quarter mile to pee." Amy grabs the flashlight off the picnic table and gets up, again obstructing his view of the fire pit momentarily. "Oh, the joys of camping are never-ending." She tramps towards the dirt path to the bathrooms beyond where they parked and down the loop road a bit.

Michael has a clear view of the campfire again, but can hardly make out the weird round rocks in the ring now. He gets up, comes around the table to within a few feet of the fire pit when suddenly a burning log topples onto the crumbling embers beneath it, sparks erupting from the blaze.

"Don't stand so close to the fire, Michael," Mom mothers.

The sparkling droplets of fire settle and the campfire's considerably dimmer. All the rocks that circle the fire pit are lit with only the softest ruby tones from the blazing embers. And none are glowing. The round rocks blend with that of the irregular stones in the ring and it's hard to distinguish one from the other.

Michael considers alerting his parents to what he's just seen, or ask his dad to come examine the rocks more closely, but then thinks better of it. He can almost hear his old man quoting Dr. Seuss: "Stop telling such outlandish tales. Stop turning minnows into whales." Mom would put her concerned face on, and then they'd bring up the Ritalin discussion, and Michael doesn't want to get into that again. No way they'll ever sell him on the notion that 'curbing' his 'overactive imagination' is a good thing.

The Activation

✳

Amy grumbles next to him as she shifts around trying to get comfortable on her blowup mat. Michael imagines floating on his as he drifts to sleep, safe in the tent under the blue plastic dome...

...then he's flying over the treetops, lying on his belly and peeking over the plastic pillow of his sleeping mat, looking down at the moonlit forest cast in blues below him. He's following an elk running full tilt through the Redwood grove. Fast and agile, it jumps over fallen tree trunks, branches, and bushes with apparent ease and amazing grace.

The massive animal clears the trees and bounds into the open ravine and then out onto the sand. A few strides and it's at the riverbank, and Michael thinks the elk will keep running, into the water and cross the river, but it stops, freezes in its tracks at the waterline.

Floating on his mat twenty feet above the scene, Michael sees hundreds of glowing softball size stones lining both sides of the river as far as he can see in both directions. The front of the majestic elk is lit from the soft glow of the stones. Its huge rack of antlers shines an eerie blue/violet as the enormous animal swings around to look behind him.

A smaller, rackless female elk emerges from the grove. She stops in the reeds a few yards from the beach, but keeps her distance from the male.

Suddenly another male elk comes bounding out of the redwood grove and into the reeds. He too, has a huge rack of antlers. The massive animal moves towards the small beach eyeing the female still standing in the reeds as he passes her. He stops several yards from the other male, holding his head high, almost proudly. A moment passes with the males eyeing each other, then the elk by the reeds bends his head, his enormous antlers aimed at the male on the beach, and charges. The attack forces the other to rise on its hind legs to avoid getting impaled. He comes down with head bent, and there's a loud cracking sound, then clacking of their antlers as the two engage in battle.

The round rocks glow brighter. They start to vibrate, almost tremble, and Michael hears their now familiar hum above the river's song.

He's riveted, awe-struck by the extraordinary scene. No fear floating on his mat safely above, silently observing. The clacking of antlers sounds like gunshots and disrupts the melodic hum from the rocks. The humming gets louder as their battle rages. The rocks glow brighter, and brighter, and Michael sees electric arcs of light crawling over their smooth surface.

The elks circle one another on the small spit of sand. Plumes of steam escape their nostrils as they both rise up on their hind legs, then come down with heads bent and smash their antlers together again with a loud crack.

Sparks flowing around each round rock arcs to connect with its neighbor, almost simultaneously connecting them all. The stones rise slowly from the water, a matrix of radiating pearls strung in a web of electricity. The dynamic system rises maybe ten feet, then suddenly scramble like pool balls struck with force, a few whizzing by Michael on the mat. Most disappear, but fifty or so realign smoothly into a perfect circle a few feet above the fighting elks. The rock ring spins slowly, strobing the elks, the river, the ravine, and the female waiting at the edge of the redwood grove. She's fixed on the spinning ring of rocks, frozen by the light, but the battling males don't seem to notice.

The rocks spin faster, their frantic, now ultraviolet pulse quickening with their pace. Michael feels his hair pull away from his skin as the blaring hum transitions into a fizzling sound, followed by a blinding flash of light. He smells something burning as he blinks back in the scene, only then realizing he's now standing on the beach. The half-moon lights the ravine in blues.

The floating, spinning circle of rocks, and all three elks, are gone.

Michael gasps, opens his eyes and deep blue fills his vision. He sighs, smiles, glad to be curled in his sleeping bag staring up at the dome of his tent. Amy snores next to him. He watches the remaining light from the campfire flicker across the thin, weatherproof fabric that separates them from the wild. His dream lingers even though he's wide awake. Michael feels scared, afraid to go back to sleep. He wishes his sister was awake and would talk to him. Even mad, she'd break the quiet space where fear lurks. He rolls onto his back on the narrow mat and accidentally nudges her.

Amy grumbles, but doesn't open her eyes.

It suddenly feels blazingly hot in his tight sleeping bag. Michael squirms to get out of it, accidentally nudging his sister even harder.

"Get off me." Amy snipes. "What is your problem?!" She practically yells. "You're four feet tall and taking up three quarters of the tent."

"I'm five foot one now, Amy. I'm not a little kid anymore. And I'll be taller than you in three years, mom says."

"Get away from me! You are such a doofus believing mom." Amy screeches as she pulls her sleeping bag around her and rolls onto her side, away from her brother. "Move over you little git!"

The campfire flares, lighting the inside of the tent in cobalt through the blue fabric dome.

Michael sits up. "You're the git!" Whatever that means.

"Grow up, Michael. Why do you have to be such a royal pain in the ass."

"Because you're such a royal bitch!" Michael growls back.

The firelight outside becomes brighter, flickers faster.

"I'm a bitch!? His sister rolls over and glares at him. "You're the one who woke me up, you pathetic piece of—"

"Shut up, Amy! Look!"

The campfire is flickering brighter than ever now. Light ripples through the blue dome, hardly dimmed by the translucent fabric.

Amy's eyes widen, then dart around the tent at the light show. "What is that?"

Michael hesitates. "I think some of the rocks you took from the river for the fire pit aren't exactly...well..."

"What!?" she shrieks.

"Rocks."

She looks at her brother like he's an idiot as she sits up. "You are so full of it, Michael."

"I'm telling you, Amy, you pulled some of the rocks we both saw glowing along the riverbank this afternoon."

His sister shakes her head at him. "It's no wonder mom and

dad want you on medication. You are delusional."

"ME?! If I'm mental, then so are you because you saw 'em too. You reached down to get one and I told you not to. You saw them, Amy. You know you did!" Michael insists.

"Shut up, Michael! Don't pull me in your warped fantasies you twisted little creep—"

"You shut up! You're the one who got those rocks and put em around the campfire, which makes you the doofas!"

Light flashes like rapid lightning strikes, seemingly emanating from the campfire. The electronic hum is back, faint but audible, and getting louder. Michael feels scared to go out, afraid of what he'll find, or what may find him.

"You hear that?" Amy's tone rises in pitch and tenor. "What the hell is that?!"

"They're the glowing rocks from the river, Amy!" Michael snaps over the increasing hum.

"Stop it, Michael!" Amy shouts, her eyes wide with fear as the hum turns to a loud fizzling buzz.

"And I think they're mad at us, or scared of us, or—"

"Shut up you maniac!" She wriggles from her sleeping bag, and moves to her knees to unzip the tent. "No one put out the campfire, and we probably just set the forest on fire—"

Campfire flares bright white and suddenly the tent is

bombarded with tiny sparks burning pinholes in the fabric dome around them.

"Oh my God! Oh my God!" Amy yells as she unzips the tent hastily, but the zipper it gets stuck on the curved corner.

"Forget it!" Michael shimmies out of his sleeping bag. "Get outta my way!" Then he's on his knees, pulling apart the opening above where the zipper is stuck.

"You idiot! You're jamming it more!" She elbows him out of her way and continues to struggle with the stuck zipper.

Michael elbows her back, harder, and continues to pull at the small opening. "You got it stuck in the first place. You're the idiot!"

Amy shoves him hard and they scuffle for position. "Stop it, Michael. NOW!"

The hairs on Michael's arms and the back of his neck raise off his skin, then a blast of heat, and light. The campfire flares so bright the tent around them literally disintegrates, the blue fabric pierced with flaring holes that extinguish to dust.

Amy screams as she brushes herself off of stray ashes like she's swatting a swarm of bugs. She doesn't stop screaming as she scrambles from the smoldering remains of the tent in her shorts, tank top and knee-high socks.

"Shut up, Amy! Stop screaming!" Michael yells after his

sister as she runs towards their parents tent at the far end of the campsite. "You're making em madder!" He covers his mouth with the collar of his t-shirt as he gets up to follow her, but pauses for one quick look at the fire pit 12 ft away.

The five round rocks glow bright ultraviolet and spin in a perfect circle a few feet above the fire pit. Lightning crawls across their surface and shoots out from their sides connecting them. Fragmented bolts fly off as electric rain from the slowly rising, and expanding spinning ring of rocks. Several sparks hit Michael's arms, but they only sting a second.

"Let's go! COME ON!" Mom can barely be heard over the now blasting fizzling buzz.

Then Dad is beside his son, shielding his eyes as he moves towards the fire pit, as if hypnotized.

"No, Dad! NO!" Michael screams, fighting the panic taking hold with the memory of his dream, and what happened to the elks. "STOP!"

"Andrew!" Mom yells, with a piercing pitch Michael's not heard before.

Dad stops, freezes actually, but is still captivated by the lightning rock ring, now six feet off the ground, spinning fast and widening slowly, the heaviest of the electric rain getting closer to them. The air twinkles with sparks, igniting the dry foliage beyond the campfire clearing.

"Let's go! MOVE!" Mom pushes Amy along, then grabs the back of Michael's t-shirt. "Andrew get the keys!" But his dad just stands there watching the rock ring. "Andrew! We need the car keys in the tent," Mom yells as she herds both kids away from the campsite towards the dirt path that leads to their car. "ANDREW!"

Dad finally turns to look at his wife, then runs back to their tent. Michael pauses, waiting for their father, but mom pushes him along. "Go! Go! Dad'll catch up. Go!"

Hot sparks of ignited pine needles whirl in the growing wind, grazing them. Amy screams, batting them away as she runs to their car. Michael can see the rock ring growing larger through the small pines lining the path. It's almost above his parents tent now, electric rain sparking some of the surrounding grove ablaze, smoke filling the crisp night air.

"MOVE! MOVE!" Dad yells as he sprints past them on the path, fumbling with the remote control on his key fob to unlock their SUV.

They come to the clearing where the car's parked and dad gets behind the wheel. The roar of the engine as his father guns it is barely audible above the crackling noise all around them now. Amy jumps in and slams the back passenger door behind her.

"AMY!" Michael, mom and even dad yell in unison. Mom

and Michael reach for the door at the same time.

"I got it!" Michael says as he pulls open the back door and gets in almost on top of his sister sitting scrunched up on the floor facing the back seat. "Move over, Amy!"

"Buckle in!" Mom yells as she gets in the passenger seat and slams the door. "Go, Andrew!"

"Make it stop! Make it stop!" Amy cowers on the car floor without moving over. Her hands are over her ears. She's trying to shut out the bizarre electric crackling.

Dad puts the car in reverse, then shifts to Drive. SUV lurches forward, and Dad barely misses rolling it as he swings around to exit the small lot. The horrible staticey buzz seems to fade with distance.

"Amy! Get off the floor and buckle in," Mom yells. Michael buckles into his usual place behind mom, pushing his sister aside with his legs to latch his seat-belt. She shoulder slams his legs. Hard.

"This is all your fault," she seethes, glaring at her brother. "We wouldn't even be here if it wasn't for you!"

Glowing embers of torched pine needles blow like snow, some smashing against the front windshield then snuffing out.

"Shut up, Amy" Michael retorts, nudging her with his legs, almost as hard. The SUV bounces along the loop road toward the park entrance. "This isn't my fault—"

"It is so! 'Michael has special needs,' so we all need to cater to Michael. It's always about you. We're here because you always get your way—"

"Stop blaming me, Amy!"

"Amy! Stop it," Mom yells without turning around, her auto-play response to sibling bickering.

"Me!? What about him, the golden child? He's the one that got us into this—"

"I did not—" Michael yells above the growing fizzling noise, suddenly audible again above their angry exchange. "YOU got the round rocks from the river—"

"Are you crazy? This isn't about some stupid rocks, you nutjob!"

"You liar!" Michael screams at his sister. "You saw the rocks glowing. Just admit it, Amy. And YOU brought em into our campsite—"

They're approaching the tollbooth at the park entrance when the windows of the small building suddenly explode. Dad slams on the brakes and swerves to avoid the broken glass. The SUV spins out of control, then screeches to a halt a few feet from the ditch along the side of the road.

"You guys OK?" Mom asks, trying, but failing, to keep the

panic out of her tone. "Everyone OK?"

Amy stares up at her brother wide-eyed with fear, but finally silent.

"We're fine, Mom," Michael says, looking down at his sister still on the floor, but behind the driver's seat now.

"We're not fine, you moron," Amy seethes, looking past her bother out the car windows just as something flashing outside catches Michael's eye.

It's raining sparks all around them, like ultra-bright sparklers, sparks are flying off the circle of 30 or more white hot round rocks now rotating above their car. Michael saw this in his dream—the glowing rocks circling above the dueling elks, then in a flash of light wiped them away without a trace.

"Why are we here? I hate it here! I hate camping!" Amy screams over the now crackling electronic buzz, her hands back over her ears. "And I hate you!" She glares up at her brother.

"And I hate you too!" Michael yells back louder, seething at his sister.

"Stop it! Both of you. Shut up!" Dad yells, as he cranks the engine trying to restart the car.

"I wanta go home! I wanta go home!" Amy's rant building in tone and temper until she's practically screaming.

"Shut up, Amy!" Michael screams at his sister. "Dad said

shut up, so shut the hell up!"

The rock circle rotates six feet off the ground, faster and faster, a dynamic stream of electricity connecting them. Sparks spin off the arcing stream, and falls around them like the Niagara river over the famous Falls, with rogue sparks hitting the SUVs windows, and the hood of their car before snuffing out.

"Oh my God—" Mom says, but is barely heard above the crackling white noise synchronizing into a deafening, yet melodic hum, and the kids incessant bickering.

The hairs on the back of his neck and his arms rise from his skin, then a searing wave of heat sucks the oxygen from Michael's lungs, and the air, then a flash of light, like a nuclear bomb suddenly illuminates the road, the trees, then bathes everything in brilliant white.

Reactivation

Eli's sure his growing headache is from allergies to the increasing wilderness outside. Dad drives the winding mountain highway with ease, controlling the sports car to hug the curves even at fast speeds. Eli sits proudly in the passenger seat, a privilege granted only because there is no back seat. Clearly, his dad hadn't purchased the Porsche with him in mind. He stares out the side window watching civilization fade away, then oaks and aspen, and then redwood trees blanket the hills. Late afternoon sun tips the treetops in bright orange, and the mountainside is lit up like a forest of fiber optics.

This camping trip is his father's penance. Mom doesn't know, but Eli heard her yelling at him on the phone through their thin condo walls for missing his middle school graduation. "You'd better set this right you sonofabitch." The next morning dad called and invited him on a father/son camp-out for the weekend.

Eli isn't too hip on camping, since he's allergic to just about everything outside, and doesn't much care for dirt, and bugs, and outhouses. He has to appreciate his dad for trying though, even if he hardly ever sees him anymore, since they stopped the every other weekend visits after Betsy moved in. The next two days Eli has his dad exclusively to himself, and he's promised himself not to complain or whine too much. He'll make this weekend so fun for both of them his dad will want to be with him, and look forward to their next trip, though Eli will try and convince his old man to book a hotel room next time.

The sun has set, plunging everything into darkness when they turn off the main highway onto the road to Hindley State Park. Eli shivers. He can't help it. The city never gets totally dark like out here, in the middle of nowhere.

"I thought there was a fire up here last year," his dad says, like he's trying to fill the silent gap between them.

"Anderson Valley has forest fires ever year but I didn't hear about any in the park. I think maybe you're thinking of someplace else." Eli doesn't bother pointing out how dense the now towering redwood forest around them with no signs of recent fire, since he's sure his father sees this too.

"No," Dad ponders as they glide around a sharp curve. "I heard it was around here somewhere." They pass the closed park entrance kiosk since his dad was an hour and a half late to pick him up from his mom's. "A family went missing during the fire," his father says. "I don't think they ever found them, or any trace of em, which is kinda weird," his dad adds, too casually to be telling a ghost story.

"They probably got eaten by bugs," Eli mumbles, but Dad shows no sign he's heard his son.

Dad drives over the rough loop road slowly. He finally pulls into a small clearing and parks. "We're here," his father says rather passively, then looks at Eli. "Ready?"

Eli was seven, the one and only time he camped up here with his parents. That was seven years ago, when they were still a family. Dad stays buckled in his seat behind the wheel and stares at his son like he has no idea what to do next. Eli's looking for direction from his dad, but his father just sits there.

"I guess we set up, Dad." Eli can't keep the disappointment out of his tone.

"Oh, right." Dad's angular face hardens. His eyes narrow and his square jaw seems even sharper with his teeth clinched so tightly. "Okay then." He sighs audibly, and unbuckles his seat belt. He runs his hand though his shoulder-length, rock star hairdo, then opens the driver's door and finally gets out of the car. "Let's get it on, and get set up."

The throbbing pressure in Eli's skull grows as he gets out of the Porsche and goes around to the back of the car where his dad has opened the trunk. It's dark, and cold, but it does smell great out here, crisp, sweet, fresh, nothing like the city.

Dad stands staring at the contents in the packed trunk, but doesn't take anything out. "Do you remember where the campsite is from here? It's all so vague after all these years." He looks around at the forest surrounding the parking lot clearing, squinting into the darkness. "Where the hell is that path?"

"We need a flashlight, Dad." Eli is trying to be tolerant. He remembers their last time here. Mom's stellar packing job meant they lacked for nothing, except Eli lost his family that trip. His parents brought him camping here all those years ago to cushion the blow when announcing their divorce.

"Damn. I think I forgot to get one of those." Dad gives his son a hollow grin.

Eli sighs, imitating his father's audible sigh. "Mom packed a backpack with a flashlight, and a lantern, and a bunch of other stuff she said you'd forget. We need to find it."

"Don't give me attitude, Eli. I'm doing the best I can here, and I don't need cheek all weekend." His father pulls stuff out of the trunk and tosses it on the ground behind him. "Find what we need, and let's get this show on the road."

Eli finds the 'back up' backpack his mother insisted he take, even though his dad had said only to bring his sleeping bag, and had promised to take care of the rest. Promises. Promises.

Flashlight in hand, Eli leads them as they carry and drag their stuff along the dirt path through the small patch of trees to the campsite.

"Slow down! I can't see!" Dad protests loudly behind his

son, disrupting the evening quiet. "Ouch! Damn it! I'm running into tree limbs here. I need some light!"

Should have brought a flashlight... Eli keeps the beam on the path in front of him so he can find their way to the campsite clearing.

"Stop! Now!" Dad yells, several yards behind him, bogged down with the tent, the Coleman stove, and the blowup mats, still in their unopened boxes. "Eli, for Christ's sake, get back here!"

Eli doesn't stop. He carries only his sleeping bag, and the backpack Mom packed. Navigating the dim path, he's sure he hears music ahead, like violins in a melodic rhythm, above his dad's whining. The sound becomes a resonant hum. He emerges into the vacant campsite and drops the sleeping bags and backpack. Wind whips his hair into his eyes, cold stinging his cheeks and cutting through his North Face jacket. Dust swirls around the rickety picnic table and the rusted barbecue. Huge redwoods rustle, and Eli realizes the hum is just the wind through the trees. He'd forgotten how nice it sounds.

"Damn it, Eli! What the hell's wrong with you?" Dad practically flings the stuff he carries down on the ground next to Eli's pile. "I told you to stop."

"Sorry, dad. Didn't hear ya." He turns to his father, shining the flashlight in his face.

"Ahh! Aim it down, fool!" Dad shields his eyes. "And don't

give me crap, Eli. I'm not your mother, and I don't buy it. Just help me set up the damn tent."

Something's shimmering in the campfire pit beyond the picnic table. Someone must have been here recently, left their fire burning. Jerks. Forests were constantly being lit up from stupid campers. Eli goes to put it out. Better safe than sorry—

"Get back here, Eli! I need the damn flashlight."

"Then you should have brought one," Eli says, thinking it's not loud enough for his dad to hear.

"Excuse me?! This is bullshit. This entire trip is bull..." His father rants while banging about in the dark to find the box with the tent.

Eli ignores him, stops a few feet from of the fire pit. No smoldering campfire. Black ash blankets the bottom, matted down from rain and snow. No one's been here for some time.

"Eli, get the hell over here with the flashlight now!"

There's a tight ring of rocks varying in shape, weathering, and shades of gray, bordering the fire pit, but five of the rocks stand out from the others.

"I swear this is it!" Dad rants on. "The last time we do anything other than share a meal for the foreseeable future, until you grow the hell up..."

The oddball rocks are softball size, and almost as round, and smoother than the normal looking stones. They're placed, what seems randomly in the near perfect circle of stones around the pit.

"...Damn it, Eli. Get your ass over here, and help me set this damn thing up!"

Eli whips around and points the flashlight at his dad. "WHY!?"

"Get the goddamn light outta my face!" His father's anger is so visceral it seems to stir the wind. Eli hears the melodic hum again, though the trees are not moving.

"You get the hell outta mine! Set up the tent. Don't. I don't care what you do! I don't even wanta be here. And neither do you!" Eli turns away from his dad, faces the fire pit again. And whether from the last of the twilight, or a reflection from his flashlight, or just his imagination, it seems to Eli as if the five oddly spherical, smooth gray rocks are, well, glowing...

✦ The End ✦

THE
MORALITY
POLICE

A fractured fairytale by

j. cafesin

The
Morality Police

These cops travel slivers of light to right moral infractions...

The Piano Man

Lush, rolling green hills all around her, Faith hears a piano in the distance. She strolls on a narrow dirt path, watching the tall grass ripple in the wind. Except there is no wind. Cloudless sky is ultra-blue, almost too blue, vibrating in sync to the haunting piano piece, rising and cascading. The song's familiar. Faith is sure it's one of Billy's ballads, but made darker.

She hears the music before she sees its source. Standing on a rise, she scans the rolling hills to horizon. Landscape is barren, only a couple of trees in the entire 360° view. Just endless rolling hills blanketed in rich chartreuse, and Faith notices the grass is swaying with the sweeping tune, like it's in sync, too.

Another quick scan and she sees the huge black, glossy grand piano, lid propped open, not twenty feet away. Piano bench is empty, but as she approaches Faith notices a man, well, sort of, more like a projection of a man sitting at the grand playing the eerie tune. He's in top hat and full tux, with tails that fall over the bench behind him. He sways with the music he creates, in sync with the vibrating sky and swaying grass. Still on the path but only six feet from the piano now, she can see straight through him, his image breaking up then solidifying like a bad video connection.

The piano man turns to her, and with a flick of his head rolls the top hat down his arm to his hand, then gives her a big, happy smile, like he's proud to have pulled off the trick. "Sylvester McBean, Morality Police, at your service, Faith Taylor." He's young, late 20s maybe, brown hair cropped short on the sides but left long on the top. He's cute in an old-fashioned, beatnik kind of way. "But first, I am compelled to present to you... *reality*." His smile fades, then he sweeps the hat toward the silhouette of a couple sitting on a blanket atop the next soft hill along the path thirty or so feet away.

She hears Billy's laugh, deep and resonant as his exquisite voice. Then hears a woman laugh, in that coy way women do when they're flirting. And suddenly Faith is next to them, still on the narrow path but only feet from their blanket now, watching Billy kiss a goth girl— black hair, black clothes, black eyeliner, probably half his age, the same age Faith was when he first kissed her. The girl fixes her dark eyes on Faith over Billy's shoulder when they separate, her china white skin practically glows with her twisted grin. Then she joins him in watching the sunset.

A sparkling animated sun with a video of a baby's face in the center giggles as it sinks behind the green hills. Only then does Faith realize the piano has stopped. She looks for it but it's gone. She looks back at Billy and the goth girl. They're gone too. Sky is blood red with the sunset, and Faith feels scared, out there all alone. Then the ground starts trembling and everything goes dark.

Faith wakes abruptly to the bed shaking as Billy slides in beside her.

The bright red numbers on the digital clock read 4:13am. Faith rolls onto her back but Billy rolls away, onto his side gathering their huge quilt around him. She considers rousing him, sure she's ovulating, but then thinks better of it. Unlikely he'll be in the mood to get it on after working all night, and likely drunk. She can smell liquor the moment he passes out and his mouth falls open. Disappointment they've missed another opportunity to make a baby, then anger. Then guilt. She's being absurd. Billy doesn't have the time to cheat on her, at least not now, in the studio practically 24/7 producing the Xone's next sensation.

She listens to his heavy breathing still chilled from her dream. It was just a dream, amplifying a fear, since Billy is a famous musician now, and still so hot, and at 31 she was so... *not* anymore, not like when she was young, fresh, tight. Faith stares at the coffered ceiling and recalls their first kiss...

Her best friend, Zoey, had presented Faith a cupcake at the Roxy for her 16th birthday during a break in the band's set. She lit the tiny candle stuck in the center of the swirl of chocolate frosting doused with colored sprinkles, but before Faith blew it out, her BF since kindergarten insisted she make a wish. But her wish was already coming true. The Xone was her favorite band, and the Roxy on the Sunset Strip her favorite club. Sure, she could have had a Sweet Sixteen party like her benevolent but clueless mom suggested, or even had a date with her pick of several classmates, but she and Zoe were *so* beyond high school boys.

The Xone came back on stage but Billy wasn't with them. A spotlight momentarily blinded her and suddenly he was standing beside her, smiling his adorable dimpled grin. He took her hand and said, "Come with me," and led her onto the stage.

Zoey whooped and hollered happy birthday wishes as Billy led Faith to the mic.

"I hear today's your birthday. How old are ya, baby girl?" Billy still held her hand but had his other around the mic on the stand.

"Old enough for you," Faith retorted, smoother than she ever imagined possible with the butterflies in her stomach and her knees practically buckling.

The audience, packed tight up against the stage laughed, but Billy didn't. He stared into her eyes as if she was the only other person in the room, nodded and smiled gently. "No doubt," he practically whispered, kept his eyes on hers for another second then looked out to the mostly young white crowd. "Let's all wish—" and he looked at her again for her to say her name but Zoey screamed it out before Faith spoke. "Let's all sing a rousing Happy Birthday to beautiful Faith here, how ever old you are, darlin."

He released her then, retrieved his black electric guitar from the stand, put the strap over his head and settled the instrument in front of him, directly over his groin, strummed it for tone then played the opening chords to the classic Happy Birthday song. Faith felt foolish but privileged while Billy, the band and the crowd sang to her. Right before the song ended, Billy stopped playing, reached his huge hand around the back of her neck and pulled her in for a passionate kiss. He slipped his tongue inside her mouth and Faith tasted liquor. But his full lips blanketed hers in warmth, his touch was gentle and made her tingle and the crowds cheering faded until he pulled back, grinned at her again, then looked back at the audience and started strumming the opening chords to *Dreamer*, one of Faith's favorites.

A bouncer came up behind her and escorted Faith off the stage. She joined Zoey, swaying with the crowd up near the front of the stage. She stared up at Billy, enraptured by the haunting ballad, his undeniable talent, and practically swooning over his brilliant prose. How was it possible for *him* to know how it feels to be searching for the perfect lover, left only to be dreaming for one...

Tears streak down the side of her face while Faith lay there staring at the ceiling. She can't recall what she thought her perfect partner would be like back then, but she's pretty sure she's not living the life she imagined. She'll be gone before Billy wakes, and back home tonight alone with him working late in the studio, pouring his heart and soul into his fifth album. She can hardly fault him for that. His passion is with his muse right now, where it must be for him to create the amazing music he does. Billy has become a rockstar.

Faith has become profoundly lonely.

Fifteen years since their first kiss on stage at the Roxy. Been married for the past ten. He'd asked her after the manic Coachella concert, when he was almost mauled by the crowd of 40,000. Billy had flown directly from the concert with the boys in the band to see her at UCLA. He had them land the chopper in Marshall's field on campus, then found her in her American Art History class in Perloff Hall where he asked her on bended knee in front of 150 students in the lecture hall to marry him.

She lay next to him now, listening to his heavy breathing, wondering if he's smoking again. Probably. He always gets self-destructive when he's cutting an album, or on tour, away from her for long stretches. She's watched him pop Desoxyn to focus, smoke weed all day to stave off the sharp edge, and drink whiskey to sleep. He ate little, slept even less for days, weeks in a row sometimes. His muse was more like a siren then, but Faith dare not mock her. Besides having no right to deny the world his magnificent talent, she knew she'd lose him if she ever got between Billy and his music.

They'd been involved since that first night at the Roxy. At the after party Billy had asked Faith for her number. He'd called her the next day. She'd tell everyone for years they talked for hours. But thinking back to that first conversation, the truth is she'd gushed and peppered him with questions, and he barely asked her anything. Through the nine months of the Xone's first national tour he called her from the road daily, galvanizing their relationship, but now Faith realizes even those calls were all about him. They broke up three distinct times over the five years before he proposed, but even knowing he was likely an addict, and truly an obsessed artist, he attracted her like a magnet, excited her like no other. And for reasons beyond her wildest dreams, Faith was the one he'd chosen to shelter him.

She gets up to pee. It's almost 5:00am, and getting light out, sagebrush and short pines on the dry hill becoming distinct through the picture window beyond the sunken tub. No point in going back to bed, cycling between disappointment, anger and guilt. On her way out of the bathroom she stops in the dressing area, pulls on her favorite worn Levi's and her torn/patched t-shirt, one of her better college designs. She crosses the hardwood floor as quietly as possible even knowing rhinos could run through the place and Billy would remain dead to the world for the next six hours.

First Reality Check
✦

Traffic's light on the 110 this early in the morning on her way into downtown. Sun is rising over the short gray/green trees amid the tangled shrubs bordering the Pasadena Freeway. At this rate she'll be at the factory by 7:30. Most everyone will have been there an hour or more already, working on the new line that has to be done for McQueen's by August, and it's already mid-June.

She catches a glimpse of the young driver of a classic teal 1960s Ford Mustang convertible in her side view mirror as it comes up along side her in the fast lane. He slows to pace her, check her out, or probably more likely to see if she's watching him. It's L.A. after all. Sun suddenly spotlights him. Adorably cute with thick dark hair cut short on the sides but left longer on top is framing a square-jawed baby face behind Ray-ban sunglasses. He flashes her a friendly smile. Jeez, he looks so familiar. She gives him a tentative smile back, trying to figure out where she's seen him before. Almost as cute as Billy. He veers away, to the right, crossing four lanes to just make the cloverleaf turnoff onto the 101 toward Hollywood.

Ah, the paths not taken... And she wonders how different she would be had she chosen someone other than Billy. She toys with the idea of being married to the classic Mustang guy, pictures their beautiful children, paints a scene of the American Dream— family, health, wealth, and happiness at the copious backyard barbecue. Back on the 110 heading into downtown, about all she's got going right now is her business, and regardless of it's critical acclaim and financial success, leaves her feeling rather... valueless.

Faith takes the 6th Street exit ramp over the freeway and into the heart of downtown Los Angeles. Tears slide down her cheeks as she moves down 6th, shadowed from the modern glass and old brick skyscrapers lining both sides of the street. She focuses on breathing, and with each quivered breath wills herself to stop crying the closer she gets to work. She's the boss, and shouldn't be a mess when she comes in.

She wipes her face on the end of her tattered T, and runs her hand through her short, thick hair a few times to tame it as she pulls into the gated lot and parks. Go straight to her office and maybe no one will notice her bloated face, she hopes, as she climbs the three flights of creaky wooden stairs to the Gilman Street Threads factory.

On the top floor of the yet to be restored 1920s brick building, Rosie, Maria and Angelina are at their stations. They don't hear her over the buzz of their machines, don't notice her until she passes them. Simon's lights are on, but he isn't in his office. Mario smiles at her from the cutting table, says "Hola, Señora." His big brown eyes reveal his gentle nature and belie his burly stature marked with gang tattoos from his youth. Faith returns the greeting as she passes on the way to her office.

She sits at her desk, opens her laptop and focuses on what needs to get done. Her mountain of work has virtually doubled recently since Valerie went on maternity leave.

Faith has been designing clothes since high school, cutting up pants, skirts and shirts then sewing them together, mixing the fabrics and creating something entirely new. Most of her threads back then were sleek, sheer, fit to her shape and a casual but feminine style. The punk/grunge thing was Billy's idea. A clothing line designed after what she'd been telling him to wear for years would not only make a fortune with his financing and endorsement but would help promote *him*.

Billy turned out to be right. Gilman Street Threads did over forty million last year, and picking up Neiman Marcus this year would lead to international fame the likes of Bono's *Product Red* campaign. Faith cringes at the notion. She's getting close to that now or never age to have kids. And she can't have them, or at least care for them running a multi-billion dollar business.

Simon taps on her door lightly. "You okay, boss?"

Faith glances at him. "I'm fine." It sounds more defensive than she meant to, and she stares at her monitor afraid if she keeps looking at him he'll see she isn't fine. "What's up?"

"Apparently not you," he says in that pissy way he does when he's annoyed. "What is going on? You look like hell. Have you been crying? Is Billy being a jerk again."

"Lay off Billy, will you Simon. I'm not up for it today. It's already been a long morning. Bad sleep last night. Bad dreams."

"Again?" Simon shakes his head. "Perhaps your psyche is trying to tell you something, boss?" He leans against her doorway threshold, tall, thin, hands shoved in the pockets of his black jeans, his tight gray tee-shirt hinting at his sleek frame under the snug black silk blazer. Chic personified. "Like it's time to cut the chord with your roguish DH."

Faith gives him a tolerant grin. "Simon, can we focus on what needs to get done here please. Do you have the sample pieces for Issac's ready to ship?"

"So, that would be a Yes on seeing something happen out of time again?"

"Simon. *Focus.*" And Faith asks again about the Issac account, and after a comment about her being snippy, which somehow translated into her not getting any from Billy again, he answers her question and they begin their workday.

Dreaming Reality
✦

The same classic teal 1960s Ford Mustang convertible stands out among the traffic in the next lane over, likely on his way home from work like Faith is. He becomes her marker for which lane's moving faster. Faith plays catch up and pass with the young male driver as traffic crawls towards the 110/101 split. He really is cute in an old-fashioned kinda way, like a 50s surfer, or a softer Elvis. He fits the car he's driving. He looks over at her, smiles when they stop side by side a moment. Flattered, Faith can't help smiling back. Traffic opens up in her lane and she moves on, losing the

Mustang behind her.

Sunset on another hot day in L.A., but the fog's finally coming in off the coast. It's after 8:00 and it's just cooling down for the night. Faith turns off the air conditioner and unrolls her window as she gets on the 210 East. The breeze tousles her hair and brushes her skin. She rolls down all the windows and the wind whips her hair around, prickling her neck, face, and shoulders. She takes a deep breath, inhaling the evening mist like a drug, focusing on experiencing the moment, feeling, being alive. For the briefest glimpse it feels like she's flying, rising above the freeway and the traffic, up into the San Gabriel mountains. But then she thinks of home, and going back there, alone, and abruptly Faith's back in her Acura in stop and go traffic inching towards the Alhambra Exit.

She checks her cell for the fifth time on the ride home, hoping Billy's texted, even knowing he hasn't. They'd spoken only once today, when he got up to go to work around 1:00 this afternoon. She was headed to a lunch meeting to negotiate with a distributor Valerie usually dealt with and couldn't really chat. Faith knows better than to call him back when he's in studio. Billy doesn't respond to interruptions in the creative process unless it's an emergency, and pretty much nothing's an emergency except death or imminent death, he's proclaimed.

By the time she pulls up their driveway off Hastings

Heights Road it's almost dark. Their seven bedroom, seven bath, three story estate home is more than Faith ever imagined, or wanted, especially for just the two of them. It looks rather daunting against the deep azure sky and the scrub trees and dwarf pines surrounding it. Growing up in a four bedroom Craftsman with two siblings in the foothills of Burbank had been tight, but cozy. Her mom and dad still lived there, still married after 42 years. Faith smiles with the memory of her father's toast at their recent anniversary party. The secret to their lasting marriage, he'd professed, was simply enjoying each other's company, and sticking it out, staying together no matter what. Well, how exactly is Faith supposed to enjoy Billy's company when they're never together anymore. And what exactly is she sticking around for?

Zoey confirming their lunch tomorrow is the only message on the house answering machine. A tearing cramp in her uterus nearly stops her on the stairs but she manages to get to the bedroom. Faith sits on the end of their unmade California King, rubbing her belly. She's ovulating for sure, can almost feel the egg moving through her fallopian tube, only to be left unfertilized and thrown out with her next period, like trash.

"Damn it, Billy. I need you." Her eyes fill and warm tears streak down her cheeks. Faith moves onto the bed and curls onto her side, wanting to roll into a tight little ball and right out of her messed up life...

...Second floor, Neiman Marcus. She's perusing the racks and hears the piano, what sounds like a Twilight Zone version of a Benny Goodman tune. The music is ominous, in a weird, boppity kind of way, and it grates. She notices Billy walking down the main aisle, which is strange because he didn't come with her today and he hates the mall. She calls to him but she has no voice, like screaming in a dream and no sound comes out.

Faith tries to catch up to him but he's moving through the department store towards the mall entrance at a clipped pace. Again she calls to him but her voice is sucked into a void before it leaves her mouth. Silence, like deafness, there is no sound. Only then does she realize the piano music has stopped.

The mall is deserted except for a very young, very hot woman on the second floor walkway strutting towards Billy. Heroin thin, in a classic little black dress and black pumps, her long blond hair blows back as if there's a stiff wind. Except there is no wind. Her perfect smile radiates white, makes her seem like she's glowing as they meet. Faith stands at the mall entrance to Neiman Marcus and watches her husband put his huge hands on the girls flawless face, and then pull her in for a passionate kiss.

Music starts again, interrupting her free-fall into despair, and suddenly Faith is back in the store. She's standing by the second floor escalators, next to the black grand piano, the store's hallmark touch of prestige. The piano man sitting on the bench is playing a ballad now, a familiar tune played differently, slower, smooth and sensual. It calms her. He seems familiar too, but Faith can't place him. Dressed in a tux, tails over the back of the bench, his slender form sways back and forth as he plays. Late 20s, maybe early 30s, short cropped dark hair, left kind of long on top—the 50s look, with chiseled features that soften with his wide grin. And only then does Faith realize he's smiling at her.

"Hey," he says casually, as if they're supposed to be meeting there then, but he doesn't stop playing.

"Hey." Faith moves to the grand piano towards him.

"Like the tune?" He watches her, his deep brown eyes sparkling with humor. His slender fingers crawl over the keyboard like dancing, long-legged spiders, and with razor precision.

Twinkling of high notes that opens the chorus and she smiles. "*Dreamer.* I love it. Billy Rogue is brilliant."

"Ah. Forever the die-hard fan. You should have fallen in love with the art, not the artist. They are notoriously self-involved, which makes for a lonely life, as you well know."

He says it gently, with compassion, like her dad would, or like he knew profound loneliness. She studies him. His gaze is fixed on her. His eyes penetrate. His full lips reveal the slightest, knowing grin.

"Do I know you? Have we met?"

"Not formally. I'm Sylvester McBean, but most everyone calls me Sal. I'm with the Morality Police. We handle moral infractions like willful ignorance, corrupting omissions, blind prejudice, costly arrogance, things like that, on the... *personal* level."

"You're a cop?" And Faith feels scared. L.A. cops are notoriously unstrung.

"Well, yeah. But not like LAPD. Their beat is crimes against humanities laws, like stealing or murder and such. The Cosmic Justice Council handles the abstract stuff, like moral and ethical violations. I work for the CJC. Passed the Ethics exams, did my centennial internship. I'm fully licensed to travel time and use magic, well, tinker with physics. And I'm here to offer you a once in a lifetime opportunity, Faith."

"How do you know my name?"

His grin becomes a broad smile. He stops playing then. "Faith." He says it like the title of a poem.

"Faith. Faith. *Faith!*"

"*Faith!*" Billy stands over her, reaches out and puts his hand on her shoulder. Faith recoils, startled fully awake. "Move over. You're in the middle of the bed, babe. I need some space here, darlin'. I really need to crash."

Faith sits up. She really is in the middle of the bed.

Billy goes into the dressing area. He strips off his tee-shirt and throws it in the laundry basket, then runs both hands through his thick, wavy hair with a heavy sigh. Still slender, his arms and chest are buff, his stomach still rippled with six-pack abs, his pelvic bones protruding on his lanky frame lead the eye right to his groin. He holds his boxers to his hips as he dribbles off his jeans then tosses them into the laundry basket.

Faith instinctively combs her hand through her hair to style it, then stretches out on her side of the bed and leans on her elbow so her contour shape is accentuated. Billy comes back in the bedroom and gets into bed without even looking at her. Feels like he hit her, and she sighs, trying to shed the weight of her disappointment.

"Oh. Sorry." Billy leans up and gives her a quick peck on the lips, then his adorable dimpled smile before settling back on the bed. "It's happening, Faith. I'm getting old, and tired. I'm burnt. We'll talk tomorrow. Catch up. I'll call you before I go to work." He rolls away from her onto his side. "Night, babe."

She sinks back on the bed, feels a warm tear slide down the

side of her face before she knows she's crying again. Lonely doesn't touch what she feels. More like blackness, a void with no light, no sound, no air, no hope. Faith lets the tears spill down her face and silently cries herself back to sleep.

Blind Faith

✦

Her eyes are puffy and her face is blotchy, Simon comments when he comes into her office, less than a minute after she's sat at her desk. "Another bad dream? Ooh, what was it? Tell me. Tell me."

"I'm fine, Simon. What do you need?"

"You ain't fine, boss. Not for a while now." He drops into one of the two chairs and stares at her across her desk. "You get into it with your DH? Mr. Rogue being roguish again?"

Simon mocks Billy often, though, like most everyone, he's madly in love with The Xone, and was glad, proud even, when they got the Tony for Uprising. But in the five years he's been Faith's social media/PR/marketing/designer, Billy hardly acknowledges him when he comes in to review a new line or go over some marketing strategy. "Billy deserves center stage being so hot. I'll even give you he earns it as a great guitarist. But your husband is a self-absorbed git, my dear, and you don't need him."

Faith rolls her eyes. Simon has a *need* to express himself. It's part of what makes him such a gifted artist. But his ragging on Billy because he feels dissed by him is tiresome, and has become rather brazen of late. "Simon, it's dangerous to bite the hand that feeds you. You are employed at Gilman Street Threads because of Billy Rogue," she reminds him for the umteenth time.

"That's bullshit. Faith. You're a talented designer. For some bizarre reason, you are one of the few who don't know that. You would have made it out of the gate with your shear vintage line from college, no problem."

"Right. Whatever." Without Billy, she'd probably be in some cruddy flat in the Valley trying to eke out a living with her useless BA, stuck in a downtown factory sewing someone else's threads. "Simon, can we please get off the what if's and on with reality, or are you just in here to annoy me?"

"I'm trying to help ya, boss. And while I love getting rich on your generous stock options package, I *know* you'd be happier designing your own lines instead of this grunge stuff."

"How magnanimous. Are we done yet?"

"Not magnanimous, sweetie. Greedy. You put out your vintage line and Gilman's valuation is only going up. If it pisses Billy off, screw him. And I'm in here to tell you we got the silk bolts from Qingdao."

Billy doesn't call or text all morning, regardless of his early morning promise. Faith checks her cell several times on the way to Langer's to meet Zoey for lunch, even knowing he hasn't, and won't call. By some gift of the traffic gods, she finds a space on the street half a block from the deli. She parks, pulls quarters from the coin cubby to feed the antiquated meter, but instead of getting out of her car she sits there, staring at the fountain in the center of the little lake in MacArthur Park across the street. Urban legend is once a year when they drain the lake they invariably find several dead bodies. Isn't surprising, given the area of mostly low income. She'd be among them if not for Billy. He'd saved her from an ordinary life. But lately it's been occurring to Faith that a simple, typical existence, creating *her* visions, and filled with kids, family and friends is exactly what she's missing, even if it means subsisting on far less.

Her phone rings and buzzes simultaneously from where it lay on the tray in the seat divider.

i love u, read the text from Billy. *miss u. us. sorry we didn't talk this a.m. wrote after u left. maybe best yet. almost @ studio 2 lay it down. Green lite. ggn. later...*

Faith smiles, longs for him right then, even knowing his text is an afterthought, an apology for not calling as promised. And she knows 'later' means she won't hear from him the rest of the day.

love u 2. Faith texts back. Ah, to hell with his immersion in the creative process. He doesn't have to answer. *can't wait 2 hear it. bring home 2nite 2 share! u n me. dinner? r kitchen. can do late as midnite. Lmk...* Send.

The clock on her phone reads 1:10 and she grabs her wallet, gets out of the car and locks it, then loads the meter with quarters for the two hour limit. Crossing the street to Langer's Deli she notices a 1960s teal Mustang convertible parked in front of MacArthur park and flashes on the one she'd seen on the 110 yesterday. Creeps her out. What are the odds of seeing the same classic Mustang in a two day spread? Probably pretty good, since it's L.A., and most all of the ten million residents have at least one vehicle.

The deli's packed. Every stool along the classic chrome-rimmed counter is taken by the business lunch crowd in suits, or local Latinos in worn work wear. Be hip to do a line that combines tailored functionality with soft, breathable, washable cottons and linens. Several men at the counter blatantly check her out. A guy with cropped hair on the sides, left shaggy on top sits among the ogling men but does not acknowledge her. He makes the whole 50s scene in the deli, like James Dean. She knows this guy, has seen him before, she's sure. Zoey waving from a booth by the windows draws her attention. Faith waves back and moves towards her but can't help staring at the young man at the counter. He doesn't even glance her way as she passes, and she can't place him with only his profile view.

Zoey gets up to greet her with a hug. Faith still feels her friend's affection and returns it before the women sit, but their exchange is tepid from what it once was. They'd drifted over the years since high school, when Faith settled with Billy, and Zoe went back east to college. She'd stayed in Boston, as a legal secretary for an entertainment firm [where she met her lawyer husband], so they'd seen little of each other over the past ten years. They'd gotten together a few times since Zoey moved back to L.A. last spring, when her DH joined Tyre, Ramer & Brown as a partner, which came with a part time position for Zoe as one of his secretaries, telecommuting, of course, to be available for her two gorgeous girls.

"You're living my dream life, Zoe," Faith confesses as their waitress retreats after placing their orders in front of them. "I wish I could get Billy on the page of having kids."

"Well, I can see why you'd want Billy's genetics, anyway." Zoey stirs milk into her coffee then looks at Faith, her hazel doe eyes brimming with sympathy. "I just don't get why you want to stay with him. He's gone constantly, works all the time, and for as long as I've known him, Billy's been more into Billy than anyone else."

"He's a gifted musician, Zoe, off the charts talented artist. And the only way to get good at anything is practice, and Billy practices all the time. And I give him the space to do that."

"And what does he give you, Faith?"

"My livelihood, for one. Without Billy's fame and money I'd be nowhere. I have a BA in Fashion Design, not a law degree like you—"

"Billy didn't give you your career, Faith. You work your ass off, girl. You built a company from scratch and made it successful. And you probably would have done great with your own line instead of pimping him all these years. I'm sorry I hooked you two up way back when. But who knew?" She shakes her head and her fine, straight, shoulder length auburn hair flows softly with the movement.

Faith stares at the five inch turkey sandwich on the plate before her but doesn't feel hungry. She feels shamed. "Zoe, you have Daniel, and your beautiful girls, and a career you can do part time, any time, however old you are and will become. I have Billy, and Gilman Street Threads. I lose one, I lose the other. And then I'm back to nothing. Only a lot older. And alone."

"That's what you keep telling yourself." Zoey's come down

on Billy before—quick quips in emails or on the phone over the years, when Faith complained about feeling lonely and abandoned, but never as direct, or cutting.

"I'm thirty-one years old, Zoe, and childless. I don't have time to start over, date however many men for however many more years to find someone I want to spend my life with. I married Billy for better or worse. I've invested ten years of my life with him. And maybe it's not all I ever dreamed of, but it's workable. His current album wraps the end of July—"

"And then he's on tour again—"

"The band's taking three months off before they tour, and they're cutting it short with this release—only major venues because they can sell out Dodger Stadium now." And Faith feels small trying to sound big.

"And Davis and Ray have new babies and want to be home."

"How do you know that?"

"Tabloids." Zoey smiles, momentarily biting her pouty lower lip. "I live vicariously. I'm the management side of talent."

"Me, too."

"That's crap. You *are* the talent, Faith. You just never believed it. And your DH doesn't exactly encourage your visions, as he's so wrapped in his own." She says it as a statement of fact, then takes a big bite of her pastrami on rye.

Zoey echos Simon. Faith softens. Her friends were like a Greek chorus, always in her corner with words of encouragement. "I possess neither the talent nor tenacity Billy does. I'm too distractible, and I want more than just a career. He wins when it comes to diligence and focus on his craft. If I can't match it, the least I can do is support it. Billy needs me. To stand behind him and hold him up when necessary. It's my contribution to our relationship, and to the world that gets to hear his amazing music."

Zoey studies her friend. "Ah, Faith, you're really still just a die-hard fan."

And Faith flashes on the piano man in Neiman Marcus saying the exact same words to her in her dream last night. She turns around to look for the guy with the James Dean haircut at the counter, recalling their striking resemblance, but he's gone.

"Do you really think Billy will ever want more than his career, and put the kind of *focus* and *diligence* into your relationship as he does to his music, Faith?"

"Yes." But somewhere in there she knows it's a lie. "Billy's never been opposed to kids. It's always just been a timing issue." She takes a drink of her ice water but still can't eat, instead moves the coleslaw around her plate with her fork. "I always come unglued when he's on an album. He disappears whether we're together or not. He's inside his head where he should be, where every great artist must be to create."

"Yet another line you keep feeding yourself."

Faith scowls at her. "Zoey, you may have known Billy as long as me, but you have no idea who he can be. He's tender, generous, perceptive, and a blast to be with when he's paying attention."

"Yeah. The trick's always been getting Billy's attention. And he may be a brilliant talent, sweetie, but I don't see him making you happy. Maybe it's time to take control of your destiny, demand what you want and if Billy can't, or won't oblige, move on and go get it before you really are out of time. I'm not trying to hurt you here, honey. I love ya, girl, have since we were seven. I'm trying to wake you up."

Faith looks down at her sandwich, lifts half with both hands and takes an obligatory bite to appear casual though she feels like crying. She chews without looking at Zoey, glances around the deli. The bite of sandwich is mush in her mouth but it's still hard to get past the lump in her throat. "The album wraps in a month and we'll have three months to make a baby. Three shots. And third time's a charm, right?" But she doesn't really believe it.

Chasing Truth

✦

Billy hadn't texted her back to confirm dinner together. But then, Faith knew he wouldn't, though it didn't prevent her from checking her cell three times during lunch, and back in her office first thing every time she left it unattended. It's after 7:00 when she leaves the factory for the night. Only Simon's still there, and probably will be for hours to come. It's where he hides when he's single, and usually his most productive time creatively, unencumbered by a lover.

Zoey was wrong mocking her perception of artists. Faith knows how it feels to immerse in the creative process, lose the world around her and solely engage with her muse, which, for her, always morphs into a siren, luring her into a life of suffocating loneliness. She needs to contribute more than clothing, or Billy's music to the world. Maybe because he's a man, or maybe he's just wired differently than her, but Faith knows Billy feels alone only in rare moments, which is when he turns to her. The problem is, she needs more than moments now, as will kids, if they ever have any.

She notices the teal, convertible 60s Mustang in her rear view, moving through traffic with narrow margins to get around the stop and go commuters on the 110. Seeing the same color classic Mustang three times in two days means it's probably the same car. *Who is this guy? Is he following her?* He's catching up to her fast, changing lanes to outpace traffic, comes up behind her and Faith stops breathing. Top down on his Mustang, she can see him clearly in her mirror—the longer, top part of his hair blowing, his angular face masked only by his Wayfarer sunglasses. He abruptly moves to the right lane. Clearly he isn't following if he passes. A new job recently probably put him in the vicinity.

Faith watches the Mustang come up along side her expecting it to pass quickly, but it slows. He paces her, though the car in front of him is gaining distance. Trapped by the Audi in front of her, she can't move her Acura except into the breakdown lane, which she'll do if he pulls a gun. Sadly, a realistic concern when driving in L.A. Refusing to look at him directly, she sees him raise his hand in her peripheral vision. Eyes now wide with fear, she looks at him as he sweeps his hand in an exaggerated wave hello.

"Not interested," she says aloud as she shakes her head, knowing he can't hear her through her closed window. She holds up her ring finger, displaying her wedding ring. "I'm married!"

He nods, more like he knows than he gets it, his rugged face breaking into a big, friendly smile. She *knows* this guy, beyond just from the counter at Langer's deli. She's seen him before. Spoken to him, in fact. *But where?*

Horns blaring behind him, Faith glances at the Mustang as he pulls away to keep pace with the accelerating traffic. She loses him as he enters the first of the four short tunnels on the 110 near Dodger Stadium.

Takes a moment for her eyes to adjust to the dimness before she sees the Mustang ahead of her by several car lengths now. She weaves through traffic to catch up to him, comes up along his left side. He looks her way as she paces him, lifts his Wayfarers and smiles gently, knowingly, as if giving her a chance to remember him.

They plunge into darkness entering the second tunnel. She flashes on the piano man in her dream, rolling the top hat down his arm in greeting.

The bumper of a large SUV in front of her is suddenly only feet away and Faith slams on her brakes, barely misses hitting it. *The piano man, on the grassy hill, and in Neiman Marcus in her dreams.* No. Can't be.

Mustang pulls away again, slides into the lane to his right and disappears in front of the guzzling Ram pickup and the absurd mammoth Suburban blocking her, surprising even herself by the anxiety she feels over losing him. She squints in the dimness to find him as traffic in her lane picks up again.

Bright sunlight again and she spots the teal convertible and the top of his hair bopping around as the Mustang crosses into the fast lane three cars in front of her. She loses him again when he enters the last tunnel. Traffic flows faster now, and she maneuvers around the cars between them inside the fourth bore, and gets behind the Mustang just as he takes the I-5 Sacramento turnoff.

Faith follows, though the 110 is her route home. Curiosity overrides the voice of reason listing why following this guy is beyond bizarre, bordering pathetic, on par with stalking. He maneuvers through traffic with the grace of a race car driver, moving in and out of lanes without making anyone brake. She follows the Mustang at 70mph around the Griffith Park hills towards the San Fernando Valley. Faith keeps up, knowing changing lanes attracts the attention of cops, more afraid of losing him then getting popped.

Was it possible this was the man in her dreams? He was a dead ringer with what she remembers of the piano man at Neiman Marcus, the chiseled, stubble jawline softened by his penetrating eyes and knowing smile. Or was she just connecting the two with the beatnik look they both had going...

He takes the 134 connector. Faith turns on KROQ to distract her from the ridiculous pursuit she's engaged in. Of course, the now infamous, *Uprising*, blasts through her stereo, Billy wailing on the electric, belting out the cry of the damned. She almost catches up to the convertible several times, but he stays just ahead, outmaneuvering her through increasing traffic, either not knowing or caring that she's following him. If he's noticing her at all, he's probably assuming, as she has, they just happen to be taking the same route from downtown.

They come up on the 170 split. Faith continues to follow the Mustang onto the 101, which is actually moving for a change. Sudden, inexplicable fear as they head west towards the setting sun on the Ventura Fwy. She tries to guilt herself into turning around and going home. But she doesn't.

She sees the flashing red and blue in her rear view and instinctively hits her brakes along with everyone else around her. The cop weaves through the congestion, comes up right behind her. *Shit.* Faith puts on her blinker and moves to her right. The cop passes her. She releases a sigh and focuses ahead. The Mustang is gone.

She watches the flashing lights on the cop car move through traffic up the freeway, and scans the scene for the teal convertible, missing the Mulholland/Valley Circle exit to turn around. Parkway Calabasas, one mile ahead just so happens to be the exit for Studio 666, where Billy and the Xone are recording tonight. Faith laughs at the irony of Entropy, that she's followed a guy she doesn't know right to her husband. Cosmic justice? More like a teachable moment. She really must be desperately lonely to pursue some guy she doesn't know, imagining he's the man in her dreams.

Zoey's words ricochet in her head. Perhaps the dream life she sought is not with Billy after all. The idea of being alone, a space she's never really known, with Billy since the blossoming of puberty, scares her to her core. Her friend's right about one thing, for sure. If she and Billy don't work at having kids soon, she'll lose the window to have them at all. Instead of waiting, and hoping, perhaps it's time to lay it on the line with her husband, remind him how much she wants a family, and of his promise they'd create one, way back when.

Since she's not heard back from him in regards to her text request, and she's right there, she'll personally deliver her invitation for Billy to join her at home for a late dinner. Just a quick in and out, won't interrupt for long. She'll talk to him in the living room, away from the guys, tell him how it is, why she needs him tonight. She'll close with the kind of kiss filled with promise of more to come, then leave, make sure to stop at the store on the way home for the meal they hopefully don't bother to eat when he gets in.

Second Reality Check

✦

She takes the Calabasas exit, then makes her way up the small hill and turns onto the long narrow driveway. Faith follows it up to the large parking lot of the abandoned fitness center, complete with Olympic pool she'd skinny-dipped in with Billy a few times, long ago, when she was his 'sweet distraction.'

Faith drives past the vacant rectangular building to the sprawling house-like structure surrounded by a mini-forest of oaks, elderberries, pines and palms at the far north end of the lot. Adobe style estate, whitewash walls with a red clay roof, her heart pounds hard and she feels it pulsing in her neck and throat as she walks up the slate path to the entrance of the infamous recording studio. Her mother, a bible-thumping Catholic, had scowled when Billy proudly announced he and the band would be recording their third album at Studio 666 during Thanksgiving years back. Had it really been only three years since Uprising? It seemed a lifetime ago. Faith was twenty eight then, and Billy hadn't reached superstar status yet. They had time. She had time.

Cameras mounted to either side of the arched wood doors track her as she goes inside. Two more cameras are mounted in corners of the lobby area. Two black and one red leather couch are set in a U- shape around the stacked slate fireplace. Framed gold and silver albums of famous bands from the Chili Peppers to Green Day lines the cork bark wall. The room is empty, and dim, with sparse recessed lighting and a couple desk lamps, and just one narrow window by the stacked stone reception desk near the entry.

Three doors lead to different parts of the studio. All locked. One left. One right. And Faith is about to go behind the counter and call inside when Jennifer comes out the middle door, perfect smile with teeth so white they practically glow, clutching several folders while managing not to spill her full mug of coffee.

"Faith. Wow! It's been ages. This is a surprise." She glances up at the camera attached to the wall near the ceiling, then her eyes walk all over Faith. "You look fabulous! Is this one of yours?"

"Well, the jeans are Levi's." She's wearing her silk and lace, spaghetti strap halter, and jeans. Jennifer looks hot as ever, her long legs in black leggings, her long blond hair and perfect, rather large breasts pronounced with her skin tight, maroon Marciano cashmere sweater. "Hey, my DH around?" Faith tries to sound casual, though she feels anything but. "Just need to ask him a quick question."

"That top is just gorgeous! Seems more your style than the Gilman Street lines. More mine, too. I'm so done with grunge. I want something feminine for once. Are you expanding your line to stuff like that?"

Faith suddenly flashes on her dream from the previous night with mounting dread. It's remarkable how much Jennifer looks like the woman Billy kissed in the mall.

Jen turns away, walks around the reception counter to her large corner desk. Faith follows, stops at the opening so not to intrude on her office space. A bank of monitors on the desk protruding a foot below the counter shows different locations of the grounds. She waits for Jennifer to pick up the phone to call into the studio, but she files the folders instead.

"Billy's in the isolation booth, laying down some vocals." She doesn't look at Faith as she speaks. "I can call back and let him know you're here, but it might be a while." Jennifer slams the file cabinet drawer. She seems to be avoiding eye contact as she goes to her desk and picks up the phone.

"How about if I just go back and listen. It's been a while since I've heard Billy sing. We haven't been crossing paths a lot lately."

Jennifer holds up her index finger to indicate 'one second.' "Hi Charlie," she says into the phone. "Sorry to interrupt. Billy's wife, uh, Faith, is here, now, in the lobby, with me." Jen gives Faith a quick smile then looks away again. "Yeah. Okay. Thanks." She hangs up, gets up and finally looks Faith in the eyes. "He says to bring you back. Come on."

Right door buzzes and Faith follows Jennifer down the dark, narrow hallway to the control room. Through the thin glass window on the wood door ahead, Faith can see people inside. She expects to hear Billy's voice coming through the control room speakers when she and Jennifer enter the room, but doesn't. She hears the high pitch but beautifully resonant voice of a young woman.

The room's dim and crowded. Ray and Davis are on the couch against the fabric draped wall opposite the mixing boards, computers, keyboards and other musical debris. Two engineers sit at the long soundboard. Faith recognizes only one. Everyone says hi, or hey, or acknowledges her in some way. She hears Billy's guitar before she sees him in the studio through the window beyond the soundboards. He sits perched on a stool with an acoustic guitar in his lap picking a fast, fantastically complex rhythm that blends perfectly with the woman singing into the mic on the stand only feet from where he sits. She's small, petite, with very short, silky-fine, almost black hair, wearing a thin mini-t and worn skinny jeans. She has a dozen or more thin black bands around both wrists and wears several silver rings on both hands in the typical goth style.

Her stunning voice fills the control room, wordlessly quavering in perfect pitch with the melody Billy plays. The tune's bizarre though, boppity but dark, and familiar, but Faith isn't sure where she's heard it.

"This is a new one," beanpole thin, spiked blond hair, blue-eyed Ray says, coming up next to her to watch Billy and the woman/girl through the rectangular window. "We're using T for the background vocals. She's got a great voice, doesn't she."

"Yes." Faith whispers, then gasps.

The girl, T, stops singing abruptly and laughs, then apologizes profusely to Billy for messing up the timing, and then turns to the window and apologizes to the engineers in the control room. Her china white skin almost glows against her black lipstick and black eyeliner. Faith knows her face. It's the goth girl, the one Billy kissed in Faith's dream a few night back.

She feels faint, thinks she may puke. First Jennifer, and now this singer, Billy cheated on her with both women in her dreams. But they were just dreams, weren't they? They were just fears manifesting in her sleep, right?

"Hey!" Ray seems alarmed. "Faith. You okay?" He puts his hand on her forearm as if to steady her.

"Yeah. I'm fine." But she isn't. She can't breathe. She has to get out of there. "Look, I don't want to interrupt. Just tell Billy I stopped by and that I'll see him at home later." And she practically runs out of there, down the hall, and is pushing the door open out into the lobby when she hears Billy calling her.

"Faith! Hold up!" He meets her in the lobby, stands facing her, his eyes half-masted. He's buzzed, tired, or both, but he looks adorable with his dark, wavy hair peeking out in tufts from under his classic flannel English cap, framing his wide face and dimpled grin.

"Hey, baby." He kisses her gently on the lips. "What's up? What are you doing here? Everything okay?" He looks at her, then at the camera on the wall, then refocuses back on her.

"Can we talk, alone, for just a minute?"

"Sure. Yeah." Billy looks up at the camera again, but he doesn't move.

"Can we talk in the living room?" Faith asks, trying to keep the tension from her tone.

"Yeah. Sure." And he takes her hand and leads her through the middle door to a large room, complete with a huge U-section leather couch surrounding a fireplace, full bar with four stools, an air hockey table, a foosball table, and french doors that led to the garden outside. Billy drops her hand, goes to the bar and pours himself a scotch. "Want one?"

He knows she hates scotch. A sharp stab of anger at him asking. "Billy, why didn't you answer my text earlier?"

"Never got it. Can't find my cell. Thought I brought it into work but I must have left it in my car." He adds two ice cubes to the short glass, and swirls the amber liquid around before taking a drink. "Why? What's the problem? Is there one?" He eyes her suspiciously. "Everyone's alright, right? Your parents? Christine and David?"

"Yes. Everyone's fine." Except Faith isn't. She just doesn't know how to say that, so she stands there watching Billy sit on a stool at the bar and sip his drink.

He feels a million miles away. He's chosen to sit by himself instead of being with her, and loneliness consumes her again. She wants to run from him, or to him, fall to her knees and beg him to be with her, stay with her, come home and be with her tonight. She feels her throat constrict, her eyes fill. She blinks and tears stream down her cheeks. And with all she wants to say, Faith can not speak.

Then Billy's in front of her, wrapping his muscular arms around her and pulling her in. She surrenders to him, burrows into him, buries her face in his chest and cries.

"My beautiful, sweet wife. I'm so sorry." Billy whispers. His body presses against hers, she can feel him breathing, his heart beating. "I know I haven't been around, and how hard this is for you. For us. On us." He looks at her, strokes her tears away with his thumbs, then holds her face with both of his huge hands. They stand almost eye to eye. "I love you, hon. Tell me how to make it better."

"Meet me at home tonight so we can try to make a baby." Her tone's pleading and she feels shamed.

Billy laughs. "Is that what this is all about?" He releases her, turns away and shakes his head, then takes his cap off, sets it, and his tumbler of whiskey on the bar then runs his hand through his hair. Then he starts to undo his thin black belt. "I can't leave now. We've only got T for tonight. That's it. She's off to London in the morning to record with InTone at Apple." He pulls the belt from his jeans and drops it on the floor then moves to Faith again. "Let's make a baby, babe." He gives her his mischievous, dimpled grin and kisses her.

Faith kisses him back but doesn't want to. His mouth tastes of scotch. His tongue's down her throat and almost makes her gag. There's nothing gentle or loving in his touch. He's almost mechanical. He nearly tears the fine lace of her top trying to get his long fingers around her breast. He backs her toward the couch, almost throws her down on it, lands on top of her and laughs. Faith doesn't. She feels like crying.

It's over in three minutes, for which Faith is grateful, though, to be fair, he's really just accommodating her wishes. He's trying to resolve her issue in his own bizarre way. He'll give her his sperm, just not much of his time right now. He kisses her on the lips, then on her forehead, then gets off of her, pulls on his jeans and zips them up, then goes back to the bar and drains the scotch from the glass. Faith pulls her pants up and sits up, straightens her shirt and notices the tear in the fine lace at the neckline.

"Well. That was fun, but I gotta run, darlin'." Billy comes to the couch and kneels on both knees in front of her, takes her hand and kisses it, holds his warm, full lips to her palm with intentional pause. He finally pulls back but holds her hands in her lap with both of his, and looks up at her with his puppy-dog expression of contrition. "I wish I could escape with you right now, follow you home, make love all night long. You are the reason I thrive. Thank you, my Faith, for believing in me." He rests his head in her lap, releases her hands, then puts his on her belly and holds them there. "And I hope we made a baby tonight."

But right about now Faith isn't so sure she wants a child with Billy anymore.

Quick knock on the living room door.

"Come." Billy commands.

Davis cracks the door open and sticks his head in. "Oh. Been waiting on ya, dude. We got like four hours before T takes off, man. Sorry Faith." He looks sorry too, his broad shoulders slumped, his perpetual stubble accentuating his strong features, and loose grunge wear hiding his massively muscular build.

"Gotta go, babe," Billy says, pulls her face to him as he rises and kisses her hard on the lips, but without passion. "I'll be in late, and wiped. And good for nothing, especially you." He slowly backs out of the room as he speaks to her. "This will end. And I'll be home. And we'll have time together. I promise. Keep a light on for me, and I'll see you when I get there. I love you. Drive safe." He puts his fingers to his lips and blows her a kiss goodbye.

"Good seeing ya, Faith," Davis says as he follows Billy out of the room.

Faith wills herself not to cry in the building, or be seen crying on one of the many camera scanning the grounds. She has to put her hand to her mouth to stop a wounded shriek escaping her lips as she drives away, past the abandoned gym, down the narrow drive, then onto the 101 and home.

Rather Be Dreaming
✦

Cameras flash, from everywhere. And for a second Faith can't see. But then the spotlights hit Cassidy as she saunters onto the runway past the crowds seated on both sides. She's wearing a casual ensemble from Faith's newest fall line, a combination between executive attire and labor wear. Straight black suede skirt just above the knees, simple, fit, hugging but not skin tight, offset by the casual sleeveless blouse of strips of worn cotton and linen woven together with thin strands of leather. Faith left the bottom edge raw, and it dangles rhythmically with Cassidy's exaggerated stride, as does her long, auburn hair. She looks like a confident pro, for almost any career, feminine without flaunting.

Faith is pleased, proud of her efforts and those of her dedicated staff. Cassidy turns around at the end of the runway and heads back. Faith goes into the makeshift room behind the Frons Scenae and directs Valerie to adjust the silk ties on Roxy's halter on her way to help Kiki get her waist length, fine black hair into a braided bun and stay there.

It's hectic, but manageable in the large changing area with four designers presenting tonight. Faith smiles when she hears the crowd clapping as her models walk the runway. Kiki goes to strut as Cassidy returns, followed by Roxy, then Kiki's back, ending Faith's part in the show. She's congratulating her staff, helping them undress when her 4 yr old daughter, Megan, comes running in with a dozen red roses, almost tumbling on the hem of her dress. John follows close behind, his emerald eyes sparkling with pride.

"Everyone loved em, mama!" Megan exclaims as she hands Faith the roses and then hugs her legs. "Everyone thinks you're new treads are just great!

Faith laughs, bends and picks up her daughter. "Whose everyone, peanut?"

"Well, me, for sure! And daddy says so too."

"Oh. Thank you, sweet pea!" Faith hugs her daughter trying to transfer her adoration, then sets Megan down who goes to sit and twirl in a make-up chair. "And daddy too," she says to John and smiles at her husband.

"My beautiful wife, you did it again. Congratulations!" And he wraps his arms around her waist, gently pulls her to him for a warm, loving kiss filled with promise of more to come.

Out of nowhere a twangy, digital version of the music to *Dreamer* starts playing, like a voice over. Faith looks around then back at John but he's gone, as is everything else.

She blinks in her cavernous living room, filled with Frank Gehry furniture that isn't comfortable, and Emil Nolde and Egon Schiele paintings that creep her out. Her cellphone sings and buzzes on the all glass Tonelli table she's always tripping over in the dark. She grabs the phone and sits up on the curvy couch that clearly isn't meant for laying down on, stands and stretches as she reads the text message.

my sweet distraction... sorry cant b w u now 2 try 4 baby all nite long ;). love u. miss u. wish i was there 2 kiss u. promise this will all b over soon.

Faith stands there staring at the screen in her hand, and laughs disdainfully. Love, like intention, is meaningless without action.

She drops her cellphone on the couch as if it's diseased. She's suddenly exhausted, done for the day and goes upstairs and lay on their huge bed, devoid of the energy to even wash up. She recalls her dream, her daughter's beautiful tawny curls streaked with shimmering gold, her brilliant green eyes lit with excitement as she ran up in that funky dress Faith had made her out of her old stuffed animal, Charlie, the life-size lion. And of course, her husband, John, tall and stately with thick, golden brown hair and piercing emerald eyes. He was there, at *her* event, and clearly proud of her, and for a second Faith felt their visceral connection, beyond anything she'd ever known with Billy.

Faith pulls Billy's side of the quilt over her, curls onto her side and closes her eyes. With luck she'll go right into that same dream. Rare, but it does happen. The heaviness in her chest creeps throughout her body and she welcomes her return to sleep. Dreaming seems far more pleasurable than the reality at hand...

Detective Sylvester McBean

✦

...Sunrise over the olympic-size pool at the abandoned gym near Studio 666. Sunlight streams in through the glass walls and makes the water sparkle, which is weird because Faith is sure they'd emptied this pool years ago when the gym closed. She is alone, stands by the vacant diving board trying to remember why she came. Mist clings to the still water's surface, though fog fills the room, making it hard to see to the other end of the enormous glass enclosure.

Rustling sounds, like wind through trees, and her hair blows with a breeze, makes her skin prickle. Haunting hum emerges from the wind. A young woman with the rich, resonant voice of a trained singer belts out the eerie melody of a siren's song. Her voice is familiar, and though beautiful, it irritates Faith that she can't place it. The curvy form of a woman at the other end of the room appears then disappears in the rippling mist.

Faith moves closer, along the edge of the pool, water now turgid, lapping over the sides. Woman's voice crescendos, then she cracks up laughing in that coy way women do when they're flirting. Clapping is coming from the vague form of a man as he appears through the thick mist, and the fog clears around him as Billy moves to the singer.

Faith stops, not wanting to be seen, noticed— bear witness to indiscretions.

The singer wears skin-tight jeans and a tiny tee which shows her belly button. *"Blind faith in me,"* she sings, *"and you will see the power you give me corrupts absolutely..."* Then her voice fades to soft laughter. "How's that?" She speaks to Billy only feet from her now, then she looks directly at Faith. Fine, short, almost black hair, deep eyes set wide, made larger by the black eyeliner against her china-white skin. The singer is T, from earlier at the studio.

"That was beautiful, baby." Billy picks her up and twirls her around, then sets her down for a passionate kiss. And Faith flashes on their midnight skinny dip at this pool years ago, when she'd called Billy to meet her, and he'd picked her up and twirled her with a kiss.

"I'm sorry, Faith." And suddenly the piano man, the guy from the Mustang is standing beside her. "But this isn't my doing. It's yours. And you must know by now this recurring theme is not a dream."

Dressed in 501s, white t-shirt and a lightweight, black leather jacket, he's at least three inches taller than Billy. He looks down at her, his gentle brown eyes, almond shaped and set wide are filled with compassion. "I'm Sylvester McBean. We've met before.

Second floor, Neiman Marcus, in your dream a couple nights ago. I'm with the Morality Police." Tufts of dark hair fall over his forehead. He sweeps them back.

Faith hears the opening of Tiny Dancer by Elton John, but does not see a piano. She looks back at Billy and T kissing, but fog is filling the room making it impossible to see them.

"Your husband has violated your contractual agreement of fidelity. He's been thoughtless, careless with the precious gifts of love and trust you've given him. Billy has created a moral tear in the continuum. And he's the reason I'm here."

'Violated your agreement of fidelity.' 'Thoughtless.' 'Careless.' His words echo in her head. She feels like crying but refuses to come apart in front of a stranger.

"I'd like to offer you the opportunity to mend a moral... *rip*, if you will. But it needs to be a conscious decision, so, wake up, Faith!" McBean snaps his fingers in front of her face.

Faith wakes with a gasp. She sits up in bed and shivers. Was she dreaming or was that a vision, a glimpse of the future? Fully awake, she isn't sure it matters. Most all of her already knows Billy has, and is likely still cheating on her.

She hears the piano resonating up the stairs and into the bedroom. Her breath catches in her throat and she stops breathing, listening. Someone is in her house! She takes quick, quiet breaths and stares wide-eyed at her open door, listening to the chorus of *Tiny Dancer*, seemingly coming from the make-shift studio downstairs. Could be Billy, though the desk clock said it was only 11:30, way too early for him to be home. And she'd never heard him play Elton John in all their time together.

She quietly scrambles off the bed and looks out the french doors for Billy's Ferrari in the circular driveway. She has to open one door and go onto the wrought iron balcony to see the classic 60s Mustang parked below her window, its polished teal blue finish practically glows in the moonlight.

Faith is sure she should run, but to where she doesn't have a clue. Her car's in the garage, and once the door opens two feet whoever is in the house will have ample time to get to her before she can back her car out. If she runs up into the hills she'll probably kill herself on the rocky terrain, or fall off one of the many plateaus invisible in the dark. The nearest neighbor's an acre away, with a six foot electric fence around their entire property, and in keeping with L.A. protocol she'd never met them, doesn't even know their name.

Call 911. And she crosses back to the nightstand to get her phone as the piano goes into the main riff again.

'Blue jean baby, L.A. lady, seamstress for the band;
Pretty eyed, pirate smile, you'll marry a music man;'

She hears Elton in her head, singing Faith's song, according to her sister, Christine.

Ballerina, you must have seen her dancing in the sand;

Now she's in me, always with me, tiny dancer in my hand.'

Faith picks the phone off the charger and holds it to her as she crosses her bedroom to the threshold, pauses a moment, listening, recalling the lyrics with the piano.

'But oh how it feels so real,

Lying here with no one near,'

She proceeds down the hall then quietly down the stairs.

'Only you and you can hear me,

When I say softly slowly,

She passes through the living room and takes a steel poker off the rack of fireplace tools. She may be dreaming, or this could be a vision, or really happening. With the last scenario, a weapon would be smart to have. The music swells, then cascades, then swells again.

'Hold me closer tiny dancer;

Count the headlights on the highway;'

The studio door is open and she can see him from the hallway sitting at the grand, playing. Dressed in a tux, tails over the back of the bench, his slender form moves like flowing water, he sways back and forth as he plays.

'Lay me down in sheets of linen;

You had a busy day today.'

He glances at her, gives her his *'look what I can do,'* grin and keeps playing, weaving syncopated harmonies and rhythms into the simple tune, finally finishing the song with a twinkling of the keys, letting their resonance drift to silence.

Faith stands in the threshold watching him, clutching the poker as he rises and moves from behind the piano. "Stop!" She holds the poker in front of her with both hands. "Why are you in my house? What do you want? You've got five seconds to tell me or I'm calling the cops."

"I told you, I *am* a cop." And suddenly he's sitting cross-legged on top of the grand. "And you're not gonna hit me with that." He glances at the poker in her hand. "And even if you tried, I have all these cool tricks I can do, like make it blazing hot, or make it disappear completely."

And the poker's gone in a twinkling of light. Just like that, her hand's empty and Faith is defenseless. She grips the phone still in her hand, puts her finger over the green button but doesn't press it.

"Hello, Faith." He takes a thin silver case from the inside pocket of his leather jacket, extracts a cigarette and lights it, except not with a lighter. A flame, the size of a Bic, comes out the tip of his index finger. He smiles, like a kid with a new toy, then looks back at her. "Glad to finally meet ya in person."

"Haven't you heard smoking is bad for you, and everyone around you?" Faith says flatly to sound like she isn't afraid of him. "There's no smoking in this house," she manages definitively.

"Thanks for the tip. Nasty habit, to be sure." Smoke comes out his mouth as he speaks but goes straight up his nose, not into the air. He flicks the cigarette away and Faith's about to scream at him but the butt vanishes into thin air with a bright fizzle, like it was shot in a video game. Again, the broad, amused smile. "I can play with physics," And his big brown eyes glitter with wonder and mischief, but then they dim. "But I can't stop cancer. I can only use magic when I'm on a moral violation inside a tear in the continuum. When I'm in my own life, the one I was born to, I'm just like you." His hair's in his eyes again, and he combs it back with his fingers but locks fall forward.

"Who are you? What do you want?" she asks, though she already knows.

"I'm Sylvester McBean, with the Morality Police." He says it like he's stating the obvious. "But please, call me Sal."

"What do you want with me?"

"It's my job to investigate moral crimes, pass judgment as it pertains to the Physics of Progressive Evolution, and then execute sentencing." In an instant, McBean is off the piano and sitting on the couch. "It's like your friend Zoey said, Billy has been into Billy as long as you've both known him. You want more. You *deserve* more. And I'm here to give you the opportunity to get it."

"Why me?" Faith barely whispers, unsure if she's spoken or simply thought the question.

"Well, to be honest, I picked your case randomly, like all the others. Every ethical infringement tears a rip in the continuum, a sliver of light that acts as a portal to the time and place the violation occurred. Slivers brighten with every subsequent offense. I noticed Billy's sliver pulsing, entered the scene in your dream, that first time we sort of met on the grassy hill a few nights ago. Your dreams have become visions, Faith, to let your conscious mind know what your unconscious already knows. Billy's sliver is one of the brighter in the dynamic matrix of morality violations. Wanta see?"

The room lights up with an intricate multi-dimensional matrix of tiny slivers of phosphorescent light moving all around, some brighter than others, brightening and fading, a never ending matrix filling the room, seemingly right through the walls, ceiling and floor.

"There. That's Billy's rip." Sylvester stands on the piano now, pointing to a bright, pulsing sliver near the ceiling a few yards from where Faith stands in the threshold. "I'm here until I mend the tear, pass sentence and execute it, but have to get back through there before the portal closes or I'm stuck here, and off the Force. And personally, I prefer living my own time with the people I love, who love me. Makes life sweeter, don't ya think?"

Phosphorous slivers slide through the polished instruments and miscellaneous equipment scattered around the studio. The matrix seems alive, slivers of light pulsing like breathing.

"Isn't it totally cool?" Sal's leaning against the wall, not two feet from her, staring in awe at the matrix. "Granted, Billy's rip isn't as bright as some others, but I'm glad I traveled this tear. Learning about you on the way from my time, you're one of the more deserving I've run across lately."

"You're from the future, a time traveler." Faith states it for his confirmation, searching for some plausible reality, other than she's dreaming. It all feels so *real*.

"I'm from the past. Born 1943. Grew up in Huntington Beach. Still live there, in fact, have a flat a block from the beach which works great since I surf almost everyday when I'm home. I enter lives when a moral rip occurs, and exit when justice has been served. When I return to my time, I come back to the moment I left. But I digress. This is about you, Faith. Not me. The moral slivers you see are limited to my time line. Morality police can only travel within our lifetime. The beauty of it is, when we're time traveling, aging slows down, which is why I look thirty instead of like the old man I would be by this date. Fixing moral violations is rewarding, and playing with physics is fun, but staying young is a great motivator to take a lot of cases. It's rather addicting."

Faith reaches out and touches a pulsing sliver, feels the pull suck her finger in. She pulls her hand back. Suddenly the matrix is gone, and the studio seems dim with only the inset ceiling lights on.

"*Ah. Ah. Ah.*" Sal waggles his long index finger at Faith. "I'm here to show you another way, not solicit you into the Force. Trust me, you wouldn't have the heart for what we do, which is a good thing. I've never been very emotionally wired, but this job has made even me rather cynical and angry. Humanity needs more compassionate, gentle spirits like you." Sal sits cross-legged on top of the piano again. "Old back injury. Can't stand around too long. Anyway, so, here's the deal. I can handle this case on my own, find a suitable sentence for Billy's crimes, which usually involves prolonged impotence or castration in an accident for this type of offense, or I'll give you the option to handle it."

"How?" she hears herself ask. She isn't about to let McBean hurt her husband if she can stop him, regardless that Billy had hurt her.

"You already know. You've seen a possible outcome in your first dream tonight. I can place you at that fork in the road, but you're going to have to choose the right path to get there."

"Where? What are you talking about?" she asks, even though she actually has a clue.

"Your daughter, Megan, is beautiful. And your husband, John, your greatest advocate, and has always been. Your choice, Faith— that life to this?" He flashes a wily smile. "A bit of magic, well, it's all physics really, in this case like a playback button, and I can make it happen."

A YouTube video of a cupcake with chocolate frosting and colored sprinkles appears on the old 55" LED flat screen mounted on the wall across the room. But the translucent Play button is two feet from her face. It pulses softly to the Xone playing *Change*, but the band can't be seen in the background beyond the cupcake.

"Here's your chance to control your destiny, Faith, my settlement to you in lieu of sentencing Billy." Sylvester McBean is next to her again, leaning against the wall.

Faith watches someone plant a tiny birthday candle in the center of the cupcake on the TV. View pulls back to reveal Zoey slipping a Bic lighter from her jeans pocket and lighting the candle. Reality mingles with memory. She can hear her heart beating with the throng of the music, reverberating in her ears, her chest, her crotch. "You won't hurt Billy?"

"Ah, I'm right about you. You really are a loyal, nurturing soul." He gives her a gentle smile, his big brown eyes sparkling. "Your maternal gifts should be shared with those who have reverence for their value. Billy does not. Don't know if he needs to. His contribution to our evolution may in fact be his music. Not my judgment call. His violations are for breaking your contractual and spiritual agreement of fidelity. Press play to mend this rip, or live with it. You're choice, Faith."

A spotlight is on her and Billy is next to her on the flat screen, taking her by the hand and leading her onto the stage. "So what happens to my husband?"

"Don't know. Not my job. Have to admit, I do hope he makes it with The Xone. They're damn good. I especially like *Uprising*. Rockin tune." He gives her another wily smile. "I can't tell the future, Faith. Not even my own. Can't travel my own time line, for obvious reasons. Morality police are not privy to personal infractions, or of anyone in our lives, past or present. The future is dynamic, created by our choices, or lack of them, as the case may be."

"Yet you dangle Megan and John before me as if they were more than a dream." Catching the flaw in his reasoning, awe turns to suspicion. "What if in not choosing Billy I end up with no one.

Alone."

"Your dream was not of the future. It was a glimpse of a probable *past*, the path not taken. Press Play, and as settlement for your husband's violations, I'm awarding you the opportunity to replay that choice."

"I might just make the same choice again. How will I even know any different?" She watches herself on the video, hand-in-hand with Billy on the stage now. He's singing her happy birthday with the crowd.

"You'll remember me, and this time-line, for a while at least. But this life will eventually fade, feel more like a dream than it ever was a reality, merely a girl's fantasy of falling for a rock star, who chooses her out of billions to love back." The room lights up with the matrix again, zillions of slivers of pulsing phosphorus light fill the space in the studio and slides through the furniture, walls, ceiling and floor. "You must *choose* to direct your destiny, or accept life thrust upon you, Faith. You now possess the knowledge to make an informed decision, and I've done my job." McBean sits cross-legged atop the piano again. "Either way, this case is closing and I have to move on."

Faith slowly moves into the room, stops near the piano a few feet from Sylvester. Slivers of light go through even her, though there's no sensation as they pass through. On TV she sees her husband kiss her onstage, remembers literally swooning. This is all too surreal. Dizzying.

"Ah. I see you've reached a decision." And a fine red laser shoots from the tip of his index finger, pinpointing a pulsing sliver of light that appears to be slowly fading.

The translucent play button suddenly floats in front of her again. Beyond it Faith watches Billy redirect his attention to the audience with the opening of *Dreamer*, seemingly forgetting she was with him onstage, not acknowledging her again as the bouncer escorts her away.

Faith lifts her hand and presses Play.

Beginning Anew
✦

"Woe, girl. You okay?" she hears Zoey say as she grips Faith's arm to keep her upright. "Was he really that great?" She looks so *young*, just a teen in the amber club light. She's commanding Faith to make a wish before blowing out the candle she re-lit since Faith's return from onstage with Billy.

Faith looks around the Roxy, the dance floor crowded with fans. Lead guitar is always center stage but Billy deserves the spotlight, wailing on his electric, like he's stroking his dick, belting out the lyrics. He looks a bit younger, though almost the same— lean, wild, sexy as hell.

She's reliving her 16th birthday. Fifteen years have been stripped from her life. She's still young, hot, single, and available. A giddy delight spreads through her. Faith doesn't need a birthday wish. Dream or reality, she couldn't ask for a better Sweet 16th. She blows out the candle with a quick "Thank you, Sal!," though no one hears her above the music.

Zoey grabs her hand and they shimmy onto the dance floor. Fresh and tight again, most every guy there is watching Faith writhe and wriggle, her long, tawny hair flowing in soft swirls around her. But Faith is dancing for Billy. She moves in perfect sync to his guitar, as if he's stroking her instead of his electric. She feels his eyes on her. She looks up at him, smiles, hoping to show him her moves, how he moves her, but he's already looked away.

She sees Zoey gyrating towards her. The two girls dance together, bopping up and down with the crowd. Faith looks at Billy again, follows his line of sight to a young girl close to the stage who's taken off all her clothes and is dancing in her bra and panties.

Mix of disgust and disappointment her husband would fall for such a cheap display. But, of course, he wasn't her husband yet. Faith calls his name to recapture his attention, but her voice is drowned out by the music. She considers taking her dress off, but it's her latest—black leather and lace woven together over a deep ruby silk bodice. She doesn't want it wrecked, or ripped off. She twirls, lets the dress flare out and brush the crowd around her.

The band finishes *Dreamer*. Billy's watching her again as he announces *Blindsided,* a new one, and the band starts playing an ominous, weird, boppity tune that's familiar but she can't place it. He's playing to her now, but she doesn't swoon like she did once. She's traveled time with Billy and he'd left her wanting. Best to fall in love with his music, not the musician.

Ray's on the bass. Davis is on the drums as usual. The band stops to let the keyboard solo the opening chords of the chorus. Instead of Jonny, Sylvester McBean stands at the band's signature triple-level synthesizer. He looks directly at Faith. Smiles his wily grin. Winks!

Then a guy, at least six feet and slender, dances in front of her obscuring her view. Hair cut short, but thick, and golden brown, stubbled cheeks that looks affected, like to show he has facial hair, but his full lips are in a broad, welcoming smile. Maybe 18 or 19, he's cute in an awkward sort of way. But it's his eyes that floor her— sparkling emerald, focused solely on her.

He leans in close. "Hey! Happy Birthday!"

"Thanks," she yells back. Faith is sure she's seen him before, or someone who looks like him, but...older. Then she flashes on her dream at her fashion show, watching her husband, John, coming towards her after the show with the exact same grin on his face in her dream as now.

"Great band, aren't they!" he yells over the Xone. "I'm John." He moves back and forth awkwardly, on one foot then the other.

Faith smiles. "I know," she says, but not loud enough to be heard over the music. She looks at the stage to find Sylvester, thank him with a nod, or wink, but Jonny is back at the synthesizer. Sal is gone, but her eyes find Billy's, back to looking at her. Then John is hovering in front of her again, his goofy grin still focused on her alone.

"Hi, John. I'm Faith. Glad to meet ya!"

✦ **Ending at a New Beginning** ✦

Kat's Dog

A dog tale by

J. Cafesin

Kat's Dog
A Romantic Fantasy Dog Tale

Adoption

🐕

Santa Ana winds are bending the tall palms lining the parking lot of the West L.A. Animal Shelter as Kat pulls in.

"Danny and I were supposed to do this together," Kat says to her boss, pulling her Civic into a parking space. "We were gonna get a friend for Riley."

"Seriously? I call bullshit, honey." Frank says in his big brother way as they get out of her car. "Danny was passing through from the day he moved in, Kat." They fall in step as they cross the lot to the shelter entrance. "He was never gonna set up house with you, girl."

"I get that, Frank," Kat says flatly. "Thanks," she adds, holding her long tawny hair from blowing in her face and feeling darkness descending. "I'm just so done with being single," Kat confesses. She pulls the scrunchy from her wrist and puts her hair in a ponytail. "Most everyone I know is married already. At *least* once—"

"Yup. And even *I* have found my prince. And you will too if you just get yourself out there in the real world." Frank shakes his head as they walk into the lobby of the shelter. It stinks of piss.

"Dating sucks," Kat says definitively. "The few guys not looking for hookups, or visas, are starving actors or musicians like Danny. Emotionally and financially stable, heterosexual men who aren't adulterers, narcissists, or misogynists aren't exactly readily available in this town, sweetie." Kat sighs.

"Come on, Kat. You can't keep hiding in your job, or your house waiting for another roommate with benefits like your last two if you want an actual life." They go through the back doors and across the gravel lot to the long, corrugated steel barracks housing the dogs for adoption.

"I'm not hiding, boss," Kat says more confidently than she feels. "I'm sheltering in place," she confesses.

"You really are your own worst enemy, girl," Frank says exasperated.

They perused the cages lining both sides of the concrete aisle. Most of the dogs look fully grown, but Kat wants a puppy. Three to five dogs in any given cage, filled with mixed breeds in various sizes, but mostly males. All are adorable, of course, but Katrina is set on adopting a female. Female dogs are known to be more loyal than males, a common gender trait among many species, it seems.

Several cages down, Frank falls in love with a fluffy tan Cockapoo-mix. Floppy ears, round brown eyes and a black button nose. He's literally gushing as he asks an attendant to open the cage and get the mutt for him to hold. Of course, they're there for Kat, not Frank, but he simply can't resist small, helpless creatures in need of affection. It's likely why they became friends beyond just workmates, she muses.

Kat waits with Frank while the attendant goes in the cage to retrieve Frank's pick. The Cockapoo, and a silky Golden Lab pup, maybe 5 or 6 months old, surrounds the stocky attendant, vying for her attention. The outlier is a Shepherd-mix pup, less than a foot tall, maybe 3 months old. It ignores the attendant entirely and saunters with the cadence of a mountain lion to just the other side of the wire fence where Kat stands.

The attendant extends the small dog to Frank as she exits the cage, shooing away the Golden to shut the gate. Frank gathers the Cockapoo-mix in his toned arms and holds the frenetic animal to his chest, lost in a love fest with the high-wired mutt.

The Shepherd pup sits, eyes on Kat through the squares of the steel mesh fence. Clearly female, she has an adorably sweet face—black muzzle with tan cheeks and Groucho Marx eyebrows. There is a perfect black diamond dead in the center of her tan forehead. She has huge ears with one of them flopping over at the tip top. The dog stares at her, it almost feels like *into* her with those big, almond-shaped brown eyes fixed on Kat alone.

"Hey, baby." Kat kneels in front of the Shepherd. She presses her hand up against the cage fencing and feels the cold wetness of the dog's nose. The puppy investigates her scent, then its warm, long tongue licks Kat's palm through the fencing.

You. Mine! Kat hears the Shepherd pup say in her head as it sits there staring at her, like they are the only two beings on the planet.

The Golden moves in to garner some attention too, soliciting a low growl from the Shepherd who suddenly lunges at the Golden with a quick snap of the pup's razor sharp teeth. Kat stands instinctively, suddenly afraid of the pup. The Golden yelps and retreats to the back of the cage.

"What's that dog's problem?" Frank snipes. He holds the Cockapoo in his oddly long fingers against his chest in a protective pouch.

"Stop that," the attendant scolds, but like a loving parent. She bangs her palm against the fence near the Shepherd.

The Shepherd pup resumes sitting in her spot near the fence in front of Kat, seemingly undisturbed by the attendant's banging. The pup stares at Kat, directly into her eyes, and stays fixed on her. *Weird.*

"Shepherds are territorial. It's in their breed," the attendant says. "But they're smart as hell, and loyal, which is more than I can say for most people." The stout woman stares down at the pup sitting just the other side of the fence. "Seems she's taken a shine to you," the attendant says to Kat. "Maybe you wanta go in, take some time with her, see if there's a match? Just give her a good smack on her muzzle if she gets rowdy again. Best to teach em right from wrong early on." She looks at Frank. "And what about you? You ready to bring home a new family member today?"

Frank snuggles his face into the Cockopoo's neck and looks at Kat with his guilty pleasure smile. "Oh, don't make me put her back in that smelly, disgusting cage!"

Kat grins sheepishly at the attendant then glares at Frank for his derisive comment about the facilities. "Honey, do you have any idea how Doug will feel about you adopting that frenetic ball of energy?" It is likely Doug won't be totally pleased with a mutt, if he wants a dog at all right now. They'd recently lost their dog of many years— Diana, a pure-bread Maltese.

He puts on his classic pout for not garnering her instant support. "How could he not fall for this face," Frank cups the dog's muzzle gently, then kisses the top of her white furry head.

"Why don't you call him and find out?" Kat suggests gently.

"I'll do that." He pulls his cell from his jeans back pocket and takes the fluff-ball with him to the exit. The attendant starts to follow, then stops.

"You know, that pup has not stopped staring at you. You got treats in your pocket, or what?"

"No. No treats," Kat defends. It suddenly feels surreal the way the Shepherd puppy is fixed on her. Until the attendant's confirmation, Kat could pass off the dog's undivided attention as her own delusion, her insane need for validation.

YOU. Mine, Kat doesn't exactly hear, but senses a bizarre familiarity in the dog's fixed stare, like the puppy thinks it knows her, or belongs to her already.

"Feel free to go in and say hi, the attendant says. "Just be sure to shut the gate going in and coming out." She follows Frank out, no doubt to help him adopt the Cockapoo.

Kat looks down at the Shepherd pup looking up at her, practically without blinking. The puff-puppy sits there with those huge ears and big brown eyes staring up at Kat, and she mocks herself for feeling afraid of this dog. Raised with a Shepherd-mix, she knew them to be a loving, loyal breed, as the attendant had confirmed.

"I see you," Kat says to the pup staring at her through the fencing. The Shepherd's big eyes are still fixed on hers. "What is it, baby?"

The puppy cocks her head to the side like she's trying to understand, her soft ears flopping over to the side with her tilted head.

"What are you looking at?"

You, Kat almost hears in her head, like an echo, or perhaps a thought-bubble she put above the dog.

"What do you want?" Kat asks the pup.

The puppy flips her head to the other side, her ears flopping too, her eyes still on Kat, but then she looks directly at the gate, then back at Kat, then back at the gate. She whines, like a half-bark when she looks back at Kat.

"You want me to come in?" Kat asks.

The pup barks two high pitched yelps. Kat laughs, surprised how responsive the dog seems. Its tail thumps on the concrete and continues to thrum as Kat goes into the enclosure, quickly closing the gate behind her. The Golden gets up to greet her, soliciting a low, gravelly growl from the Shepherd puppy.

"*NO!* Bad dog! Stop that!" Kat commands as the attendant had done, though she has no intention of hitting the dog per the attendant's rec. Her heart is racing. The Golden, weary of the Shepherd pup and likely Kat's outburst, lays down against the far wall again. "You be nice!" she says to the Shepherd with more command than she feels.

The puppy's huge ears droop. Her Groucho Marx eyebrows draw together, her muzzle downcast, her big brown eyes watery as she looks up at Kat. The change in the dog's demeanor from aggressive to submissive is palpable. She doesn't take her eyes off Kat. It's all rather bizarre, really, the way the pup watches her, like the dog is trying to talk to her telepathically.

The Shepherd pup gets up and saunters over to where Kat stands, then sits in front of her, within inches. She raises one of her big paws and extends it to Kat, soliciting a handshake.

"Well, look at you," Kat kneels on the surprisingly clean concrete floor in front of the Shepherd. She takes the dog's paw and lets it rest in her hand so the puppy doesn't feel trapped. "Hello beautiful. Nice to meet you, too."

The puppy retracts its paw, then stands and moves to Kat, gingerly nuzzling her entire body along Kat's side like a cat.

Ooo... Ahhh... Again Kat is sure she hears, or more like feels the dog's immense pleasure as she rubs up against Katrina, then circles behind her and rubs up against her other side.

Kat glances at the Golden. The Retriever pup watches them, occasionally thumping her fluffy tale on the ground but does not come over to join them. Figures. Golden's aren't known for their boldness. Not exactly the best guard dogs.

The puppy locks her big brown eyes on Kat again, with a familiarity of family. *YOU. My pack,* Kat hears that weird echo in her head again. *'Home.'* The Shepherd looks at the gate, then saunters over to it. She looks back at Kat and whines, like she is asking to be let out. *Lead the way,* Kat is almost sure she hears the dog say in her head.

"You wanta come home with me?" she asks the pup as she stands. The dog barks a high-pitched yelp. Kat is almost sure the Shepherd pup is responding directly to her query, then mocks herself at her own folly— anthropomorphising an animal that isn't even hers. Yet.

About Face

Kat christens her new puppy, Killer Dog Face. Killer, as in cool. Dog, because she is one. And Face, after a term of endearment her mother used to call her. She figures the pup deserved three names, like most everyone else has, but Kat calls her by her last name most of the time.

Her beautiful Face.

Dog Face, Killer, Facerelli, Relli, Rel, Kat adopted many terms of endearment in the seven months they've been together. Her puppy is close to a year old now, and has grown into a sleek, 67-pound Shepherd-mix, slender hindquarters with a high arch similar to hunting hounds. She'd retained her puppy looks with her huge ears and paws so she doesn't look fierce exactly, but Face is a Shepherd, which gives Kat comfort when the dog accompanies her, which is just about everywhere.

"This dog is a great diet aide," Kat says to Frank and Sarah in her office at their Friday wrap-up. She tosses Face the last of her powdered donut. The dog catches the treat from where she lay in her beanbag bed and swallows it in one bite. "Yum!" Kat says to Face as the dog licks the white powder from her muzzle with her long pink tongue. Face stares at Kat, then whines, mooching for more. "No more. Sorry kid. Can't be scarfing a lot of crap," Kat says tenderly. "My best buddy needs to stay healthy. Yes you do."

"Honey, do you hear yourself?" Frank asks, sitting next to Sarah on the other side of Kat's desk. "Do you know how cringy you sound right now?" Frank and Sarah look at each other then back at Kat.

"He's right. You do sound rather cringe, sweetie," Sarah says in her crisp British accent, her silky brown hair in a casual pixie bob belying her compulsive need for order. Her otherwise petite frame looks like she is carrying a watermelon in her belly at almost eight months pregnant. She sits primly next to Frank, her tablet faced-down in her lap, hands folded over it. "I'd say it's downright sad how much of your free time you spend exclusively with that dog. You certainly must interact with more people, Kat, or you'll end up an old, well, *dog* lady."

"Hey, at least Face always makes me feel appreciated, and respected, and safer, and for sure not so alone," Kat retorts, wondering who she's trying to convince. She looks at her dog and flashes a tender smile. "Isn't that right, beautiful."

Face gets out of her bed, comes to Kat and puts her head in Kat's lap soliciting strokes.

"OMG! Seriously?" Frank chimes back in. He glares at Kat's dog, now frozen in rapture, like Face is under a spell from

Kat's touch. "You really need some actual *human* contact, my dear. You work 14 hours a day reading about real relationships while you've been exclusive with your damn dog since you got her." Frank propped his tablet on her desk and spun it to face her. The dating app, Spark, is on his screen. "It's time you get back out there—"

"Is this like an intervention, or what?" Kat says, annoyed. "I thought this was our weekly wrap up. What happened to that?" She sighs, stops patting Face and looks at Frank, then Sarah. "And for the record, I have no interest in a dating app. I'm fine on my own, just me and Facerelli," but as her words register in her head they sound rather pathetic.

Face looks up at Kat and whines. *'I'm bored.'* Kat hears the now familiar echo in her head, though she often passes it off as knowing Face well enough to recognize her cues. Face saunters to the door, then her big brown eyes find Kat's, connecting them again. She whines again. *'Can we go now?'* Kat practically hears her dog say in her head.

Kat stares back at Face. She shakes her head at her dog's request. Face seems to get it because her ears droop and her tail drops as she saunters back to her beanbag and huffs as she lays in it.

"Honey," Sarah says to Kat. "You know we aren't wrong. Face is your *dog*, after all."

"I get it," Kat finally admits solemnly. She'd feel more miffed at them for this intervention, but she'd whined to them enough about being single and she understood they were just trying to help her. Face *is* a dog, and in being so she could never fulfill Kat's unrelenting ache for real intimacy.

Kat glances at the homepage of Spark on Frank's tablet propped on her desk. Two cellphones against a black background have streaming shots of ultra-attractive men and women, then the pictures stop on two single images. A sparkler ignites between the two phones and it says "BAM!" below the sparkling, then "Spark a Match Today." A bright red button under the headline reads, "Join Us Free!" She rolls her eyes.

"I knew she'd go there," Frank says to Sarah exasperated. "I told you! And voilà!" He sweeps his hand towards Kat.

"Well, you can bring a cow to water," Sarah says, the word 'cow' in Britain meaning 'stupid woman.' She grunts as she gets up, holding her baby belly and her tablet. She looks at Kat sitting behind her desk. "I love you, honey. I'll even admit, after watching your fur baby grow up, you have a good mutt there," and Sarah looks at Face who stares back at her from where she stands by the office door. "But Face can not join you in making fun of a lame movie. You and your dog can not laugh together over a shared meal, or cry together from bad news. She can't hold you at night, or fulfill your fantasies of a home filled with family. She'll never be more than a dog, Kat." And with that, she leaves the office.

Frank is standing now, too. He picks up his tablet from Kat's desk and looks at her. "It's been almost a year since Danny. A *year*, honey! Time to get back out there or you'll end up like Sarah says— an old dog lady." He keeps his eyes on hers for a moment, then glances at Face and leaves Kat's office.

Face gets up, stretches and yawns, wide and long as if in slow motion, then saunters over to Kat soliciting strokes. Kat obliges, but the silky touch of her dog's soft fur doesn't soothe her. She feels like crying. She doesn't want to end up an old dog lady —childless and alone. "I'm gonna try and get out more, Facerellie, likely to places you can't come. You're gonna have to stay home and hold down the fort."

Face sits down beside Kat staring up at her, tilting her head to the side with Kat's words, her big brown eyes suddenly watery, like she is about to cry. When Kat goes silent, Face stands and whines.

'No. Stay home,' Kat hears, or more like saw the concern in her dog's expression, her eyebrows drawn together, her ears back, tail down. *'Come!'*

Face puts her head in Kat's lap. "Ah, Rellie. I wish you were enough." Kat gently strokes her dog, swallows hard to suppress the lump rising in her throat but manages to hold back her tears. Face stands frozen in bliss. "My beautiful Face, I promise you, if I find someone I like, I'll bring him home to meet you. And you can tell me honestly what you think of him," she adds. *If only...* Kat muses. It'd be great to have an trusted oracle to guide her to 'The One.' She already knew how Face would feel about anyone she dated. Accompanying Kat most everywhere she goes, and around people as much as Face is, Kat is sure her dog genuinely likes most everybody.

Psychic Guard Dog

"I can't believe you broke up with him. There is not a planet in our galaxy, possibly our universe, where Ryan would not be hot."

"That's a double negative, Frank," Kat says. "And I thought you 'absolutely forbid them.'" She sighs. "And we were never together, so we didn't break up. I just stopped seeing him."

"You sure got moxie, girl, walking away from that baby face, those pecs, his *abs*,'" Frank's says, gathering his tablet, his Diet Coke, and his electronic pen from the huge, polished wood conference table. "Oh, the things I could do to that hard body," Frank says salaciously. "If I wasn't with Doug, of course."

Kat and Frank are the last of their colleagues to leave the Friday debrief in the Fishbowl. The conference room has three glass walls enclosing the meeting space, and the fourth wall gives a floor to ceiling view of the Plaza Towers, with glimpses of the Hollywood hills between the concrete and glass monoliths of Century City.

"He's an actor," Kat says. "Ryan has to stay in shape for his job. You, too, can have a body like his if you spend 4 hours a day working out." She leads the way out of the Fishbowl.

"Honey, I could spend every day, all day working out and I ain't never gonna look like that," Frank insists, matching her quick pace down the hallway. "I just don't get why you let go of that fine piece of machinery after possessing it for four straight months, longer than anyone you've seen since Danny."

"Ryan and I spent a total of six weekends together in those four months, when he flew in from wherever he was shooting, and that one time I met him on set in Maui for a few days."

"He's a *successful* actor, hon. How many of those are you going to find in L.A.?"

"You're just starstruck, Frank," Kat retorts as they near the open glass door to her office. "I want more than weekend flings. Regardless, Ryan is too into himself to be with anyone else." Kat grins at him, then slides the glass door shut between them and goes to her desk.

Frank slides the door open and comes into her office. "You're too picky."

Face gets out of her beanbag bed, stretches as if in slow motion then saunters over to Kat and solicits strokes. Of course, Kat obliges.

"Hey, Baby," she says as she strokes Face.

"Sarah would back me up on this if she were here," Frank adds.

Sarah is on maternity leave, tending to her beautiful two

month old daughter, living the life Kat longs for.

"OK. Enough. Go on," Kat says to her dog.

Aww, Kat hears in her head, sensing the dog's disappointment, but Face takes the hint and sits by her bed in the corner of the small office space. The dog watches them, alert, eyes wide, looking from Frank to Kat as each speaks.

"And I bet Face thinks you're too picky too."

Face watches Frank and shakes her head right then. Then she looks at Kat and shakes her head again. Then barks, one high-pitched yelp. She stares at Kat with adoration.

Mine. Brave. Strong. Perfect, Kat is sure she hears Face in her head, her big brown eyes glistening, her rocket ears straight up. *I love you too,* Kat says in her head, hoping Face can at least feel her deep affection. But as much as she loves her dog, Face won't ever understand she'll never be enough, as Kat seemingly is to her.

Frank watches Kat's dog with furrowed brow. "Creepy. Ya know, sometimes I think your dog is psychic or something."

Yeah, me too, she thinks but doesn't say for fear of sounding crazy. "And I'm not too picky, Frank," Kat defends. "I'm *discerning,*" she says more to herself than Frank. "Look, Ryan is fine—"

"Fine?" Frank mocks as he plops in the chair across from her.

"Well, he is... was. He's famous and gorgeous and as long as he has a script, he knows exactly what to say."

"Ouch," Frank scrunches his face in a smirk. "Well, Face liked him."

"Face likes everyone, Frank." Kat says, then opens her laptop to get to work.

Frank takes the cue to leave and stands as Face curls back in her beanbag bed. "You know, if you insist on being so '*discerning*,' you're going to have to up your game—get out there and date a *lot* more. If you want to create a family, and I know you do, you're out of time to continue indulging in casual because it feels safer than working at finding something real."

"Thank you, Sigmund," Kat says. "Hope you and Doug have a great weekend with Liza. See ya Monday."

"She's so pushy," Frank says to Face who watches him from her bed. He goes to the threshold of Kat's office but stops just inside and turns around. "Go home and have a bubble bath if you have nothing else going tonight. Then give Spark another try. Promise me you won't stay here reading all night."

"Face is with me. I'm fine, Frank. Go have fun this weekend. Go home!" Kat focuses her attention on the large curved monitor in front of her.

"She commands," Frank snipes. "So, I'm the dog now, Facerelli,'" he quotes Meg Ryan in *When Harry Met Sally* to

Face who watches him passively. "I'm being dismissed." He huffs, then leaves her office. "Make this weekend memorable, my dear. You only get this one life, honey. No use sitting alone in your room," Frank says and whistles *Cabaret* as he walks past her office back to his.

It is close to 5:30 p.m. and everyone is leaving. Kat has no plans for the weekend. She'll likely take Face to Zuma beach, which is fine. But picturing another Saturday night alone scrolling through her socials while watching TV makes her feel rather hollow inside. She could be with Ryan, wherever he is this weekend, and she feels a stab of regret for breaking it off with him. He's said he wasn't surprised 'the talk' was coming, only that she'd stuck it out for so long. That six liaisons over four months is a long relationship to Ryan is another reason she'd called it quits with him.

Face growls, low and long, and at first Kat thinks her dog is dreaming but she lay sphinx-like in her beanbag, her eyes open wide, her rocket-ears up. She's looking through the frosted half of the glass door at a shadow approaching Kat's office.

Over a year with this dog practically 24/7, and the only other time Kat heard Face growl was at the Golden Retriever in their cage at the pound.

"Shit," Kat whispers when she stands up and recognizes Dean Reynolds approaching through the clear glass half of her office wall. Of course, she'd heard less than flattering rumors about the talent agent. Groper. Misogynist. Pervert, to name a few from several of her female co-workers in the five years she'd been at CTA.

Dean waves as Kat comes around her desk to greet him. He is a literary agent, repping book authors, and above her position as a script analyst. Screenplay contracts go to film agents at Creative Talent Agency, so they'd had few interactions to date, mostly polite exchanges at corporate events.

Face growls again, deep and grumbly. "Stop that. Stay in your bed," Kat commands softly as she pulls her office door open. A rancid stench of liquor on Dean's breath and she suddenly feels afraid. Her heart races, now thumping in her chest.

"Heelloo," he says, thick and slurred. "What are you still doing here?"

"I'm just getting ready to leave," she says simultaneously, overlapping his question. They exchange polite smiles for speaking over each other but Kat does not move her position of effectively blocking him from entering her office, and directly seeing Face.

"Well, I'm glad you're still here. I've been meaning to talk to you about your coverage report for *Threshold*." Dean's name suits him. He has the whole ivy-league preppy thing going on, even though he is closer to 50 than college age. Steel blue eyes. Light-brown hair cropped short on the sides but sticking up on top. He is short, but lean, compact.

"Is there a problem?" Kat asks, holding her ground.

"Your actual report is fine," Dean says. "Stellar as always, from what I've heard—"

Face is suddenly at Kat side. She growls at Dean, mouth twitching, a mohawk of fur gathered along her back, tail straight out like she is ready to pounce.

"*Whoa, what the hell...*" Dean takes a step back as he glares wide-eyed at Face standing beside Kat in her office. "Call off your dog, Katrina! *Now!*"

Her teeth bared, Face growls angrily then ramps to barking at Dean.

Kat grabs her dog's leather collar. "*Stop!* Now! *Leave it*, Face," Kat commands, dumbstruck her dog is acting so aggressively. Face instantly calms with Kat's touch and switches to intermittent growling as Kat pulls her dog behind her, putting herself between Face and Dean. "Go in your bed and lay down," she says loud and deep with all the command she could muster, and surprisingly Face does, with a begrudging grunt.

"I'm really sorry, Dean," Kat says, hoping to quell his hostility. "She usually loves everyone—"

"Why is your *dog* here?" Dean asks, moving in closer to her office but not crossing the glass door threshold. He keeps his eyes on Face in her bed, hindquarters under her, paws over the edge of the beanbag like she is itching to get out of it. "This is a place of business and we could get sued if that bitch bit anyone. She shouldn't even be here. CTA has a no-pets policy."

"Well, not exactly," Kat says, knowing she is about to cross a line with her superior but not much caring anymore with Dean referring to her bestie as a bitch, though technically, of course, she is one. "CTA has *no* pet policy. None at all. I asked HR when I first started bringing her." She looks back at Face in her beanbag, head up, ears up, eyes wide and alert watching her and Dean interact.

"Fine. Just keep her away from me." Dean watches the dog watching him.

"So, I'm unclear how *Threshold* ended up on your desk when I got the script from Eileen." Kat turns away and goes to her desk to collect her things and show him she has every intention of leaving. She shuts her laptop and shoves it into her large black SmartBag.

"Yeah. Well, Eileen is out for a while. Someone died of cancer, or she's got cancer. I can't remember."

Kat manages to keep her mouth shut but is unable to contain the slight shake of her head.

Dean catches her response. "*What?* I don't have the bandwidth to get involved in the lives of my office mates when I have to babysit my roster of neurotic writers day and night." His eyes kept shifting from Face to Kat. "Anyway, in your synopsis of *Threshold,* one of your comments says something like, 'a clone of the last ten thousand superhero films.' And it got some of us, like me, wondering if we should pick it up at all."

"Isn't that up to Eileen, well, and now you?" Kat says as she puts her TBRs for over the weekend into her bag, then zips it closed.

"It is. But Eileen isn't here, and since she clearly values your opinion, I'd like it on this one too. CTA has producers lined up for *Threshold,* and until I read your report, I had a vision of the perfect actor for the lead to virtually guarantee a potential blockbuster." He stands in his spot near the door, pries his eyes from the dog and looks at her. "I think maybe you could use some of your feminine wiles to convince Ryan to play Mindmelder."

Finally, here it is—the reason Dean came to talk to her. Not to get her opinion on picking up *Threshold,* and adding the screenwriter to CTA's roster, but to get her to solicit her ex, presumably with sex, into playing the lead in yet another Marvel movie. It seems everyone at CTA knew she'd been dating a movie star, a la Frank. They clearly hadn't heard she'd called it quits yet. She stares at Dean for a second, then slung her heavy bag over her shoulder.

"I'm meeting Ryan right now for the weekend," she looks him straight in the eyes as she lies. Telling Dean she is newly single right then doesn't seem wise. "I'm already late, so I gotta run, but if you think he'd be great for a role in *Threshold*, by all means you should call his agent." She stands eye-to-eye with him because now he is blocking the doorway. "We have a pact never to talk business when we're together."

Dean seems flustered by her abrupt change in demeanor. "Uh, OK. I guess."

"Come on, Rel," Kat says to Face. Dean startles when the dog pops up from her beanbag bed and he quickly moves aside to let them both exit. Face's muzzle twitches into bared teeth and she growls as she passes Dean who stands frozen against the frosted glass wall.

"Knock it off, Face," Kat commands, and her dog does. Ears back, tail down, eyes suddenly watery, she follows close behind Kat.

"That animal shouldn't be in this office, Katrina," Dean says loudly. "I'm going to talk to HR about this."

It is the last bit she hears Dean say before the elevator door closes with her and Face inside. Her dog hates elevators, especially going down. She splays her paws out as soon as it begins dropping and has her tail between her legs the entire ride.

Even if Dean reports Face as vicious, most everyone would likely defend her dog. She frequently visits the cubicles and offices with open doors mooching for attention and strokes. Most everyone at work loves her around. She's the office 'comfort animal.' Those who don't like dogs, Face got the message after her first visit and never visits them again. Of course, Dean could give her a hassle about bringing Face to work, but CTA isn't firing her any time soon. Kat, and her boss, Frank, knew she is easily one of their best script analysts, putting in the hours on a crappy salary, with reviewers virtually quoting her synopses and comments on any given script nine out of ten times after the film released.

"The prick was trying to pimp me out," Kat says aloud, unable to contain her outrage after she and Face cleared the glass doors to the office tower and are halfway up the stairs outside. It is dark out, and quiet, with a discernible chill in the air. It would feel creepier crossing the quad to the parking structure on her own if Face wasn't with her, walking beside her now.

"Dean Reynolds is a scumbag. He's a Hollywood cliché," Kat says, talking to herself more than Face. "*God*, I'm so sick of the sexist *crap*." Her voice, and low-heeled ankle boots clacking on the concrete floor, along with the clicking of Face's nails, echos in the mostly empty 2nd floor of the underground lot as they walk to her car. Kat sighs heavily, feeling darkness, loneliness descending as she opens the hatchback and watches Face gracefully leap into the back of the Civic.

Stop and go traffic up on the freeway doesn't help her mood any. What should be a 20 minute ride home will now be 50.

Doesn't really matter. She has nothing going on. *Ouch!* Kat feels the lump in her throat and swallows it back, determined not to cry. Ah, to have someone waiting for her...

And the notion soothes her. He'd be in the kitchen cooking a great meal, but would stop for a moment when she comes in. He'd put his hands on her face, draw her in and kiss her passionately but quickly, and she'd join him in preparing dinner while they shared their days...

Kat spends the drive imagining the partnership she's so ready for: a *'safe-harbor for each other,'* her mom used to say about the 25 year union her parents had shared.

"What is your deal with Dean, Rellie?" Kat asks Face, now laying in her sleeping bag bed near the back of the hatchback. Face tilts her head to one side while eyeing Kat in the rear-view mirror. "You clearly had a problem with him before he even got to my office."

Face centers her head, her giant rocket-ears straight up, eyes clear and locked on Kat's rear-view reflection.

"I thought you love everybody. What happened to that?" She exits the I-10 into the heart of Santa Monica. "You freaked me out back there, Face."

The dog's ears goes soft, her Groucho Marx eyebrows gather just below her diamond-crested head. Her eyes seem to get larger, and sadder, and wetter, like she may cry, her canonical response to being called out. Yet still, Face's doleful expression guilts Kat out as she stops at the red light at the bottom of the freeway ramp.

"Oh, come here. You're my good girl."

Face moves behind the driver's seat on the folded passenger seats creating a flat open space for her in the hatchback. She rests her head on Kat's shoulder. Kat scratches Face's muzzle with her free hand.

"Dean's a jerk. Glad you noticed. Good to know you can sniff them out," Kat says, though she doesn't feel glad. It freaks her out a bit that Face had been so aggressive towards Dean. It *is* possible her pound-hound is becoming a bit unhinged as she reaches adulthood and could arbitrarily attack someone else when Kat isn't there to stop her.

Face snuggles her muzzle into Kat's neck. *'YOU. Mine. Pack,'* Kat hears in her head, or more like feels in her heart with her dog's loving gesture. Light turns green. Face retreats as Kat proceeds, goes to the rear window and whines. Kat is familiar with this particular request and rolls down the back window two-thirds of the way. Face sticks her head out and takes in the chilly evening air. For the next couple of miles going home, every light they stop at and many cars they pass or pass them the drivers and passengers smile, wave, and/or yell out their window for Face's attention.

Kat pulls into the one-car driveway of her inherited California adobe Craftsman and waits for the electronic gate to fully open. She stops in front of the detached garage, turns off her car and surveys the long stretch of lawn she'd grown up playing in. Flash memory of the peach playhouse with aqua-green shutters her dad has built for her 7th birthday. Kat sees her mom kiss him, lift her hand to his face and draw him in lovingly. He'd responded in kind. Kat smiles with the memory, something she could not do when she thought of her parents for years after their plane crashed.

The Oracle Face

It's Friday night and Kat does not feel like reading yet another iterative script. Face is in her beanbag bed by the triple-arched windows a couple yards from where Kat sits cross-leg on her parents' bed. She doesn't want to move back into her childhood bedroom. She isn't a child anymore. Nor does she care to move into the guestroom, or convert her dad's study into a bedroom. Moving back to the house she'd been born and raised, now without her parents there, Kat doesn't have the impetus or energy to remodel their home.

Face yelps and continues to grumble. She is deep in a doggy dream, eyes closed, mostly, but darting about in REM sleep, her limbs jerking, probably dreaming of chasing a squirrel, Kat muses. TV is on as background noise to fill the silence of an empty house. She's been scrolling her socials on her cell for a while now and suddenly feels disgusted she is doing so, again.

She should be writing a script instead of just reading them. Problem is, she's lost the impetus to write anything but coverage reports and personal journaling since her parents' death five years ago.

Katrina was sure she'd be a movie maker when she was ten

and dreaming of her adult life. She should be producing and directing her own screenplays by now, living in the beach house her architect husband built for them, with a couple of chaos generating children. She never pictured she'd be a senior script analyst at 32, aka *reader* for the Creative Talent Agency in Century City. Nor did she imagine she'd be an orphan, still single and childless, with zero proposals and no real prospects. She looks at Face again, now still and silent, and easily the best bit about her life.

Kat sighs, annoyed with the war inside her head between the part of her that doesn't want to get online and go through countless disappointing dates in hopes of meeting someone she'll sync with, and the part of her that feels hollow, empty, so very alone back in her parents' home with her folks gone. She could sell the house, buy another, even in the area, but then their memories may fade without the reminders, and Kat isn't ready for that.

She exchanges her cellphone for her tablet on the night table. Kat unlocks the iPad and pulls up Spark. First time logging on in six months. She'd gotten on the platform after Sarah and Frank's little talk about her social life being with her dog. Less than a week into engaging on the app, Kat met Ryan at a Talent party CTA threw late last spring. He was funny, witty, well read, and hot, for sure. And right there, asking her out. She'd been harsh in her critique of him to Frank. Ryan had been kind to her and Face, trying to fit them into his busy life. She'd had fun with him, for the most part. Casual fun. And the longer they dated the more obvious it became that it'd likely remain casual with Ryan. Frank was right. Kat is out of time to indulge in casual anymore.

Her first experience on Spark wasn't *bad*, per say. She'd watched a ton of videos, Liked a few she thought may have potential, but no one really excited her. Most every guy said the same things: how successful and happy they were; in great shape, and at a great space in their lives. All they wanted (not needed, as Kat does) was someone to share their wonderful life with. They'd all seem fine, not psychopaths, or even clinical narcissists. The men were more… *typical*— all about themselves all the time.

According to her dashboard, Kat has 156 Likes and 5 Matches of guys she'd Liked back who'd Liked her. She'd spoken to none of them since she stopped using the app while dating Ryan. It's easy to get Likes but most of them are from guys looking for hookups. Kat isn't into that. She wants her next lover to be the last man she'll sleep with. Her 33rd birthday looms. In eight months she'll be *in* her mid-30s, and on the clock for having children. Kat passionately craves a family of her own, to create a home like the one her parents had gifted her. She'd been privileged to witness their deep affection for each other. Growing up with the best of what marriage can be, Kat wants no less than what her mom and dad had shared together.

"Dating is a numbers game," Kat's mom used to say having married somewhat late for her day. Katrina feels as ready to play as she'll ever be. She quickly swipes left through her Likes, but lingers on her Matches trying not to get her hopes up. She stops on "Michael P." Full head of dark, wavy hair. Deep brown eyes, and a wide, perfect smile made brighter against his brown skin. Next to his name at the bottom of his profile pic shows he is only 27. She'd be robbing the cradle, Kat muses. His one line text description says, "I am becoming the doctor your mom always wanted you to marry." Within 3 seconds of her lingering on his page, his personal video message to her begins without prompting.

"Hi Kat. I'm Michael, or Mike, or M as my sister calls me," Michael says to camera and flashes a shy smile with the thick ruby lips of youth. "Glad we Matched." He is dressed in green scrubs, at least his shirt is. He holds his cell pointing upward so behind him is a florescent lit ceiling haloing his head. He is as cute, if not cuter on video as in his profile pic. "I'm finishing my residency at UCLA Medical next May. But fear not," Michael says, and smiles broadly. "I'm second year and the grueling bit is behind me now so I have some time for an actual life, which is why I'm on this app."

Kat startles when Face jumps on the bed. She lies next to

Kat, tilting her head to one side then the other as if trying to understand what Michael is saying.

"How about you, Kat?" Michael asks on his video. "Why are you here on Spark?"

Face often does the tilting head thing when she hears people talking through a phone, monitor, or TV screen. She used to whine, or bark at the screen when she saw another dog running or playing as if she was trying to get their attention. It didn't take her long to figure out they weren't going to notice her, so she mostly just watches now, alongside Kat.

"Shoot me a quick video and let me know," Michael finishes with a wave goodbye and his profile video stops, replaced by his profile pic and intro data.

Face whines then suddenly barks, startling Kat again. "Whoa. You got a problem with Michael P.?" Kat studies her dog lying next to her. Head up. Ears up. Her classic smile, lightly panting, black nose twitching, eyes fixed on Kat's, then Face looks at the tablet screen Kat holds in her lap. Kat can only assume her dog is responding to Michael P's pic which is prominent on her tablet. Face barks again, not angrily, more like, 'Play with me,' like she used to do with dogs on TV.

"Knock it off," Kat gently commands, and Face does, but she starts panting as if stifling her voice makes her anxious. "OK. What?" Kat asks her dog. "You wanta meet Michael P., Facerellie?"

Face looks a her tablet again, presumably at Michael P's pic, and whines then barks, just once.

"Is that a yes, or no, Rellie?" Kat asks her dog jokingly, since, of course, Face doesn't really know what she is talking about, only that Kat is speaking to her. Her tail thumps rhythmically, vibrating the bed as she stares up at Kat with her classic happy grin, the one she wears most every day they go to play Frisbee. Kat's dog stares at her a moment, then back at the tablet, and whines again. Is there any reality to the notion her dog is directly responding to Michael P's pic and video?

Kat scoffs, dismissing the notion as anthropomorphisizing her dog again and focuses back on her tablet. A red button prompting *Record Your Reply* floats over Michael P.'s profile pic. The app is entirely video except for the minimal bio text. No hiding behind pictures. And to avoid scams and spam, everyone has to record through the app, in real time, no filters, no photoshop, no edits, no do-overs.

"Hello Michael P.," Kat says aloud then presses Record. A moment later her tablet camera is on, recording her. Kat laughs nervously. "Wow. This is *so* awkward. I've never done this before. I got on Spark six months ago, was on it less than a week and met someone, at a party, not on the app, but it didn't work out, obviously... so I'm back... on the app..." She smiles to hide her embarrassment for rambling on and divulging so much so quickly.

Kat feels her face flush with heat that quickly travels to her chest. She runs her hand through her hair to pull it from around her face and neck while taking a breath then sighs. "Hi. I'm Katrina, like the hurricane. But most people call me Kat, which has a certain degree of irony because I prefer dogs, as you know from my profile video," and Kat angles her tablet to show Face lying next to her, now resting her head on Kat's crossed leg. Face lifts her head, ears up, eyes on the tablet Kat holds in her lap, presumably at Michael's image. She smooshes her nose into the screen like she is trying to smell him. "No! Gross," Kat puts the camera back on herself and rubs her screen clean with her shirtsleeve. "Sorry. Anyway, hope you're good with dogs." She smiles broadly. "If you'd like to level up to live chat, I'm in. Reach back out if you are."

Kat stops recording. *'Level up to live chat?'* How cringe is that? "I suck at this, Facerelli!" Face lifts her head off Kat's leg and looks up at her, then kisses her cheek with a quick wet lick when Kat bends her head to look at her tablet again. "*Ah,*" Kat says, heartfelt. "And yuk! Dog slobber." She wipes her cheek dry with the long sleeve of her oversized flannel night shirt.

Face rests her head on Kat's crossed leg and watches her swipe left on the next few profiles. Kat stops on Mark C., a 35 year old sandy blond, blue-eyed rocket scientist, literally. It says he's working at JPL in Pasadena currently on the newest Mars rover project. His bio text is under his profile pic for about 3 seconds, then his video reply to their match begins without prompting.

"Hi Kat. Nice to virtually meet you," Mark C. says, but then just sits there, long enough for Kat to assume the video froze.

"Great name," Marc C. finally says. Face lifts her head and looks at Kat passively, then back at her tablet. They both watch Mark C.'s video, likely shot from his laptop, as he shifts in his office chair. "I have a cat, a blue-eyed Siamese. I do prefer cats to dogs since they're much easier to take care of, but I don't see that as an issue betwe—"

Kat swipes left and moves on. She passes several more Matches then stops on Arthur S., 34, who looks strangely similar to a young Elvis. Again his video reply begins without prompting.

"I'm glad to see we Matched, but I don't see a message from ya, Kat. Did I miss it?" Arthur asks in a subtle southern accent. "Guess I'll play the roll of the classic gentleman here and reach out to you first. Don't mind, really, I'm kind of old-fashioned anyway. I'm just hoping you're not among the many women on this site that uses Likes as click-bait."

Face growls, gravelly and resonant, emitting a long, low vibration the likes of which Kat has only heard from her dog once, with Dean Reynolds, the scumbag agent at her office.

"Anyway," Arthur continues. "I'm a successful real estate developer. I'm at a great space in my life..."

Kat angles the tablet for Face to see the screen clearly. Her dog's eyes stay fixed on Arthur's video as she growls again, mouth twitching intermittently baring her teeth, and it is clear she is not trying to initiate play.

"...All I need is someone to share the journey with," Arthur says.

"What is it, Rellie? You don't like this guy?" Kat asks her dog, rhetorically, of course, stroking the Mohawk strip of fir raised along Face's spine.

"... If you're ready for the real thing," Arthur continues. "Reply with times you're available to virtually meet. Or meet up in person, if you dare." He smiles a hugely wide, white grin, and his video ends.

Face looks at Kat, then back at the tablet and bares her teeth in her twitchy way, then growls that deep, angry growl again.

Kat looks at Arthur S. pic on her cell. "Well, he looks fine to me. Cute, actually."

Face abruptly lifts her head all the way up, rocket ears straight up. She's fixed on the windows then bolts off the bed. Kat can not see what Face can since it's dark beyond the triple-arched windows, but it's likely there's a squirrel or raccoon in the backyard. The dog runs from the bedroom, her claw nails tapping in a quick, rhythmic pace down the hall towards the kitchen.

Kat goes back to perusing Spark. She hears the doggy door flap as Face goes out to chase whatever is invading her yard. She does not consider her dog's opinion, or seriously consider Face *has* an opinion about the four men she eventually chooses to reply to.

[Mostly] Before Face

"Arthur Simms tried to assault me on our one and only coffee meet," Kat says, exasperated. "I don't think that's 'avoiding commitment.'"

"I'm not talking about Arthur Simms and you know it," Sarah says during lunch at The Apple Pan. "You know what I mean, Kat." The diner is packed, every seat at the counter, which wrapped the cooks on three sides, is taken. Her six month old, Cassidy, is with them. Sarah is feeding her spoonfuls of banana cream pie, which, if she does not get instantly after consuming the previous bite, she starts fussing in her hook-on high chair. "Since you broke up with Danny you've rejected Ryan, the actor. Then there is Michael, the doctor you met on Spark. He was 6, or maybe 8 weeks before you broke it off with him. Then Shemesh, Shameem, I can't remember. The IT guy at work. How long was that. Like a month?" She feeds her daughter another mouthful. "And now this other guy from Spark, Jay, is it? You go out with him, what, three times and call it quits. Gotta ask yourself, do you really want a relationship, Kat?"

"Jay's a corporate attorney looking for an arm piece," Kat defends. "In three dates he asked me maybe ten questions, and I'm pretty sure he still doesn't know what I do for a living. I, however, can tell you the names of his kids, how long he's been divorced, and his issues with their marriage, which, of course, are basically because she's a greedy bitch."

Creamy sludge oozed out of the baby's mouth and looks disgusting, but Kat feels jealous of Sarah anyway, now wiping Cassidy's mouth with wet-wipes.

"Michael is finishing his residency and is way too busy for anything beyond occasionally," Kat continues in her defense. "He's great on Facetime, but I want more than an online relationship, or last minute texts that he's been abruptly assigned to Emergency rotation and can't meet me." Her friend and colleague has no clue what online dating is like. "And Shemesh went to work for Microsoft in Seattle, so, not my fault."

"It's not about fault, sweetie. But while you're hoping to model some glorified version of your parents relationship, time is fleeting. You want a family then you best get on that. Or maybe, you want to look into having kids on your own?"

"I want a father for my children. It's sheer arrogance to believe that I can ever be all they'll need," Kat says, Want pervasive now watching Sarah rub noses with her beautiful daughter. They both giggle in delight.

"Then maybe you should lower your expectations just a tad," Sarah says in her clipped British accent. "Isn't it possible your folks are like most couples who struggle to stay together?"

Sarah's husband Malcom has adored her since college. "Are you struggling to stay with Malcom?" Kat asks, maybe wrongly assuming they are good as always.

"Sometimes." Sarah sighs. "It's *hard* sustaining an intimate relationship for most anyone in them." Sarah eyed Kat like she is stating the obvious, then gets up to attend to her daughter. "It takes *work* to support and share the best of each other, especially with jobs and kids."

Kat swallows the lump rising in her throat as she picks at her slice of coconut cream pie. Sarah isn't trying to be mean. She is direct as always, cuts straight to the chase without filtering, and she is right, of course. Kat has had three relationships her entire life that lasted more than a year.

Sarah wipes Cassidy's hands and face again with a wet-wipe from the pack she keeps in her baby tote-bag. "Thing is, we're social creatures by nature," Sarah continues. She straightens and unbuckles Cassidy from her clip-on seat. "We all crave that flippin amazing feeling of synchronized connection, unmitigated acceptance, security... *love*." Sarah picks her daughter up. "But it's a double-edged sword, right?" She holds her baby girl to her and gently taps Cassidy's back to solicit a burp. "The more you love, the more abhorrent even the thought of losing that spectacular connection." Her daughter snuggles her face into Sarah's neck, and Sarah bends her head and rubs her cheek along her child's. Their exchange of love is palpable, beautiful, and painful for Kat to witness, Want so visceral now it is hard to breathe. "Love is costly, Kat, as you well know. But you're gonna have to be willing to risk loss to fully partake in love, girl."

Ouch. Kat bites her lip, hard, hoping the pain will stop her from crying. She craves something solid, connected, intimate, like Sarah has, or at least someone in her life to give her the ground her parents seemed to for each other. They'd left her alone, untethered, floating when they died. As Greg had when he proposed to Allison instead of her a month after she buried her folks. Her eyes blur with tears. She blinks and they slide down her cheeks.

"Oh god, I'm sorry, honey," Sarah says as she tucks a tendril of Kat's hair behind her ear. "I'm sure you're trying. If you keep at it, maybe even ramp it up a bit, I'm sure you'll find someone soon." She offers up platitudes as she bounces her daughter up and down while continuing to tap her tiny back.

Kat is haunted by Sarah's critical commentary of her dating progress as she drives home that Saturday afternoon. Can it be she's spent the last five years avoiding intimacy, too afraid of losing it as she has her parents? And Greg?

Sitting in stop and go traffic on the I-10, Kat considers the two relationships she's had since her folks' passing. Marc, sweet Marc, had started out a roommate, someone to fill the void in the house when she moved back home, but they became lovers nine months in. Marc was pure fun, got Kat hiking, camping, even singing again. She was the vocals to his prolific range on the guitar, but Marc didn't know the difference between Plato and Play-Doh, and didn't care to learn. Kat knew they'd never be more than friends with benefits, but they were together almost two years, until he was accepted into Berklee School of Music in Boston, Kat having pushed him to apply.

She met Danny at an office party for Academy Award nominees that CTA represents. A composer and a skilled pianist, he was up for *Best Original Score*. He didn't win, but Kat thought his music was hauntingly melodic, and the best thing about the vapid, ghostly love story in the movie.

Danny was wonderfully romantic, a great snuggler, always held her hand when they were out and about, like he was proud to be with her. They did the L.A. scene, attended film openings, popular plays, private clubs, got back-stage passes to sold out concerts of musicians Danny knew. At first it was fun, full of glitz and glamour, but it was also overwhelming— loud, crowded, so very... *public*. Kat preferred their quiet times together, hanging out at home with his dog, Riley, an enormous, 4 yr old English Mastiff/Shepherd mix.

A year into dating Danny and Kat had had enough. She stopped accompanying him to most events and shows, even his own band. She preferred hanging with Riley, the huge dog's head in her lap while she sat on the couch reading or watching TV. And the more Danny was gone on evenings and weekends, the clearer it became that they were on two different paths, and at different stages in their lives, so she kissed him goodbye when his band went on their first global tour. Kat had no interest in being part of his entourage.

Fall in love with the artist, not his art, Kat hears her dad warn when, at 13, she'd expressed her undying love for some teen pop idol. She didn't listen. Sadly. Kat admired talent, and passion, only recently discovering that artistic obsession really means narcissism.

She inches along on the freeway questioning the wisdom of meeting Sarah in Culver City. Sarah's gone through her six months of parental leave. She's currently debating coming back to work but Kat knows her well enough to know Sarah would not be satisfied being a stay-at-home mom. Kat misses her, which is why she'd initiated lunch at The Apple Pan. Sarah is the closest girlfriend she's had since high school, though they rarely speak outside of the office, especially now that she has Cassidy. Taking Frank's lead, Sarah has been on Kat about meeting someone, though she doesn't ask about her dates, or seemingly care about the details. To be fair, it isn't like Kat is forthcoming in talking about her life, and Sarah probably gets tired of soliciting her to go beyond Kat's brief responses. Most people do. Kat has never been chatty. She's always been an observer, a listener, and became even more so with the sudden deaths of her parents. And losing Greg.

Kat slams on her brakes to avoid hitting the white BMW that suddenly moves in front of her in the fast lane. "*Asshole!*" she yells then flips him off hoping he sees her give him the finger in his rearview mirror, then lets her hand fall back in her lap. And her ire turns inward. She is a month from 33. *Thirty three* years old, still stuck, *going nowhere*, Kat hears in her head and feels her chest cave in, aloneness consuming her. Again.

"Screw you, Greg," Kat hears herself say aloud before it registers in her head. She feels her ire rise again, but this time from a deeper place than some asshole BMW driver. Her body flushes with heat, and an almost violent anger is gaining momentum inside her as she sequences her life with Greg.

Next door neighbor and BFF since she was five until their early teens, then her boyfriend through high school, Greg was her first lover, and her sole confidant beyond her mother. He was her best friend, often her only friend through much of their formative years. He got into Harvard for his DBA in accounting. Kat went to UCLA's for her MFA in Screenwriting, but they stayed a couple with visits on holiday weekends and summers together in

Boston or L.A., until three months to the day after Kat's parents were killed. She was home, handling her parent's estate, but Greg's email was crystal clear. He'd not be joining her in California as planned. He'd proposed to his Cambridge roommate and was staying in Boston, at school, his job, his established life, and soon to be wife.

Sarah is right. Love is risky in the extreme.

Kat sighs shakily as she exits the freeway, her anger deflating to exhaustion. Clear blue sky and bright out, the western horizon glows gold with the arching afternoon sun as she pulls into her parents' driveway.

No. That's not right, Kat thinks. *My* driveway now, and mine alone. And with the notion she crosses the event horizon into the black hole of grief. She sits behind the wheel in *her* driveway barely breathing, watching the electronic gate open in what feels like slow motion. Face appears in the fenced yard beyond the backyard gate, rocket-ears up, panting with her happy smile on and wagging her tail.

With Face safe in the fenced yard, Kat pulls her Civic up in front of the detached garage and turns off the engine but then just sits behind the wheel. Moving right then feels like a monumental effort. Sarah accused her of avoiding intimacy, and Kat has to admit this is likely true. Since Greg, she's chosen relationships likely to go nowhere.

Face greets Kat with whines of joy and a wagging tale when Kat finally comes through the fence gate. "Hey baby," Kat says, Face nuzzling up against her, swishing her tail in delight that Kat is back. "Glad to see you, too, Rellie." Kat strokes her dog along her spine then she steps onto the porch and moves towards the backdoor of her empty house. Loneliness is descending and even the love of her dog cannot stop the overwhelming cascade of desire for more.

Frisbee Dog to the Rescue

Face drops the Frisbee in the sand at Kat's feet. She stares up at Kat smiling, her long pink tongue hanging out of her mouth and dripping with saliva. Even with sunglasses, the setting sun is blinding as Kat throws the disk down the beach with as much force as she can muster to keep it level with the westerly winds ushering in the nightly Pacific fog.

"*Oh!* Great catch!" Kat says after Face leaps off the ground and plucks the Frisbee from 4 feet in the air.

"*Score!*" a runner along the shoreline several yards away says and puts his arms up like a ref after a goal seeing Face catch the Frisbee too.

Kat smiles. She loves that Face spreads joy. On their way to the beach from work this afternoon her dog must have made a dozen people stuck in traffic smile seeing her dog's head stuck out the car window happily taking it all in, experiencing the moment, as most of us only wish we could.

Face is back and drops the Frisbee at Kat's feet again. As she bends to pick it up she sees Bruno, the horny chocolate pitbull mix barreling towards them across the sand. Face catches site of him and takes off towards the shoreline.

"Damn," Kat says and runs to the shoreline where Bruno is trying to mount Face from behind.

Face keeps running away to keep Bruno off her. She's growling and snapping at him when Kat gets to the dogs. Bruno's owner is on his cell a few yards away, laughing at whatever he is so engrossed in. Kat steps in front of Bruno, blocking his path to Face.

"Go on, Bruno!" Kat yells at the bulldog trying to get around her. "Get outta here! *Go!*" She dances in front of Bruno in and out of the shallows to keep him off Face. Face stays behind her for the most part, on the sand, away from the waterline. Shepherds are not water dogs.

"Ya here to neuter your dog again?" the middle-age incel says, finally looking up. He stares salaciously at Kat. "Bruno's just tryin ta give your bitch some lovin. Looks like you could use some too," he adds.

Face growls at Bruno coming at her when the brown bulldog sprints around Kat. "My dog's not interested," she says harshly, again trying to get Bruno away from Face. "And neither am I."

"Why don't ya let em have some fun, honey bun?" the incel snipes. "You ain't their mama."

"And she ain't your honey bun," a guy says as he approaches them. "Control your dog, or leash it, or leave."

Kat feels simultaneously empowered, diminished, and enamored by this guy stepping in, and maybe even a little afraid of him, like he's angling for a fight. The two men stare at each other and she feels the tension between them. They're about the same height, but Bruno's owner has an enormous beer belly. The other guy is slender, with a tight build, and easily 10 years his junior.

"Bruno, come," the man finally says without taking his eyes off the younger guy. Bruno ignores him. He focuses his attention on his dog. "I said *come* Bruno!" he commands harshly, then tromps over to his dog, grabs Burno's chain metal choke collar and drags him across the sand towards the parking lot.

"Thanks," Kat says to the guy. "But I was handling it, ya know." She can't help herself from making it clear she isn't in need of saving.

Face stands panting by Kat's side. "Go get your Frisbee," Kat commands her dog, and Face does.

"I know you didn't need to be rescued," the guy says, like he is reading her mind. "Knee-jerk reaction when I see someone getting harassed, I guess. I'm sorry if I overstepped."

She looks at the guy who she now notices is rather, well… *hot*. Studies him as he seems to be her. Deep brown skin, full head of wavy brown hair cut short on the sides but left longer on top, he has striking green eyes, full lips and a gently-square jawline. His sleeveless black t-shirt exposes his toned arms and pecs, his loose black running shorts revealing his muscular legs. "Bruno's owner's been a jerk since he started coming here a few months ago. It was nice having your backup. Thanks."

He smiles this adorably humble dimpled grin. "My pleasure." He nods, his lean body folding into a slight Asian bow. "I'm Aidan. Aidan Tilden." He reaches out to shake Kat's hand.

How retro, Kat thinks as she takes his hand in hers. No rings on any fingers, either hand, she notices. "I'm Katrina. Kat," she clarifies, but doesn't offer her last name for obvious reasons.

He releases her hand and steps back. "Well, I'm off, back to my run. Have a good evening, Kat," he says as he turns to run and almost trips over Face coming back with her Frisbee.

Kat's dog drops her Frisbee in Aidan's path. He turns back to Kat before bending to pick it up. "May I?"

"Sure. Go ahead,"

There are many runners and shoreline strollers every time Kat and Face play Frisbee on the beach. But in the countless times they've played to date, her dog has never dropped her Frisbee in front of anyone besides her before.

Aidan tosses the Frisbee further than Kat has ever thrown it. Face bolts after it.

Face catches it mid-air again.

"*Score* again!" Aidan says excitedly, putting both arms up

and turning back to Kat with a huge smile. "Got yourself one hell of a dog there, Kat," he says, then waves as he turns away and runs towards the shoreline.

Face comes back with the Frisbee dangling from her mouth along with her long pink tongue. She stands on the sand in front of Kat but doesn't drop the Frisbee. Instead she looks around, like she's looking for something she does not see, then whines. Face looks at Kat and whines again. She follows Kat's line of site and sees Aidan, already quite a ways up the beach running along the water's edge. She whines again, practically mirroring Kat's disappointment Aidan continued his run instead of choosing to stay with them.

—

The wind is whistling through the doggie door's rubber flap in the short time it takes Kat to fill Face's food and water bowls, choose her own meal and put it in the oven. Face takes a few licks from her water bowl then curls in her gray puffy mat near the back door. With her food always available, Kat's dog dosen't feel a need to scarf her 'dinner' when she isn't hungry.

Kat sits in the sunroom off the kitchen and opens her mother's 8 yr old laptop, glad she'd not given it away. She likes her fingers touching the same keys her mom once did. She pulls up her email and checks her inbox on the 27" monitor connected to the laptop. Sarah has sent her, Frank, and a bunch of others an animation of pics showing Cassidy getting up off her butt and toddling along, ostensibly her first time walking. Frank followed up to Kat, Sarah and others with a video clip of their Cockapoo, Liza, finding Doug's keys that had fallen between the cushions of their modular Bellini couch.

Still waiting for her mac and cheese to heat up, on a whim she looks up Aidan Tilden. Can't find him on Insta, or TikTok, or X, or even Facebook, though no one she knows is on Facebook anymore. Finally finds him on LinkedIn. Featured pic in his header banner is a beautiful house, contemporary, lots of wood and glass, windows reflecting the ocean. Great pic of him outside somewhere in the circle below the header. He looked younger on the beach but by his profile pic Kat guesses he's in his late 20s maybe. Under his picture and name his one-liner says, 'Builder of Things.' Under that his location is Pacific Palisades, California.

Under About it says: 'Architect by day and I build furniture by night. Diverse background in architecture, construction, real estate development. Co-founder and partner of MTS Architectural Studios.'

Kat smiles, ostensibly her fantasy man coming to life on the screen before her.

Face whines. Kat turns to look at her dog. Head up, rocket-ears up, eyes wide, Face looks at Kat then the monitor from her gray mat near the back door.

Kat returns to looking at Aidan's LinkedIn page.

Face barks.

Kat startles. "Stop that!" Kat commands, and Face does. Ears down, for about a second. Then she gets up and stands near Kat's chair, ears up, eyes wide and staring up at the monitor. Then Face whines and barks again.

Kat glares at her dog. "*What!?*"

Face stares up at her, ears back again, her big brown eyes watery and fixed on Kat, then back on Aidan, then back on Kat. She starts panting and circles a few times, clearly agitated, then Kat's dog looks back at Aidan's page on the screen and whines again.

Kat listens closely hoping to glean her dog's problem. *Squirrel!* she hears Face in her head as her dog spots something through the sunroom's french windows and bolts out the doggie door into the backyard. Hard to see what's out there in the twilight of the encroaching night.

Aidan Tilden's image stares back at her from the screen. He'd been kind today and she kinda reamed him for it. *Bad form, Kat*, she chides herself. He's clearly a runner, and she wonders how often he's at Will Rogers, or the odds of him passing by her playing Frisbee with Face with ten miles of unfettered beach from the Palisades to Marina Del Ray.

Dog Envy

About a month after Kat got Face from the pound, she was playing with her new puppy on the beach. Half the size she is now, someone threw a Frisbee over her and she bolted after it, then leaped 3 feet in the air and caught it. The guy with the Frisbee was kind enough to gift the disk to Kat's dog after Face returned it, to Kat, her razor teeth having punctured several holes in the thick plastic.

She's taken Face for Frisbee most every day since. After work on the weekdays, mostly to Will Rogers, or Ginger Rogers State Beach a bit south but still far enough away from Santa Monica to avoid the sunbathing hoards, the beachcombers, and the shoreline wanderers. Times and locations vary on the weekends. Sometimes Zuma, or Leo Carrillo to climb the rocks and watch the surfers.

Both Saturday and Sunday Kat goes to Will Rogers beach to play Frisbee with Face at the same time she did on Friday afternoon when she'd met Aidan. Both days he's not there. Neither is Bruno and his dickhead owner.

Monday after work she's back at Will Rogers, same time as always. While she sees many runners, she doesn't spot Aidan the entire half hour she's out there. Face returns the Frisbee, drops it at Kat's feet then stares up at Kat with her happy smile. She's foaming at the mouth, her jaw trembling, Kat's cue it's time to quit for the day. Face will play till she has a heart attack.

Face's ears pivot back and she suddenly picks her Frisbee off the sand, turns around and goes a few paces to the man approaching them. Tail wagging wildly, she drops the Frisbee at his bare feet.

"Not yet, buddy," Aidan says, and strokes Kat's dog just once then joins Kat.

Face picks up her Frisbee which Aidan has passed, brings it to where he stands in the sand and drops it at his feet again.

Aidan laughs. "May I?"

He has a great laugh— rich, resonant. Kat smiles at him. "Of course."

He picks it up and hauls it straight up the beach, again further than Kat ever could and Face takes off after it.

"*Oh! Score!*" Aidan yells as Kat's dog leaps off the sand and catches the Frisbee four feet in the air after running full-tilt half the length of a football field to retrieve it. "Beautiful catch!" he exclaims as Face comes trotting back towards them with the Frisbee in her mouth.

"She loves playing, and it keeps her in shape," Kat says. "Look at her prancing back. She's looking around to see if anyone saw her catch it. If she misses it, she'll only look at me when she's bringing it back." Kat strokes her dog now literally leaning against her legs and panting heavily. Face keeps the Frisbee in her mouth, her cue she needs a moment before another toss. "You can totally tell she feels proud of herself when she catches it," Kat babbles on, suddenly realizing how cringe she must sound.

Aidan laughs. "O*K*..." he says doubtfully.

"No, seriously—"

Face whines. She's dropped the Frisbee at Aidan's feet again but he hadn't noticed. He picks it up and holds it. "You ready?" he asks the dog. Face circles the two of them standing in the sand a couple times, then he hauls it again, his form perfect, showcasing his muscular arms and lean build in his sleeveless emerald green T. Face takes off after it.

"Watch her," Kat instructs. They both watch the dog pluck the Frisbee out of the air feet off the ground again, land, and immediately look around, but other than the two of them there's no other audience near by. "See," Kat says with a soft smile.

They both laugh as Face prances back to them, eyes bright, her panting pink tongue dangling to the side of the Frisbee in her mouth.

"She's beautiful, Kat," Aidan says with a hint of awe.

So are you, Kat smiles at her thought. "Thanks." His green t-shirt accentuates his bright green eyes. He's tall, close to 6'. His black running shorts are loose-fitting and hang on his hips just right.

Beyond the salty sweet Pacific breeze, Kat smells the sweet scent of attraction emanating from her skin. They stay on the beach talking and tossing the Frisbee to Face until after sunset. He asks her questions, and answers hers without hedging. He often turns them around, as so few she'd dated had, or do. Most men like to be interviewed. The conversation flows from their jobs to their dreams smoothly. They share intimate details about their lives, at times shockingly familiar.

Takes about 40 minutes for Face to go from enamored to annoyed with Aiden. To Face, his mere presence takes Kat's focus off her, both of them sometimes ignoring the fact that she's come back with the Frisbee and dropped it at their feet because they're so immersed in talking to each other. Kat's dog gets so miffed by this she refuses to let go of the disk and walks past Aidan and Kat standing on the beach towards the parking lot, indicating she's done playing for the day.

"Face, stay with me," Kat says to her dog.

Face stops, looks back at Kat, but then saunters a few paces across the sand.

"I said, *stay with me*," Kat now commands, and gives Aidan a bashful smile, her cheeks blushing with her dog's bratty behavior.

Face stops but does not come to Kat with now several yards between them.

"If I were you, I'd stay," Aidan says directly to Face. The dog stares at him, practically glares at him. "Seems like you have a nice setup with Kat." Aidan glances at Kat, flashes her an awkward smile. "Your dog is done with Frisbee for the day I'm guessing," Aidan says to her.

"Yeah. We usually play for half an hour and we've been out here for almost an hour and a half," Kat says, but immediately regrets it, afraid she's just sounded like she didn't want to be. "Thanks for joining us today."

"It was a pleasure chatting with you this afternoon," he says to her.

"Likewise," Kat says, but can think of no followup.

"Well, I'm gonna get back to my run. Hope to see ya out here again soon."

"Me too," Kat says as she lets Face lead her away from him, off the sand and towards her car with the Frisbee in her mouth. As she trudges across the sand after her dog Kat is ready to make meeting Aidan again more than just a hope but a reality, regardless how Face feels about him.

No Fury Like a Bitch Scorned

🐕

"Frank told me you have some issue with your new beau," Sarah says, sitting at her kitchen table adjacent to Kat. "This is the architect with the house in the Palisades?"

Kat nods. "Aidan. His name's Aidan," she clarifies, though she's mentioned him a couple times already, including her last time at Sarah's a couple weeks ago, or is it a month already?

"So, do I have to pry it out of you or are you going to tell me your issue with this guy," Sarah says. "Frank says he's… what was it exactly?" She pauses trying to recall. "Mic's David come to life."

Kat smiles. "Not exactly. But he's pretty cute, I have to admit." She feels her cheeks flush with heat, and looks down at her cup, then sips her tea.

"How old is he?" Sarah asks, looking at her daughter. Cassidy is snuggled up to Face on the quilted blanket in the makeshift playpen Sarah constructed out of rubber-coated wire shelving on the floor in the playroom. "And where's he from?"

"He's 36, but he looks way younger, like he could still be in college. And he's native L.A., but more nerd than hip, slick, and trending." Kat stops gushing and sips her tea.

"Then what's your problem with him? He sounds rather lovely," she says in her clipped Brit way.

"My issue isn't with Aidan. It's with Face—."

"Cassidy, *no!* Let go!" Sarah says and she suddenly gets up. "Face is not your teddy bear." She steps over the 2 foot enclosure just as Face pulls her tail from Cassidy's tiny fingers. "You're almost a year old now. You should know better."

Face jumps the improvised fencing with ease as soon as her tail is free. She goes to Kat for strokes, ears back, tail down, Groucho eyebrows furrowed, unsure if she's done something wrong.

"It's fine, baby. You're my gentle lass," Kat assures her dog as she strokes her. "You're a good girl, Relli."

Ahhhh... Kat hears Face in her head, like a long luxurious sigh of relief.

Cassidy melts down now abandoned by Face. She sits on the quilted blanket and wails.

"OK," Sarah says as she picks up her daughter. "Nap time."

Cassidy continues screaming and reaching her tiny hand for Face who stands by where Kat sits at the kitchen table passively watching the scene. Kat's dog is unfazed by the infant's outburst, though Face is somewhat familiar with them by now having been to Sarah's several times since she started working hybrid.

"Be right back," Sarah practically yells as she takes her wailing daughter from the playroom, Cassidy's screaming echoing down the hallway.

Kat strokes her dog, a reflex now whenever Face stands next to her. Face glances at her with her dreamy face on, her rocket-ears slack, her huge, brown almond-eyes soft— *ecstasy*.

It's astounding to Kat how gentle her dog is with Cassidy, regardless of how the baby treats her. She's been around Cassidy since birth, Sarah's daughter snuggling up to Face at just 5 months old. Always gentle with the baby, or even around her, a few months ago Face started smooshing her nose into Cassidy's belly or neck to solicit giggles, like the two of them are playing a game. And every time Sarah brings her daughter to the office, Face lays by her portable playpen like a guard dog.

"Hey Facerelli," Kat says gently as she continues stroking her dog. "You're my maternal beauty. You certainly are."

Cassidy is still wailing, now from the bedroom, likely in her crib. Face whines, looks back at Kat, her Groucho Marx eyebrows drawn together again, then stares at the hallway, her rocket-ears straight up.

Help! Kat hears Face in her head, not exactly like *Squirrel!*, but has the same immediacy. Her dog takes a few steps towards the hallway threshold and looks back at Kat then whines again, louder this time, like a yelp, and again Kat hears *Help!* in her head.

"Go," Kat says to her dog a moment before Face struts out of the room. Her paws clickety-clack on the wood floor as she goes down the hall. Moments later Cassidy stops crying.

Face went in to soothe Cassidy, had told Kat she wanted to help, and *did*. Aidan was right. Kat's dog is truly amazing, one-of-a-kind. Even growing up from 5 to 19 years old with her family's Shepherd mix, as adorable and loving as Pepper was, she was nothing like Face.

So, then what's her problem with Face that Kat just alluded to Sarah before she left the kitchen to put Cassidy down? And a memory of that first time on the beach talking with Aidan plays…

…"You really do have an amazing Frisbee dog, Kat," Aidan had said. "Ever thought about entering her in a competition?"

"Nah. I want her to keep loving it, so I don't wanta ever turn it into a chore."

"Yeah. I can see that," Aidan said.

Face was back, panting heavily. She dropped the Frisbee in the sand inches from Aidan's feet. She was drooling, which was a bit embarrassing, and kinda killing the majestic vib Face often has going.

"Her smile is infectious," Aidan said and laughed as he

bent to pick up the Frisbee. He looked at Face staring at him, crouched like she's ready to pounce. "Ready?" he asked Kat's dog directly. "You're gonna have to hall ass," he added, still addressing Face directly.

Face was standing a yard or so in front of them frozen in anticipation of Aidan's disk toss. Kat is sure she saw her dog's big brown eyes twinkle with delight. Listening carefully, Kat heard nothing from her dog but she did pick up a vibration, like another heartbeat to her own, but this one's faster than hers, and inside her head.

Aidan hurled the Frisbee half the length of a football field straight down the beach even with the westerly winds coming off the ocean.

Kat looked away so he wouldn't see her smiling. Again, it was hard not to notice his fine form, muscular arms and tight body.

They both watched Face running after the flying disk, her form also impressive— ears back, head down, tail straight, wide stride, muscles taut in fluid motion.

Face snagged the Frisbee out of the air about half a foot before it hit the sand.

Aidan howled a cheer. "She's grace personified," he'd said, almost to himself before turning to Kat standing next to him. "What's her name?"

"Killer Dog Face." Kat told him her dog's full name to see his reaction.

Aidan laughed. "Killer name." He smiled. "Killer as in 'cool,' right?"

"Yup," Kat said, smiling back at him.

"Dog, either from that John Wayne movie where he has a dog he calls 'Dog,' or because she is one."

"Second reason." Kat couldn't stop smiling at him.

"And my mom used to call my younger sister 'Little Face' when we were kids, so I'm guessing it's a term of endearment?" Aidan looked at Kat for confirmation.

"Seriously impressive," Kat had said. "Most think her full name is funny but no one's ever guessed the origin, or ever asked." She gave him a tempered smile. There was an awkward silence while they watched Face trot back to them. "Her name's Face," Kat says. "Everyone calls her Face, even me most of the time."

Aidan nodded and smiled this adorable dimpled grin. "I've seen you here playing Frisbee with Face quite a bit. You live near by?"

"Yeah." Kat turned south and pointed to the bluff of Santa Monica. "Up there." She turned back to face him. Lots of runners the nine months she'd been coming to this beach with her dog, but none she noticed details. "What about you. You live around here?"

"Just moved to the area," Aidan said. "Built a home on the hill up there," and he turned east and points to the homes on top of the bluff.

"Are you a developer?" Kat asked. She already knew he was an architect, but she didn't want him to know she'd stalked him.

"Architect," he said. "And developer, I guess. I've been a partner at MTS Studios for the last eight years." He paused, focused on me completely as if to gauge my reaction to his profession. "What about you, Kat? What do you do?"

"I'm a senior script analyst for the Creative Talent Agency."

So, you're a writer then?" Aidan asked sincerely.

Kat flushed with heat, blushed. "I have my MFA in screenwriting from UCLA but I haven't really written anything besides course assignments yet."

"Why?"

Face barked. Aidan and Kat looked down at her dog staring up at them, from Kat to Aidan. Her Frisbee was in the sand in front of both of them and she was clearly agitated neither of them had picked it up yet. Face barked again when neither bent to pick it up. Kat's dog plucked the Frisbee out of the sand and threw it at Kat's feet.

Aidan and Kat looked at each other and laughed at Face's overt display of frustration. Aidan picked up the Frisbee and threw it down the beach. Face bolted after it. They both waited to speak till she caught it. "*Nice*," Aidan said when she did, his enthusiasm naturally toned down having witnessed her Frisbee dog in action several times already.

"Annie, my Husky, wouldn't fetch no matter what I did," Aidan said. "Even fed her out of a Frisbee when she was a pup but she never retrieved anything. If I threw a Frisbee or ball, she'd look at me like, 'You threw it, *you* go get it.'"

Kat laughed. "Growing up I had the same exact thing going on with our family dog, Pepper."

Face whined, then barked. She'd dropped the Frisbee by Kat's feet, but Kat hadn't noticed while talking with Aidan. She picked it out of the sand and tossed it about two thirds of the distance that Aidan did. Face went after it.

"Was Annie your family dog growing up?" Kat asked him, since he spoke of his Husky in the past tense.

The mood seemed to darken with Aidan's weighted sigh. "She died in a car accident, along with my mom and little sister five years ago." He looked at Kat, flashed a sad smile then looked back at Face coming back with the Frisbee.

"Oh my god," fell out of Kat's mouth. "I'm so sorry..."

"Thanks. It's a while ago now," he said reverently. "But I still miss them every single day."

Face barked, startling them both. She'd dropped the

Frisbee at Kat's feet again and was waiting for her to throw it. Kat looked at Aidan. He was watching her, his head slightly tilted to one side, as if looking for cues to how she felt about his news. Face barked again. Aidan broke eye contact, looked down then bent down, picked up the Frisbee and threw it.

Face hesitated, stared... no, more like *glared* at Kat a second before taking off after it. She missed catching the Frisbee by quite a bit. She did not look around as she retrieved it and cantered, not pranced, back to them with the disk dangling from her mouth, and she wasn't smiling.

Kat hadn't shared her personal tragedy with most of the guys she casually dated. The more people that know her parents are dead, the more real they're gone forever becomes.

"Is your dad still alive?" Kat dared ask, knowing she may be getting too personal too quickly but curious if Aidan was an orphan like her.

"He is. And he's an amazing dad, before and after my mom and sister died. I'm lucky. Growing up I got to witness the best of what a partnership can be with a front row seat to my parents' marriage." Aidan gave her a pensive smile. "What about you? Your parents still here?" He looked at Kat, his eyes focused on hers instead of scanning the beach, or checking his cell.

Face barked again, and again startled them both. She continued barking this time, her eyes on Kat, then down at her

Frisbee then back at Kat.

"Stop that," Kat commanded, a bit embarrassed her dog was being such a brat.

Face looked down at her Frisbee, used her front paws to aide her picking it up in her mouth, then basically threw it at Kat's feet. She looked up at Kat and barked a few more times, and Kat hears the now familiar resonance of her dog inside her head: *We're here for* Frisbee. *See!*

Kat bent down, retrieved the Frisbee and threw it. Face bolted after it. "My parents were killed in a plane crash five years ago." She looked at Aidan. his eyes on hers, connecting them, the glass wall of acquaintance dissolving between them sharing such intimate disclosures. "I have no siblings, so I'm kind of an orphan now."

"Wow. Sorry to hear that," Aidan had said, and Kat felt as if he really was sorry, not just platitudes but like he knew her pain. "Been wondering lately, when, well, *if* I'll ever get used to them gone," he said, almost to himself.

"Know what ya mean." Kat certainly did, still aching daily for her folks, and the family she once loved. "On the upside, like you, my parents had a great relationship, a true partnership that I was privileged to witness growing up. On the down side, it set the bar pretty high for the kind of relationship I'm looking for."

Aidan nodded. "Same here," he stared at her, felt like into

her. "I'm sorry for your loss." His eyes drifted to Face coming back to them, Frisbee dangling from her mouth. He frowned to himself, then looked back at her. "Seems we have a lot in common, some of which we may both wish—"

Face barked, her Frisbee at Kat's feet again. Kat bent down, picked up the Frisbee and handed it to Aidan. He smiled, nodded, took it from her and threw it hard, and far. Face just stood there, again what felt like glaring at Kat.

"Go get it!" Kat commanded. A second pause, and almost as if she couldn't help herself, Face succumbed to the command and bolted after the Frisbee still gliding 15 feet in the air. It felt to Kat that   Face had cooled to Aidan in the 40 minutes they'd been out there, though she had no clue why.

"I get the feeling your dog isn't so enamored with me at the moment," Aidan said flatly, like a point of note but not concern.

"Yeah. I noticed." Kat said, surprised Aidan had. Face missed the catch again, picked the Frisbee out of the sand and came back to them with her hangdog face on. "She's acting very weird. She likes most everyone, even you at first. I've never seen her so... *fickle* before."

"Annie was skittish around new people till she got used to them and included them in her pack. Face'll get used to me," Aidan said confidently.

Kat smiled inside and out at his suggestion they'd be seeing each other again, and nodded. Face came back with the Frisbee but didn't drop it. She glared at Kat, and ignored Aidan entirely as she walked past them standing in the sand and headed towards the parking lot, her cue she was done playing for the day...

...."Ah, thank you, Face. A moment's peace," Sarah says as she comes back into the kitchen minus Cassidy. She sits at the table adjacent to Kat again. Her body sags in the chair and it looks like it takes effort for her to lift her teacup. The house is quiet. "You have a brilliant dog, Kat. One-in-a-million. So what's Aidan's problem with her?" Sarah cradles her tea mug in both hands, staring at Kat expectantly.

"It's the other way around." Kat hesitates. It sounds stupid to say aloud. "Face doesn't like him."

Sarah's dark eyebrows furrow. "So?" she asks, perplexed. "You do, right?"

"I do," Kat answers before the words register in her head. And they're true. "He's easy to be with. We have an even exchange, like he actually asks me questions and *listens* to my answers. And not just surface stuff. We talk about everything. He's not afraid to get intimate, be vulnerable." Kat pauses, feeling awkward for revealing so much. She sips her tea again, its warmth spreading through her body, like thinking of Aidan.

Sarah sits there grinning at her. "Well, bloody hell. It's about time," she says and shakes her head, smiling at Kat. "You're smitten."

Kat blushes, looks down at her tea, almost empty. She does not confirm or deny Sarah's assertion.

"How do you know Face doesn't like him?" Sarah asks. "Does she growl at him? Bite him? What?"

"None of that," Kat says. "She basically ignores him when we're all together. She'll only drop the Frisbee in front of me even though I consistently give it to Aidan to throw. And I swear she glares at me when I hand it to him," Kat says, exasperated. "But most of the time she can't help chase it once he throws it." Kat smiles at her dog's simplicity: *Frisbee! Get it!'* "Doesn't matter who throws it, she still only drops it at my feet." Kat rolls her eyes at Sarah. "We constantly catch her sleeping on his couch, even his bed lately. She'd never pull that kinda crap at home. And yesterday, when Aidan and I were making dinner at my house, she goes into the laundry basket and appropriates my leggings as her new chew toy."

"Hell hath no fury like a bitch scorned." Sarah raises one brow at Kat.

"You're not kidding. Aidan picked me up for our first official date and Face went berserk while we were out and ripped the shit out of the living room. She tore up the couch *and* the cushions, put deep gouges in the front door and in the parquet entry like she was trying to dig her way out to be with me."

"Yeah. Frank told me about that," Sarah says, and shakes her head with a quick grimace. "Kat, you've been attached at the hip to Face since you got her. Practically every time you leave the house you take her with you, even though she has a fine backyard." She gets up to put the kettle on. "I'll bet she was pissed you left her behind." Sarah continues. "She's just jealous. Little *brat.*"

"I know, *right!*" Kat agrees, though she feels small that Face's bratty behavior seems a reflection on her subpar training. "But maybe she's trying to tell me something about Aidan," Kat adds, even knowing how cringy she sounds, like some hippy horoscope lady.

Sarah shakes her head, stares at Kat like she's being as stupid as she feels right about now. "Honey, dogs can't detect good people from bad. Hitler loved his dog, and his Shepherd, Blondi, loved him back," she says matter-of-factly. "Dogs love anyone who cares for them. Relationships are a bit more complicated with actual people." Sarah sighs then looks towards the hallway listening for Cassidy but her daughter and Face are silent, likely sleeping.

Sarah's right, of course, Kat thinks. She's being foolish.

Her dog isn't trying to warn her off Aidan. Face hasn't come at him like she did Dean Reynolds, nor snapped at him like the Golden in the pound which are the only two times Kat has ever seen her dog aggressive. Makes total sense she's just jealous of him. It's been months since Kat dated anyone for more than a few weeks and it's likely Kat's dog feels herself slipping from the top position in Kat's hierarchy of needs.

"So, what's the damage to your house going to set you back?" Sarah has returned to her usual platitudes.

"My lowest estimate is several grand to get it all repaired." Kat frowns.

"Ouch."

"I can't afford this kind of crap." Kat finishes her tea and sets the empty mug on the table. "If Face is jealous of Aidan, then why wasn't she jealous of any of the other men I've dated. She adored them all. She tolerates Aidan, at best."

Sarah leans against the kitchen counter near the stove top and smiles, to herself mostly. "Kat, honey, you were *playing* with those other men. You didn't take them seriously. Not really, so neither did Face. They were just additional playmates to her. Maybe she can tell you're serious about Aidan, like smell it on you or something— your pheromones maybe?"

Interesting notion, Kat thinks, that Face has been responding to her all along from the smell of her hormonal releases with anyone she engages with, online or in-person. Regardless, she still has an issue with her dog's response to Aidan. "She liked him at first, like she does most everyone," Kat muses aloud. "She was ecstatic that first time he played Frisbee with her... until he and I started talking, and stopped giving her our undivided attention."

"There ya go," Sarah says, nodding. "You're dog's being hella bratty, Kat. You gonna let her get away with that?"

"Face really has been beyond bitchy to him," Kat admits. Her disappointment in herself for inadequately training her dog is being overshadowed by her rising ire towards Face. "Aidan goes out of his way to engage with her. Even after she ripped apart my place, he still welcomes her into his custom-built home on the Palisades bluffs filled with his hand-made furniture."

"Impressive." Sarah raises an eyebrow. "Ocean view?"

"Yup," Kat says, trying not to sound like she's bragging. But really, the home Aidan has conceived and built really is impressive. "Five bedroom, four bath, and the entire house runs on solar and captured rain and recycled water," Kat can't help but tell her workmate and budding friend, but clearly Sarah isn't as impressed by sustainability because she starts preparing her next cup of tea. "And the view from the living room is spectacular," Kat adds.

"And from the bedroom?" Sarah asks nonchalantly as she

retrieves the milk from the fridge. The kettle whistles. She looks away and turns off the burner.

Kat blushes. Sarah turns back and looks at her.

"Ah. So your answer is clear, with that blush of new love, my dear." She cocks her head to the side, examining Kat, kind of like what Face does when she's trying to understand.

Kat scoffs, but she can't help smiling. "Nope. We've only been dating a month. But I'll admit, I'm having a hard time seeing any glaring warning signs, except for Face."

"I thought we just went over that. As long as she isn't aggressive towards Aidan what's the problem?"

"I can't have her ripping the shit out of my house every time I get together with him and she's not invited."

"Then leave Face in her quarter acre backyard and shut the doggy door so she stays there. Problem solved."

Kat thinks about this. "Well, she's always had run of the house. I'm concerned she'll freak out if she's locked out and bark incessantly, or dig her way out of the yard..."

Sarah fills the white, porcelain tea pot with hot water and brings it to the table. "Kat, you seem to really like Aidan. Don't use Face as an excuse to wreck what you've got going with him. Just... *stop it!* Let yourself fall in love, and *be* loved by someone other than a bloody dog."

How to Convert an Adversary
🐕

Kat's starting to feel sick as Aidan guides his jeep up CA 18, aka the Rim of the World Hwy. The roads been dry so far, but as they climb the curvy mountain she can see snow on top of the hills ahead.

It was Kat's idea to go up to the cabin Aidan just finished building on Big Bear Lake. But now they're here, Kat's wondering how great an idea it was. It's mid-afternoon and sunny out but the road has icy patches and is slick. Aidan's jeep more glides than steers around several curves. Face is in the back, the bench seat down to give her more room to move. Her head is out the window, which Aidan keeps down enough for her pleasure though it's only 49 degrees outside and dropping as they zigzag up the hill making it chilly in the jeep even with the heat blasting.

"I hope you like it," he says to Kat tentatively, almost shyly. "It's contemporary, like my place, but it has more of an Art Deco feel—"

A deer is standing on the road in front of them as they come around a sharp curve towards the top of the Rim of the World. Kat gasps. Aidan brakes hard and the jeep goes into a slide towards the cliff's edge.

"I got this," Aidan says. And he does. He manages to veer the jeep away from going over the cliff by putting the car into a full spin towards the mountain side of the road and somehow avoids hitting the deer as he straightens out the jeep getting the wheels in full contact with the highway again. He pulls into a scenic outlook across the road, puts the jeep in Park and turns to Kat who is stroking Face trying to calm her dog panting in the back.

"Everyone OK?" Aidan asks looking from Kat to Face then back to Kat.

She nods, sighs, and almost smiles. "That was masterful driving," Kat gushes. "And as an L.A. native, I deeply respect great drivers," she adds playfully.

Aidan flashes his adorable grin as he turns left off Big Bear Blvd and onto a small road covered in snow though tire tracks have cut 2" grooves into the white ice. It sparkles with sunlight, as does the snow still lingering in the stubby ponderosa pines and gathered on the roofs and blanketing the enormous lots of the sprawling homes lining the road.

"It's beautiful," Kat practically whispers, awestruck by the scene. She isn't a skier, so seeing snow is a rarity for her. It's like being in a cartoon the way the pure white contrasts everything not covered in it.

"I know, right," Aidan says as he cruises slowly along the grooved snow-covered road. "My lot is only a quarter acre, but it's flat, and has a great view of the lake."

The moment he says 'lake' the cabins are gone and the view opens up on a Big Bear lake.

Face pulls her head in and sneezes, likely from the cold. She smooches her nose into Kat's sweater to warm it. Kat would turn to stroke her dog but the scene is so magnificent she reaches back awkwardly and pats Face's muzzle instead.

The water and sky are irradiated blue against the snow-covered white out. A moment later the lake is gone and they're back to housing on both sides of the road. The jeep glides around a curve then up a small hill. The tires take a minute to grip the road since it's mostly ice now, and it's melting and slushy on the hill.

"We're almost there," Aidan says when Kat gasps for the tenth time like every time the jeep slides. The road flattens out and is more water than ice now but snow still blankets the landscape. Glimpses of the lake below radiate blue through the snow-laden lodgepole and ponderosa pines.

Aidan turns right, towards the lake onto a small snow-covered road without tire tracks. The jeep's tires sound like someone eating cornflakes in loud crunching bites. Kat spots a couple of deer grazing on the only grass able to grow with snow melting along the side of the road, and she tenses. While they're beautiful creatures, they are seriously unpredictable, like most people she's known, truth be told.

Face sticks her head out to investigate as Aidan cruises slowly to the end of the road, then onto a driveway and alongside a naturally finished cedar-sided garage. Creamy white trim around two double-hung mission windows match the two creamy white garage doors, one of which is opening as they wait to pull into the elegant structure. Behind the garage, the same creamy white covers the stucco wall of a house with the same mission style windows under a gently pitched earth-green tiled roof.

"It's only 1860 feet but it has 3 bedrooms and 2 full baths and a great cooking kitchen," Aidan says, and Kat notes a bit of pride in his tenor as he pulls his jeep into the large garage and the door shuts behind them.

Face pulls her head in the car and noses Kat. *Trapped!* Kat hears her dog in her head and senses Face's panic as the garage door shuts completely.

Aidan turns off his car and looks at Kat but keeps one hand on the wheel. "OK," he starts, then pauses with an awkward smile. "You ready for late 20s to mid-30s Deco retro? Not the early stuff with a lot of Victorian cliches, but later, when it got clean, like Bauhaus, only with style."

"I love your style, honey." And she does. "You don't have to convince me your brilliant." Kat flashes him a gentle smile, then reaches out to him, puts her hands on his face locking her eyes on his then pulls him in for a long, passionate kiss.

Until Face whines. Not her *Give me attention* whine. More like *Let me out!*

They separate and look at Face, then at each other and smile like tolerant parents.

"OK," Aidan says again. "Let's go," and he gets out of his jeep and goes around the back to let Face out.

Kat gets out and joins him around the back of the jeep. She tells Face "Come," after Aidan lifts the hatchback.

Face looks at Kat before jumping out and whines again. *Let me out!* Kat hears in her head and she understands that Face needs to 'pick her spot,' like *now.*

"Face needs to go out," Kat tells Aidan as she follows him up the two steps and onto the smooth concrete landing as he opens the door to his 'vacation' home. Face follows them through the spacious mud/laundry room, complete with a deep sink and detachable faucet nozzle for easy cleaning of soiled clothing and shoes.

"She can use the backyard," Aidan says as he leads her into his kitchen. "It's fenced to the waterline. She should be fine back there," he adds.

The kitchen is stunning, a chef's dream. Creamy white

granite countertops, a stainless steel hood over a 9 burner gas range cooktop, a large center island with a huge sink. Floor to ceiling windows grace a large, half round space off the kitchen that sports a river table that easily sits twelve.

"You make that table," Kat asks.

"Yeah," Aidan says casually as he continues through the kitchen. "Like it?"

"It's stunning," Kat says, and means it. But the open dining/living room beyond the kitchen is even better. "Oh my god," she exclaims. "This is beautiful, Aidan."

The space has a glass wall its entire length showing off the 180 degree view of the lake. Huge redwood support beams are exposed across the creamy white plastered ceiling. A 5' fireplace is against the back wall. It's see-through into the playroom off the half-round contemporary turret off the kitchen.

Aidan goes to a sliding glass door across the dining area and opens it for Face to go out. Blast of cold air takes Kat's breath away for a moment. The backyard is flat for a few hundred feet, then gradually slopes to the shoreline of the lake. It's covered with snow, but there are patches of grass coming through, making it obvious the snow isn't very deep.

Face moves to the glass threshold and stops. She's never been in snow. Kat isn't used to it either, but confidently encourages her dog to go out and pick her spot. Face looks at Kat, her Groucho eyebrows furrowed, her tail down and slightly between her legs.

"It's OK, Rel. It's just snow, baby. Go pick your spot and you can come right back inside," Kat says to her dog.

Face looks back outside. Then her rocket ears go up, her tail goes out behind her and her body freezes into a full point. Kat and Aidan follow her line of sight and both see the deer in his yard as Face bolts from the house onto the porch then down the hill towards the shoreline after the deer eating the hedges likely marking Aidan's property line. Face isn't used to the water either. Shepherds aren't water dogs.

"Shit," Kat says as she follows Face outside, running full force across the yard and down the hill. "Face! *Come!*" Kat yells but her dog is already in motion after the deer which bounds in the shallows around the hedges that ends at the beach shoreline. Face follows around the hedge and disappears from view. Panic the likes of which Kat hasn't felt since the loss of her parents rises like a bullet from her stomach to her chest. "*Face!*" she screams again as she slips and slides along the snow-covered hill until falling on her butt.

"I got ya," Aidan says as he grabs her under her arms and lifts her off the ground. "You OK?" he asks and he helps her stand still holding her hands.

"Yeah," she answers before she even knows if she can walk,

yet alone run. "Please help me get her," Kat practically begs him.

Aidan releases her and takes off after Face. He splashes in the shallows and disappears around the hedges.

Kat's ankle is tender but she can jog, so she does. When she gets around the hedge to the neighbor's snow-covered yard it's empty. Neither Aidan nor Face are anywhere in sight. The yard goes up fairly far to a huge, sprawling mansion but the lot falls away on the left side less than 30 feet from the house. That's where Kat sees the top of Aiden's wavy brown hair.

"Kat!" he yells and Kat rushes over to him. He's standing on a narrow embankment about 5' below the edge of the snowy lot. Below his embankment is another, about 6' down the side of the hill. Face is standing on the narrow ledge. She's whining, shivering, stuck on the ledge unable to get up the steep hillside, and below her embankment is a sheer 20' drop to a small inlet of the lake. "I'll get her," Aidan assures Kat, though she can't see how.

He shimmies down the hillside on his butt sending snow and dirt falling onto the embankment Face is on. She crouches down, her tail between her legs. Her entire body trembles.

"It's OK, Face," Kat says to her dog. "I'm right here, Relli. Stay there. Aidan's coming to get you," though Kat still doesn't know how he's going to get her up the 12 feet of steep hillside.

"I'm here," Aidan says to Face as he sets foot on the

embankment she's crouched on. "It's OK, Face. I'm right here."

Face practically crawls to him and buries her muzzle into his legs. She's still crouched with her tail between her legs, and she's still trembling.

"Should we call for help?" Kat asks Aidan, even knowing the ask is a non-starter with the ledge so narrow. One misstep and Face is gone.

"I think I got this," Aidan says, but he doesn't sound sure. "Let's get you outta here," Aidan strokes Kat's dog then bends down so he's eye level to Face. "You're gonna have to work with me, buddy." He puts his hand under her muzzle so she looks at him. And Face does. Eye-to-eye. "I'm gonna lift you onto my shoulders and we're gonna crawl back up this hill," he says to the dog.

Face looks up the hill at Kat standing at the top looking down at them. Aidan follows Face's line of sight.

"I got this, Kat," Aidan assures her a little more confidently than before.

"OK..." Kat says.

"Hey buddy," Aidan says to Face, pulling her muzzle to him so she looks him in the eyes again. "I'm gonna pick you up. Ready?" And he slips his arms under Kat's close to 70 pound Shepherd-mix, then slips his head under her body and lifts himself and Face, now on his shoulders, to stand.

Kat's heart is beating so hard she can feel it reverberating in her throat. "It's OK, Rel. You're my good girl. Be still," Kat keeps repeating like a mantra as Aidan shimmies back up the hillside with Face on his shoulders, slipping and sliding backwards a few times before finally pulling himself and Kat's dog onto the embankment over 5' below her.

Face is whining but she's still as Aidan lifts her off him and holds her up a bit so she can use her legs. She does, standing briefly on his shoulders to hop over the side of the hill and onto the snow-covered lot. She runs to Kat, smooshing herself into Kat's legs, her tail no longer between her legs but she's panting hard, her long pink tongue hanging out.

Kat kneels down and strokes her dog as she watches Aidan scramble over the top of the ledge and onto his neighbor's snowy lot. He's wiping off his jeans and black hoodie as Kat goes to him, puts her arms around his neck and pulls him in.

"Thank you," she whispers in Aidan's ear. "Thank you," she repeats, then again.

Aidan returns her hug and they stand together, body to body. Warmth envelops her. Face comes over to them and sticks her muzzle between them trying to moosh her way in between their legs. They separate and laugh, tension dissipating into the cold air like the steam from their breaths.

"I'm sorry," he says to Kat, his brows furrowed, his full lips frowning. He strokes Face standing with them. "She hates the water, which is the only place that isn't fenced—"

"Not your fault," Kat assures him, holding his face in her hands. "She may hate water, but she can't resist a good chase. And you saved her. Thank you," she says again, then kisses him, quickly, but heartfelt. She releases his face, drops her hands down and strokes her dog, then lets her free hand fall into Aidan's as they start back to his house, hand-in-hand.

Face prances in front of them like she's leading her pack. Not a care in the world or thought in her head. She's on to her next adventure. Kat is still trying to slow her heart rate.

"Ah, to be a dog..." Aidan says and sighs.

Kat smiles, squeezes his hand. She may just be falling in love with this man. Crunching on icy snow as she walks along side him she feels protected, grounded with Aidan, unlike anyone before him. "Do you believe in *the one,* 'like one right person for everyone?" Kat blurts.

"I do not," Aidan says flatly. "I believe relationships take work to flourish. The longevity of any build is dependent on the quality of care in maintaining it."

Kat smiles again. "You do have a way with words, honey. Like Yoda."

He laughs, then shakes his head. "Nope. It's an architect's meme." He looks at her, cocks one brow, smiles. "Guess I'm hoping for a safe harbor in each other," he says with all seriousness and gently squeezes her hand.

Kat draws in a sharp, cold breath, dumbstruck that Aidan just said the very words her mom had said to her regarding the longevity of her marriage.

Your dad and I are a safe harbor for each other, her mother had told her at her parents' 25th anniversary party.

And *a safe harbor* is the partnership Kat's been holding out for.

The Scent of Love

"Where's his toothbrush and razor? Your house or still at his?" Frank asks, sitting in his high-backed black leather chair behind his desk in his office. "Or should I be asking where *your* razor and toothbrush are these days?" He raises an eyebrow and his playful grin emerges.

"Once again, we're not living together, Frank," Kat says. "Most of his clothes and toiletries are still at his house, hon." She sits in the only clean chair across from Frank's polished wood desk piled with folders filled with pages clipped together with large black metal clips. His laptop and monitor are about the only clear spaces on the desk. "How long did you know Doug before he left his razor and toothbrush at your house?" Kat turns Frank's question around, a simple avoidance technique which he consistently falls for. Frank loves talking about himself, as most seem to.

"Let's see. It was so long ago," he says, pondering. "I think it was like six months into dating, and I left mine at *his* house, for obvious reasons. His B-Hills address is so much *more* than my mere hovel was in Brentwood," Frank says. "Though I have to say, Doug's sense of feng shui is on par with Liza's. At least the dog knows a proper bolster bed when she sees one."

Face lifts her head from her curled position on Frank's office floor at the mention of her dog-friend, Liza, the frenetic fluff Cockapoo Frank adopted the day Kat got Face.

"Doug's house is impeccably designed, right out of Architectural Digest, Frank," Kat says, a bit bewildered what Frank thinks of as feng shui. "The decor is totally chill, clean but warm with cushy couches that welcome lounging, and a kitchen built for a master chef."

"That's all me, honey. Five years of revamping his pedestrian mess."

Face gets up and shakes off, then stretches— front paws forward, butt in the air, elongating her body with a grumbly grunt.

"So, when do we get an invite to see your gorgeous new crib?" Frank asks.

Face comes over to Kat and puts her head in Kat's lap soliciting strokes. Kat obliges.

"I told you, Frank. We're not living together. And anyway, we're at my place most of the time." Kat looks down at her dog, big brown eyes half-mast, she's fully sated by Kat's touch. "I can't trust this little monster not to rip his house apart." She pats her dog in a dismissive way with a few quick, flat-handed taps on her head. "Aidan can't replace his custom creations like I can my parents' Ikea couch and coffee table."

"Speaking of your little brat," and Frank narrows his brows at Kat's dog. "Is she being any nicer to Aidan now?"

Face lifts her head off Kat's lap and stares back at Frank. She glances at Kat with a rather smug expression before the dog turns away, tail curled in a soft U as she saunters out of his office, likely to wander the floor and mooch for strokes from colleagues.

"Does she still snub him?" Frank asks.

"Not anymore. Aidan's her new BFF since he saved her up in Big Bear. She greets him almost with as much enthusiasm as she does me. And she mooches for more attention from him than me." Kat smiles to herself. "But Aidan gives into her more than I do."

"*Ooh*, I adore that gushy look on you, girl," Frank says. "Is Aidan as enamored with Face as she is with him?"

"Seems like it. Aidan took her for Frisbee without me when I had to stay for the last quarterly all-hands. First time just the two of them."

"And how'd that go?" Frank wants to know.

Flash memory, where scenes unfold in real-time but only moments have passed in real life. A few weeks ago she and Aidan were getting ready for work when he offered to take Face for Frisbee since she had to work late. She'd watched him slide on his jeans and zip them. They hung on his tall, lean frame just right.

Kat smiles. She recalls Aidan came to her, stood before her, inches taller, drew his long fingers into her hair and rested his hands on her neck and cheeks. Kat remembers the way her body buzzed with his touch. She'd looked up into his green eyes. "Trust me," he'd said softly. And she did. Then he bent his head and kissed her, his full lips radiating warmth into hers. The sweet, musty scent of attraction seeped through her pours then, and now—

"...*Hellooo!*" Frank is snapping his fingers towards her. "You off in la la land with your boyfriend, sweetie?" He shakes his head and sighs heavily but there is a soft smile on his face.

"I'm right here, Frank," Kat defends, trying to focus her full attention on her boss. "According to both of them, they had a blast playing Frisbee without me."

Another flash memory of coming home late after the All Hands last month to Aidan and Face on the couch in the family room with Face's head in his lap. They were watching *Marley and Me*. Neither got up to greet her as she came through the kitchen, but Face's huge ears went back in submission knowing she was doing the wrong thing. And Kat was sure even Aidan knew the dog was not supposed to be on the couch with all the sand and grime and whatever else may be buried in her fur.

"I get she's not supposed to be on the couch," Aidan had defended. "But I gave her one hell of a workout this afternoon, so I figured it'd be nice if she got a soft place to land for a bit tonight." He stroked Kat's dog along Face's spine.

Ooh... Ahh... Kat heard her dog in her head again, the dog's pleasure amplified by her soft grunts. Face looked Kat in the eyes like a defiant child as Aidan continued to stroke her.

"...smart dog," Frank is saying. "Better to gain a playmate than challenge a competitor for your affections." His expression softens. "Aidan has clearly won your heart, Kat, and I'll wager that Face knows it, likely before you did, or had yet to realize. Maybe dogs can sense true love."

Another sudden flash memory of she and Aidan cooking a stir-fry in her kitchen last Sunday night. Face had gotten the Frisbee from the entryway credenza, and with the disk dangling from her mouth she started whining for Kat to take her to play. Kat told her, "Not now. Later," but she kept whining. Kat told her to knock it off, but instead her dog went to Aidan standing over the stove top stirring the veggies in the wok, and rubbed her body against his leg like a cat, and continued whining. When Aidan gave her the same answer as Kat, the dog smooshed her muzzle with the Frisbee into his free hand.

"Jeez, what an opportunist," Kat had said, a bit miffed her dog was acting so pushy.

"Maybe she's getting used to the idea that I'm gonna be sticking around," he'd said. And Kat recalls the heat rush to her cheeks then the warm tingle spreading over her body, coupled with the sweet, thick scent of desire with his declaration he wanted to be with her, stay with her and her dog. And for the first time since her parents had passed, that hollow space, that black hole that nothing, not even Face seemed to fill, was gone—

"I don't know that dogs can sense love," Sarah says as she entered Frank's office. "Whatever 'sense' means. But they likely can smell it." She'd been back at work a month after their conversation in Sarah's kitchen when Kat first started dating Aidan nine months ago. "A dog has something like forty times more smell-sensitive receptors than humans do," she continues as she relocates the pile of books and clipped scripts on the chair next to Kat's and sits. "I think Face can smell our chemical releases. And feelings of love either trigger, or are triggered *by* some of the most powerful chemistry humans produce," Sarah says. "Right up there with fear," she adds flatly in her posh British accent.

Is she really in love with Aidan? Kat ponders. He's not said he loved her yet, and neither has she him. She thought she was in love with Danny, though it's likely she loved the musician more than the actual man. And while Kat can't claim to ever have been in love with Marc, she surely did care for him deeply after living together and spending most of their free time with each other for two years straight. And Greg may not have been the same as adult love, but he was her first and longest relationship, even if he turned out to be a cheating narcissist.

Kat looks at her colleagues, first Frank, then Sarah. "How do you know when you're in love? How did you know Malcom was the one?"

Sarah shakes her head. "There's no such thing, Kat. Or 'Happily Ever After.' That's a fairy tale, and a destructive one at that. For relationships to work all parties involved must continually work at communicating, and compromising, in equal measure."

"Letting yourself love, and be loved, takes a leap of faith," Frank's delivery is akin to a preacher. "Believing not only in your partner, but yourself, trusting that you can be there for each other, and God forbid, even be able to endure their loss."

"I've never been any good with faith," Kat practically whispers.

"Then use Reason," Sarah suggests. "Make two lists. One is what you adore about Aidan. The other what you don't like. You know the drill."

Kat does. She does it in her head all the time now—ticking off check-boxes of Aidan's characteristics. He's kind, her number one requirement in a partner. He's smart, even wise at times. Creative, and massively talented. She feels her smile broaden, and blush. Aidan is the most responsive lover Kat has ever been with. His touch is soft, gentle, teasingly tantalizing. Sex with the seven other men she'd been with was typically ten to twenty minutes topping out. She lay with Aidan for an hour or more exploring each others pleasure centers most every time they make love.

The last few months she and Aidan had been co-inhabiting most weekends and has extended that to Friday and Monday nights too. Kat loves him there, feels safe with him next to her in her parents bed. And she adores watching him walk around in just his drawstring sweats, shirtless, or getting dressed in the morning sliding on jeans and a cotton shirt over his toned biceps and stacked abs. She loves talking to him first thing in the morning, sharing a quick bite and their plans for the day before they leave for work. And he's tidy. He vacuums Face's dog hair more than she does. He is glad to do the dishes when Kat cooks, and even when he cooks, which he does at least once a week—Mediterranean feasts of garlic shrimp over couscous, Italian bruschetta dripping with mozzarella, or old-fashion barbecued chicken and corn, Aidan certainly knows how to cook.

"OK. Enough chit chat," Frank takes on his managing analyst tone of curt efficiency. "We all have places to be so let's get this meeting going."

Face stands at Frank's office door whining. They all look at her.

"Stop that," Kat commands. And Face does, for about a

minute, then starts whining again when Kat and Sarah turn back to Frank. Kat turns back to her dog. "*What?* What is your problem?" she says, making her frustration clear with her sharp delivery. But even as she asks, she already knows what her dog wants.

Face stands in the doorway threshold, ears up, nose twitching, eyes wide and focused on Kat. She half-barks, then continues with a grumbling commentary which only she understands.

"Wait!" Kat commands. "I'll be with you in a bit. You have to wait."

The dog stops her whiny grumbling, but stays rooted to where she stands blocking Frank's office threshold. Kat turns back to Frank and Sarah. "Every time I talk about Aidan, or even think about him these days, Rellie is underfoot, mooching or whining for my attention."

"Or, she wants to go home, like I do," Frank says flatly. "So let's get this on, shall we?"

———

Her head out the window Face is oblivious to the musty sweet scent of arousal seeping through Kat's pores as she drives home, anticipating her evening with Aidan. It's likely he'll already be at her place, and Kat pictures walking into the kitchen with Face, the scent of sizzling onions and garlic wafting through the front door as they come in. She imagines how Aidan will likely stop what he's doing to kiss her, his hands holding her cheeks, his fingers buried in her hair. She sees herself helping him prepare dinner as she so often does when she gets home. Aidan's at the wok, quick frying its contents with a high flame. She hands him the cutting board with the diced red bells. Instead of taking it, he pulls her in front of him standing at the stove. Holding her around the waist with his free hand, he presses his body against hers, kisses her neck. Kat's body tingles with the image of him guiding her hand holding the cutting board over the wok and sliding the diced peppers into the pan with his long wooden spoon.

4 Steps to
Better Relationships

Kat requires something more personal than click and buy, which is why she met Sarah at the wholesale Jewelry Mart in downtown L.A.

"So, how did he ask you?" Sarah wants to know as they take the crowded, rickety elevator up to the 11th floor of The Mart, the height of the building a modern marvel when it was built in 1910.

Kat's face flushes with heat and she tries, but fails to suppress a coquettish smile recalling Thursday evening with Aidan. She and Sarah peruse the shops on the 11th floor, with a plan to go down the creaky wooden steps to the 10th then 9th and so on until she finds what she's looking for. Kinda feels surreal, as if Kat's in a dream walking the floors of sparkling jewels and describing to Sarah the details of Aidan's marriage proposal...

Aidan had already taken Face for Frisbee when she got home from work. He'd prepared his famous Mediterranean feast, which was stellar as always. Over dinner they talked about their respective days, how work went, projects that were progressing, or not. They'd shared intimate stories of their pasts to their hopes for the future. Conversation flowed, one topic to another without pause like usual. Casual, connected, a shared charge of energy plugged into each other.

Aidan whistled his low-to-high pitched whistle for Face as they were finishing the dishes. "Face!" he called loudly but kept his eyes on Kat. "Come!" He had tossed the dish towel in the empty drying rack and moved to Kat standing next to him at the kitchen sink. Aidan gathered her face in his hands, pressed his body into hers and kissed her passionately, but rather quickly. She'd looked at him quizzically. An adorably mischievous smile extended across his face.

Kat heard the doggy door flap open and close, then her dog's claws clicking on the kitchen's hardwood floors as Face came around the butcher-block island to Aidan.

"Good girl," Aidan praised her dog. He knelt down so they were almost eye-to-eye. Face looked at him. "What do ya say, Facerelli?" He scratched her behind her ears and around her neck then stroked her along her back. Face stood frozen in bliss. "You good with adding me to your pack?" Aidan had asked Kat's dog.

Face tilted her head to the side like she does when she's trying to understand but kept her eyes on Aidan's. She moved to him then, nuzzling her muzzle into him, and then rubbing her body alongside his. Aidan resumed stroking her but he looked up at Kat again, his broad smile infectious.

"I'd say she is fairly definitive," Aidan said, his green eyes clear. "So, with your dog now on board, I'm on bended knees here, asking you, Katrina Miller, to marry me."

"...And then he pulls the ring from his pocket," Kat says to Sarah as they walk the hallway of shops on the 7th floor. Both she and Sarah look at the ring of diamonds on her wedding finger as she grips the handle of the door to the boutique jewelry manufacturer that has just buzzed them in.

"How may I help you ladies?" the ancient jeweler behind the glass cabinet filled with sparkly things asks.

"I'm looking for a man's engagement ring," Kat says for the 50th time since noon. "Something unique, maybe one-of-a-kind, hopefully."

"Like he is, I'm guessin," the old man flashes a knowing smile, revealing his yellow teeth and deep wrinkles on the sides of his eyes and mouth.

Kat looks at Sarah not sure if she's just been dissed. Sarah shrugs. Kat looks back at the jeweler. "He's an architect, and a builder." Kat keeps her eyes on the old man, softening her stance and her delivery. "A creator, much like yourself, so superior quality and superb design matter."

"So, do you have anything like she's talking about," Sarah interjects, clearly annoyed. "Something different than the last 40 shops on the four floors above you had to offer?"

"Something modern, clean, but with some style, and

warmth," Kat says, igniting a flash memory of Aidan on his knees two nights ago, his tousled brown hair framing his young face, the certainty in his green eyes, like he had no doubt. "But masculine. Cut, not soft. Have anything like that?"

He does. Beveled squares of platinum with thin bands of 18k gold down the center of each square connecting them. "The ring is flexible, not rigid, so it moves with the finger, but fits snug, like a part of the hand," the old jeweler says. "Here. Here." He reaches out and takes Kat's hand, then slides the ring on her right index finger.

She can hardly feel the ring at all with it fully seated. Kat holds up her hand and examines it.

"Wow," Sarah says. "It's stunning."

"I know, right?" Kat takes the ring off and puts it on the glass counter in front of the old man. There is an awkward silence while she stands there, reconsidering her desire to give Aidan an engagement ring as he has her. "Do you think it's weird for me to give him an engagement ring?" she asks Sarah.

Sarah sighs heavily again. "Kat, honey, we've been over this already. That's why I've met you here. We could have gone to a spa and gotten massages today. Instead we've spent the entire day in downtown L.A. walking in circles floor to floor looking for an engagement ring for your betrothed in every jewelry store." She stares at Kat, practically glares at her.

"Sorry," Kat says, looking down at the ring on the counter.

"I'm just..."

"Scared," Sarah says.

"Of what?" the jeweler asks. "I'm married 55 years come April, and I'm telling you, it ain't all that complicated. Four simple steps. My wife came up with em our first year of marriage, which, I'll admit, wasn't wedded bliss. We practice them every day, and I'm pretty sure my wife would agree we've shared a good life together since I started living by em."

Kat and Sarah watch the old man and waits for him to continue, but he doesn't.

"OK, give. What are these four steps?" Sarah asks. "I've been married ten years now and I'm still trying to figure out how to... *motivate* my husband to listen to what I say."

The jeweler smiles. He holds up his hand and index finger. "One. You both must recognize you are a team, always a team, on the same boat sharing tasks and decisions." He holds up two fingers. "Two. Ask yourself, 'What does *my partner* need?' Caring about your partner's needs often before your own provides a safe harbor in each other, assuming they too are following the steps."

Kat draws a sharp breath and stops breathing. *A safe harbor in each other,*' he said. She sighs, then smiles, to herself mostly. It's at the top of her list too.

The jeweler holds up three fingers. "Three. Ask yourself, 'What do *I* need?' Doing so will insure neither builds resentment for never getting what they want." He holds up four fingers. "Four.

Compromise," he says with some force. "So both partners get something, even if it's a future give." He holds his four fingers up for a moment longer then drops his hand to the counter and picks up the engagement ring.

"That's all?" Sarah wants to know.

"That's it." He smiles broadly, his face crinkling with lines again.

Up on the 101 freeway on her way home from the Jewelry Mart, it occurs to Kat that she has been actively engaged in the four steps with Aidan, and even Face, giving both what they needed, and getting what she did from each of them from the beginning. The old jeweler's four steps are indeed a recipe for successful relationships.

Lessons from Canine Love

Face comes over and puts her head in Kat's lap.

"Hey, baby," Kat says softly, stroking her dog who stands statue still with her touch. She can hear her mom in her head, *'Get that animal off your dress this instant!'* If her mom was there, they'd have had a scuffle about it, but Kat would have let Face nestle her muzzle on her silk gown anyway. She needs her comfort dog, her canine best friend right then. She'd welcomed that argument with her mom now, especially today.

At the moment, no one but Face is in the small dressing room off the non-denominational chapel down the hill from the main building of the Heritage House, just south of Mendocino. Kat sits on the cushioned seat in front of the huge mirror and looks at herself as she absently strokes her dog. Sarah has done her hair and makeup. Masterfully. She'd somehow curled Kat's hair to cascade over her shoulders in soft, golden waves. Her skin is smooth, her blue eyes seem wider, her lips are subtlety red, yet it is hard to tell she has makeup on at all.

Sarah has gone to see if Frank is ready to begin. A married, conservative rabbi in another life before coming out, Frank is officiating the ceremony. Kat takes a deep breath and releases it slowly to calm her pounding heart. She has butterflies for sure on this day, but no doubts, she assures herself. Face looks up at her. Her dog's clear brown eyes are fixed on Kat's, and suddenly flash memories of her time with Face come so fast it's hard for Kat to delineate them…

Kat sees her adorable Shepherd pup the very first night she was home, her huge ears wet and flopping over at the tips, her fur soaked and matted down, her soft whines and clear big brown eyes begging Kat to end her bath in the kitchen sink.

Ten months later Kat's on her 10-speed peddling full-force down her street clocking 25 miles an hour. Face paced her on the sidewalk, ears back, tail straight out, limbs extending with every stride. She landed on the asphalt only once as she cleared the 20 foot intersection of a side street. She truly was grace personified.

Face looking regal on the rocks at Zuma beach, waves crashing against the shoreline, ocean spray sprinkling over them as they watch the surfers from the rock hill.

Kat curled on her parents' bed crying, grieving, still. Loneliness holding her captive in darkness she could not escape until Face came along side the bed and mushed her wet nose into Kat's cheek. "Eww," Kat exclaimed, but she couldn't help smiling as she sat up and stroked her dog.

The cascade of memories continues of countless times Face nuzzled her or mooched for her attention, making her feel valued, like she mattered to someone, even if just her dog. The consistent and unalterable display of affection Face lauded upon her had, in fact, taught Kat it may be safe to trust something, maybe even someone outside herself again.

Kat strokes her dog with intent to please, focusing her attention on rubbing Face's favorite spots— behind her ears and along her back then on her hind quarters. Regardless of her dog status, their relationship has been one of the most stable, even exchanges of love and respect Kat has ever known.

A soft tap on the door. Face's ears go up, eyes wide, fixed on the closed door. She does not growl but Kat can see her nose twitching a mile a minute.

"Come in," Kat says as she stands and turns towards the door.

"Hope I'm not disturbing," Patrick, Aidan's dad says as he enters the dressing room. Tall and slender like his son, he looks a decade younger than his mid-60s. Full head of more reddish-pepper than salt hair, cut short on the sides and left a bit longer on the top. Aidan had introduced Kat to his father at his house on Thanksgiving last year. She and Face were the honored guests. Aidan and his dad had cooked a traditional and elaborate meal.

Patrick is hard not to like. Witty, smart, even handsome in a hipster sort of way. A professor of Economics at UCLA, he seems passionate about education, politics, and food. And he's a great cook. Like father like son.

Face goes to him and nuzzles her muzzle, then her entire body against his pant leg mooching for attention.

"Face, *no!*" Kat says, afraid of dog hair sticking to her soon-to-be father-in-law's dark gray silk suit. "Leave him," she commands, but Face ignores her.

"It's fine," Patrick says, bending to stroke Kat's dog. Face preens with his touch, as she has every time they've met. "I want to personally welcome you to the Tilden family," he says, straightening. "Well, both of you." He quickly and lightly pats Face on her head then moves around her so he stands closer to Kat, without the dog between them. He hesitates, possibly trying to frame what he wants to say but keeps his focus on her. "You look beautiful, Katrina."

"Thank you, Patrick." Kat gives him a gentle smile.

"My son is lucky to have found you." He pauses, his eyes suddenly distant, like he's remembering. "I got lucky too, with his mother. Liz and I just... fit." He smiles pensively. "Don't get me wrong, we had our issues, but for the most part we were in sync." He nods, to himself it seems, his smile fades, and Kat feels the weight of his sadness lost in her memory.

"I'm so sorry never to have met Liz," Kat says softly. "And that both of you will never know my parents." The notion lingers a moment too long until Kat realizes she's stopped breathing, overwhelmed by the cascade of her conflicting feelings on this day. She takes a breath and releases it slowly. "I got lucky too," she says to Patrick. "My parents had the same thing going on— a marriage worth modeling." She gives him a tentative smile. "I just wish they were here, especially today." Kat's eyes fill with tears. She looks down at Face standing beside her— poised, attentive, ready for Kat's instruction. "Never imagined my dog would be leading me down the aisle. I grew up picturing my dad escorting me." She bites her lip to stop herself from crying.

"Actually, that's what I wanted to talk to you about," he says gently, and hesitates again. "I assumed you had a relative walking you down the aisle, but Aidan says Face is manning that helm." He keeps his green eyes on her. "How would you feel about me escorting you to your wedding today?"

It is such a kind offer, and right then Kat realizes that her marriage to Aidan comes with the beginning of the family she's longed for. She suppresses her impulse to kiss his cheek, but cannot stop her tears of gratitude from flowing over the brim of her eyes and sliding down her face.

"Oh, no," Patrick says, brows furrowed with concern. He touches her arm, his long fingers over the sheer lace of the long sleeve. "I'm not trying to replace your father or anything like that, only—"

"No. No. It's not that," Kat assures him. She goes to the vanity, grabs a tissue and dabs her face dry. "Patrick, I'd be honored to have you walk me down the aisle. Thank you."

Sarah comes in with 2½ year old Cassidy in her flowy pink

pageant dress. "Ready?" Sarah asks Kat while trying to stop Cassidy from throwing the red rose petals in her basket onto the floor. "Not yet, Cass," she tells her daughter, plucking petals from her tiny fists and putting them back in the basket.

Cassidy squeals with delight seeing Face, lets go of the basket of petals which spills on the floor as she runs to hug the dog. Face patiently sits in front of her, Cassidy and Kat's dog now eye-to-eye as Cassidy gently strokes Face's muzzle, then down her back like her mama and Auntie Kat had shown her. Sarah puts the petals back into the basket and holds on to it as she straightens.

"Ah, the joys of parenting," Sarah says in her posh British accent. "You ready for what comes next, Kat?" She looks Kat in the eyes.

"I am," Kat says to Sarah, holding her rather piercing gaze hoping to communicate the certainty of her feelings for committing to a lifetime with Aidan today.

"Ok, then," Sarah says, and takes Cassidy by the hand while holding the basket of petals just out of her daughter's reach. "It's time for Auntie Kat's wedding, baby," she says to Cassidy. "You get to throw the petals soon," she says as she guides her daughter out of the small room.

"This is it, Facerelli," Kat says to her dog.

Face stands, her eyes on Kat's.

"Ready to add Aidan to our pack?" she asks her dog.

294

Face barks. Once.

Patrick smiles at Face's response, then puts his elbow out towards Kat. She slides her arm around his with a grateful smile. He nods.

"Lead the way, Relli," Kat tells her dog.

Face does, her tail continuing to swish back and forth. She prances proudly through the open door leading Kat and Patrick down the short hall to the chapel. She practiced the previous day and seems to have learned her role well. Face saunters in front of them with the cadence of a mountain lion a few feet behind Cassidy throwing tiny handfuls of rose petals as Sarah guides her daughter down the center aisle.

Aidan stands near Frank at the end of the glass enclosed room, the sparkling Pacific coast in the distance. He's wearing his dimpled smile and looking fine in his dark gray suit and her favorite pale green tie that accentuates his eyes. Frank's dressed in classic black— slacks, button-down shirt, blazer. Only his skinny tie is silky ruby red. Less than 20 guests, mostly Aidan's family along with a few friends and workmates. When Cassidy's basket is empty Sarah guides her daughter into her lap as she sits in the front row alongside her husband Malcom. Face moves a bit left of Frank, like a groomsman they do not have.

Kat joins Aidan. He flashes his dimpled smile at her, slides his hand in hers and squeezes softly. Kat squeezes his hand back and holds it, probably too tightly, and flashes him a quick smile then looks at Frank and Face in front of her and Aidan.

Face looks regal, her fluffy fur around her collar makes it look as if she is wearing a mink stole. She sits a few feet from Frank, rocket ears up, big brown eyes crystal clear and looking from Kat to Aidan and back again.

'My pack.' Kat hears her dog in her head and Face fixes her eyes on Kat. *'You. Leader. Mine.'* Kat's dog glances at Aidan than back at Kat. *Aidan. You. Me. My pack.'* She stares at Kat with overt adoration, her almond-eyes watery but she's panting lightly with her happy smile on.

'My beautiful Face,' Kat says in her head, hoping Face hears her, or at least *feels* her deep affection. *'Thank you for being my friend.'* Kat's dog gifted her a safe harbor to love freely and be loved sincerely through dogged devotion and unconditional acceptance. And if not for her magnificent Frisbee dog, Kat would not be standing here getting married to Aidan today.

'Frisbee?' Kat is certain she hears Face ask. *'Now?'*

Kat smiles. *Ah*, to be a dog...

🐕 The End 🐕

About the Author
❖

"Writing fiction is intoxicating. Fully engaging. Hot. Sexual. Physical. Mental. Spatial. Virtually touching real as I enter the scene. And I'm a million miles from Lonely."—JC

Jeri Cafesin is a bestselling author of modern, 'genre-diverse' fiction filled with complex, compelling characters so real they'll linger long after the read.

Her debut novel, *REVERB,* about a musician who learns to love someone other than himself, quickly became a bestseller in Contemporary Romance on Amazon.

Ever fall for someone you *knew* you shouldn't?… Other works by J. Cafesin include her 'novel memoir' *DISCONNECTED,* an "exquisitely honest view of women's roles in 1992 L.A., and even still today."

Fractured Fairy Tales of the Twilight Zone, Volume 1 and 2 are collections of fantastically edgy short adventures, each with lessons that'll stick for life.

More of Jeri Cafesin's books, including new releases, are available on Amazon. Upcoming releases and sneak previews are available on her website: jcafesin.com. Many of the essays from her ongoing blog have been translated into multiple languages and distributed globally: J. Cafesin on Medium

A Stanford entrepreneurship educator, and recent empty-nester of two gorgeous, talented, spectacular kids, Jeri lives in the San Francisco Bay Area, on the eastern slope of the Oakland hills, with her husband/BFF, and a loudmouthed, big-eared Shepherd pound-hound. Find her at jcafesin.com.

www.ingramcontent.com/pod-product-compliance
Lightning Source LLC
Chambersburg PA
CBHW070558260626
47161CB00002B/643